PRAISE FOR

# AS FRANCESCA

BY MARTHA BAER

"This masterful erotic thriller is both literary and as smutty as a dime-store flip book. The cybersex scenes Baer conjures up are fresh and well-written, and her glib take on the workaday world is dead-on."

—*The Advocate*

"Entirely engrossing. . . . A deep and delirious mystery."
—*Denver Post*

"Baer's novel is highly innovative, combining resonances of Poe, Hawthorne, and performance art in a tightly structured, ultrahip, high-tech erotic thriller."

—*Seattle Times*

"Baer builds the suspense craftily [with] whodunit overtones worthy of Agatha Christie."

—*Newsweek*

"Martha Baer is a fine writer—terse, insightful, sensual, provocative. She has found the place where intercourse (sex) meets intercourse (conversation)."

—*Lambda Book Report*

"Baer . . . has written a tribute to the headiness of ambition, the mysterious tangle of love and work, sex and power.

. . . But though she initially seduces us with graphic sex talk, Baer knows how to hold us captive in a story. She keeps us wanting more, asking for it, begging for the climax."

*—Women's Wire*

"Both a playful whodunit and an examination of sex and fantasy in the computer age. No matter what you expect, this sly, smart novel will surprise you."

*—360 Mag* (on-line)

"A genuinely, compellingly erotic (and funny) novel that connects sex to the rest of life."

*—Newsday* (New York)

# AS FRANCESCA

## MARTHA BAER

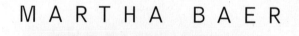

BROADWAY BOOKS

NEW YORK

**BROADWAY**

Broadway Books titles may be purchased for business or promotional use or for special sales. For information, please write to: Special Markets Department, Bantam Doubleday Dell Publishing Group, Inc., 1540 Broadway, New York, NY 10036.

BROADWAY BOOKS and its logo, a letter B bisected on the diagonal, are trademarks of Broadway Books, a division of Bantam Doubleday Dell Publishing Group, Inc.

First trade paperback edition published 1998.

*Designed by Claire Naylon Vaccaro*

The Library of Congress has catalogued the hardcover edition as:
Baer, Martha.
As Francesca / Martha Baer. — 1st ed.
p.  cm.
ISBN 0-553-06754-0
I. Title.
PS3552.—A3315A8  1997
814'.54—dc20      96-31231      CIP

ISBN 0-7679-0127-4

98  99  00  01  02  10  9  8  7  6  5  4  3  2  1

FOR SARA MILES

# CONTENTS

# AS FRANCESCA

# 1

## THE

## DRAPES

**N**o one had ever brought me to my knees like that before.

"Get . . . down," she would say. The lights were dim, the heavy drapes closed, absorbing the smells of wet soap or melon. The walls were blanketed with shadow that dipped and folded around the moldings. And there'd be a moment, right about then, when I'd start to hear my own breathing. I was indecent. I was incorrigible. My back would arch and my shirt pull away at my chest a half an inch further and the streetlights from below would edge in under the curtains and melt into the glow from the monitor.

I would stare, hard, into the light that was cupped in the darkness of the room. I would stare at each ready, blank line as if I were peering through a filthy grating, peering into an incalculably deep space whose bottom may have been just a foot below or may have been fathoms. The waiting made me despicable.

And then, long breaths later, the letters would spill across the screen. They'd come quickly, like fingers executing a musical scale.

"Get down on your knees and shut your mouth," they said, the last words each to a line,

"and

"don't

"move."

Now I was making sounds with each breath. I was supposed to comply.

"DON'T MOVE," they said, bigger. But I would slide my hand down inside my clothes.

The next day I would feel refreshed. After all, short of the most predictable morning-after effects (heaving self-hate, sickening remorse, abject shame, et cetera) bright-eyed affability seemed the next most appropriate. The kettle would pipe up, flutes and reeds would pipe in through the vents from the neighbor's downstairs, the wind would play against the windows, and I'd feel full of energy, alert and focused, like some exemplary bank clerk who's congenial from dawn till night and never seems to lose steam. I felt blessed with intelligence. There was work to be done, mounds of it, but as keen as my mind was, as steady my sentiments, it would be a cinch to complete. Everything seemed manageable—no trace of doubt, nary an epistemological wrinkle.

That was the fall. All through the city, dead leaves circled the signposts and flipped their undersides upward on the air. The weather was cleansing and prescient, and I felt for the most part it treated me well. Every now and then, the winds would pester and divert me temporarily, like a grating mendacious politician making headlines on the twenty-four-hour news, and particular gusts would suggest some cosmic disregard for my value as a citizen. But through it all, through the sometimes battering wind and through all my dark judgments of our town's material distributions, I was forward-looking most of all. I was alive to everything, sweet or ill. And most notably, during that satisfying passage in my life, now several years back, I was always capable of seizing upon goodness. I could build in my imagination, brick by brick, a palace of rewards. Pouring my thick black coffee in the morning, penciling in a thick black brow, or zipping a black jersey around my neck, it was as if I had a bull's-eye view of a future, and somehow it all looked good.

At work, I felt magnanimous. I was liked and I liked everyone in return, particularly Roberto and Kay. For four good solid months—and I mean that, "good," "solid," in several ways—I would stop by Kay's station in the mornings, where the lacy lamp she'd bought for her desk lit her cubicle with its anomalous yellow glow, and I'd apprise her of my long-term intentions, my well-conceived solutions to yesterday's problems, my plans for the day ahead. I'd listen to her opinions with fastidious regard. We were voluble, but never excessive, and Kay was loyal and smart. She would lean back and watch me gesticulate, the expression on her face knowing and bemused, her arm sprawled across an open file drawer, and I always knew my pronouncements would be met by some sort of witticism or affection.

In those months, it seemed, Kay had grown even more likable than she already was. Or at least my fondness for her had grown more acute. I remember one morning, for instance, when a wash of such deep appreciation came over me I made a conscious note of it to myself. I shook my head and smiled. She was dressed as usual in a long liquidy dress, her bony frame and girlish outfit contrasting with that vigor, simultaneously athletic and intellectual, that I admired; and standing up close to her, murmuring, I was underscoring my contempt for Gerald, our division head, with another outrageous anecdote illustrating his dearth of enthusiasm. Kay laughed and motioned with her hand, a gesture that anyone with even a slightly versatile imagination would have read as a grab for the genitals of an adversary male; I loved the way this delicate girl never abandoned her sweetness even in moments of total vulgarity.

"King Gerry," she said, and I saw, as she leaned in to grin with me, the glass beads of her earrings casting pools of multicolored light on her neck. She was laughing, the muscles of her face shifting over her jaw. She whispered something else flip, like, "He's the worst dressed version of Satan to emerge in this millennium," or, "He must have got his brain implant from Dow," and then leaned back once more. I looked at her for a moment, with the unspeakably lifeless carpeted wall behind her, that supremely unimaginative padding all the cubicles had, and I registered in the vivid contrast of it what an uncommon young woman she was.

This hadn't been obvious to me right off. For years I'd lost touch with Kay altogether, after a brief stint as friends in undergrad calculus, and it had never occurred to me to track her down. She'd been the kind of acquaintance you easily hit it off with but in a sense had met too late, having already collected a pretty full slate of companions. We were both in our last semester in college, ready to move on, but both liked doing math, particularly if it included the element of speed. And so, shortly into the course, the two of us sank into the pleasurable routine of doing problems side by side in the library and swapping solutions while racing the clock. Kay wore the same exact sort of dresses back then, though her face was less narrow, and she exuded the same kind of roguish warmth. We laughed at length in between assignments and sometimes while walking out of class, but we'd lost touch nevertheless a month after completing our finals.

When I ran into Kay at Poplar—it must have been more than five years after—circumstances for both of us were different. Clearly, like me, Kay wasn't drowning in pals anymore, nor was she likely to replicate here in the office that sense of familiarity and social abundance she'd been able to drum up on campus. In this incarnation, our attachment bore the added incentive of a little bit of need. We were elated at seeing each other. I have no doubt the look on my own face was precisely the one I saw on hers, when, in the middle of Marissa's giving me a tour of Domestic Sales and Fulfillment, on my third or fourth day on the job, we spotted each other simultaneously. It was as if we were not only surprised at the coincidence, sensing with relief that our respective isolation might be lifting, but we were also electing each other immediately, hands down, as Most Favored Workmate, as Best Office Friend. Even despite Kay's frequent moods, despite how off-putting she could be in her dark spells, I probably would have cast that same vote every day for my next three years at Poplar.

But tempered optimism, reasoned determination, heartfelt camaraderie, good breakfasts—my *own* mood, in those days, persisted. It wasn't just the mannish silk jacket or the fashionable platform shoes, and it wasn't just the orderly office with the plaid curtains that in my daily life signified purpose. There was also the way I interacted with colleagues and friends, from His Highness Gerald to nervous Jean Fine and Vera the artist from Bogotá. I was about as well liked and organized as a girl could be for that salary and I was always willing to be more so. More salaried, certainly, but more trusted and admired as well.

There were only the mildest intrusions into my confidence and my constantly upbeat bootstrap energy, and these were hardly even discernible. Just for a second as I was taking a coffee in the stairwell where I'd hide with Roberto to talk, or heading home in the evening alone, one other mood might once in a while intervene. It was a flash only, always, and a feeling bearing not the slightest resemblance to the feeling of the day. Along Frederick, say, it might happen that a wind would shove the debris along the foot of the buildings. Some empty bag would catch my eye as it rose suddenly upward, and following its path toward the parlor floor of a row house, I'd glimpse an open window. Drapes, heavier than those in my own windows but similarly fleshy and crimson, similarly slow to billow and then rest, would fill up with air. They'd swell, creating an opening between their velvety hem and the ungiving ledge underneath them. In that dark opening, just then, where the folds peeled away from the private darkness of the room's interior, I'd see the insides of my own nights. It was a glimmer only, a spark. I would have been hard-pressed to describe it in even the vaguest terms. At best I could have called it a physical sensation, stirring up whatever substances were otherwise settled in my stomach, my knees, my thighs. It was a hum or spin. Behind my eyes I felt a drawing inward, a physical subtraction that brought all my sensations, all perception, down to one tiny, dense, and living center, which, could you ever reach into it, grab it, in the hot and nebulous place of feeling where it lived, and know its name, there would be no other word for it than the one hushed iteration: "sex." It was the thing itself. And following that small and potent instant of satisfaction, there was a fleeting image that passed in my mind as quickly as a fish under water. Replacing the bulging drapes was an image of a hand, the hand of "Inez," coming violently across my face.

All this would take no more than a second to pass, and without even altering my expression, raising my brow, or shifting my eyes, I'd proceed to turn the corner onto Stuart. There was no need to notice even, really. One extraordinary wave of lust that opened up all my mental and physical passages on a quiet walk home—it had zero effect on my competence. What was significant, I noted, as I adjusted my black scarf under my collar, was how readily I left it behind and seamlessly returned to the absorbing concerns of my busy and wholesome day-to-day life.

## 2

## CROWNS

## AND STARS

At night, my whole world fell to pieces. Once, for instance, I went to sleep so dizzy and distraught that I dreamt of being taken away by ashen-faced paramedics who repeated over and over close to my ear, "she's wanton," "she's unruly"; there seemed no chance I'd manage to carry myself respectably at work the next day. That night, I'd eaten a quiet dinner at the corner café—spinach in a garlic sauce with one or two other ingredients I can't now remember. At eleven I'd taken off my shoes and dimmed the lights, and at three past the hour, I'd logged on as "Francesca."

Immediately I scanned the names of the members on-line. Most of them were familiar and of little interest, but I was confident "she" would be there momentarily. At six minutes past, the system announced a new log-on.

Of all the times I'd encountered "Inez," that time was one of the most damaging, or at least it was one of those meetings that caused the greatest fear and the strongest sense that I had lost contact with the feelings and sensations that our culture, in its lavish literary and moral traditions, has always called "normal love." Of all the wretched and thrilling encounters, it was one of those which, as it was occurring, had me thoroughly convinced I would never return.

Inez wasted no time. I was already pinned up against the wall with my hand between my legs by the time my software had finished building our private screen. "Your back is cold against the plaster," her words said, "but your fingers are hot like oil."

I moaned and slid down in my desk chair, slouched like a boy in class.

"You're feeling in between the folds," she kept on. "Do you think I don't know? Do you think I can't smell it? What do you feel there? Tell me now."

My pants were unzipped and slipped down around my hip bones.

She grew impatient. "I said what do you FEEL?" she wrote again. She waited for me to write out the answer. But I didn't. I knew I could get away with a few seconds more.

"WRITE IT NOW," she commanded. She reverted to lowercase and added a new line: "And get the spelling right."

Then when I did, when I'd yanked my hot hand from under me with a sound deep in my throat, a complaint that barely escaped the dense wanting clogging up my mind, when I'd made my hand work again this other way, and it had slipped around the keys like a tongue against teeth, and I'd written out almost angrily the dirty details, begging by now, "OK, I want you, let me come," and she'd made me go back and retype where I'd fumbled or misspelled something, then when I'd finished, she said, "OK. Enough."

"I'm holding you," she said, "by the neck."

I imagined now my arms dropping to my sides. My breath was short and ragged. I knew we hadn't even gotten to the real part, the part where, every single time, she would do something new. And that was what I wanted and feared. That was what made my chest tighten, my head rocking back on my shoulders, drawing that arc at my throat that alluded to some kind of exquisite servility and to dying. My bowed neck was far too revealing despite how hard I resisted. I was craving and hating what she'd do to me next.

"Now," she said. "Suck on your fingers."

I did. They were salty and rancid and sweet. They were all the way crammed in my mouth.

"I suppose you think you can rest now, that I'll soften now and stroke you nicely. Do you think it's over? Do you think we're done?"

I imagined her up close, her hand wedged under my chin. I could feel her breath on my mouth and the vise of her body tightening against me.

"You're not done until I pin you down, until I turn you over. You're not done until your spine melts under my knee and your skin starts to glow and you feel like a million people trapped in the darkness, counting the seconds till daylight. . . .

"Look at me, girl, I'm talking. What are you doing with your fingers?"

She knew. Both my hands this time were jammed down my jeans.

"NOW," she said,

"TAKE

"IT," and I knew just what had happened. Inez was going to beat me on-line. I could imagine the hard warm palm meeting the bones of my face.

"You're not done until my hand burns."

Just the idea of that impact made my right eye close, and the edge of my monitor twist and then jerk back into focus. The stinging hummed like acoustic feedback in the halls of my chest and my arms. The smack of that hand forged in my body an opening that grew wider and hotter as each second passed. I leaned back in my chair, riding on my own fingers.

"Your face . . ." she said, "your face . . ." as if those words signified great heights, as if they expressed coming itself, all at once, then she dropped to a new line.

"TAKE IT AGAIN."

And again, this time from the other direction, I felt the impact—my head snapped to one side—like breakage, the cracking of rock, running all the way from my cheekbone to my spine. I felt it down my neck. There were long sounds in the room, which, only at the edge of my mind, I knew were my own. "AGAIN," said the words. And my hand kept lunging, harder and harder, as I took the third, fourth, fifth blows, my jaw clenched, my whole face catching fire.

Sometimes I wonder just how Inez always knew I'd come before I had the time or the wits to say it. Maybe it was simply good guessing, or maybe it was in timing how long it'd been since I'd typed my last response. But really I think it was her ability to judge just which orders, out of the scores she fired at me over the months of our meetings, were the most effective ones, the most elegant and demoralizing. Through some uncanny wisdom, Inez could tell that "Bend your knees" wouldn't be the one, nor "On your stomach," but that "Don't touch me, girl, don't even look" was enough to bring me into a huge mental darkness and "I know it hurts, slut, it hurts you" would finish me off.

And I remember that particular night, she did it. She broke me—not just in that she made me eventually wither and relax, snapping the tension that held me in place like a beam fourteen hours a day, but, too, she broke me off from something. She intercepted my knowing the world—its gradual, irreversible history, its slowly accumulating facts. She made me feel that whatever it was I'd just gone through, it had no counterpart in the rest of my life.

As usual, I woke up fresh. I opened my eyes and stretched my legs down into the day-warm sheets and everything looked promising. I smacked my lips, breathed deep. The dishware, the drapes, the salmony Formica around my kitchen sink and the patterned bath mat I'd recently bought with its whimsical crowns and stars reminded me of all the ways life was various and of all the opportunities you had to improve. I was even a bit startled by just how airy and fragrant the bedroom seemed, as if, while I slept, it had grown cleaner.

And that was the day I first sensed it for sure: in my very bones, I could feel a promotion coming on. I knew it. There were gold stars ahead for this sharp doer on the company's master scorecard. I could feel it when I walked through the brick corridor—as we informally called it, on account of the old walls recently exposed—into which the two conference rooms emptied out department heads and other midlevel big guns from their weekly meetings. Passing through these dust devils of company influence, I got knowing nods and startled greetings pregnant with coincidence—"Ha! we were just speaking of you," they conspicuously didn't remark, but I could hear it. I lowered my eyes demurely, because I *was* demure in all honesty—I'm fearful of attention en masse— and sped up my gait. Modest, I am, not grasping, but not stupid either: that day I knew there was something concrete to be gained, as if I'd hit a spot in the game where my teammates began saying "warmer . . . hot" at a gradually increasing pitch. I knew I was about to put my hand on the hidden object.

I felt I *had* to. Over the course of four months, out of a long spell—a lifetime in fact—of hesitancy, a curious urge to be promoted had been mounting in my otherwise quiet mind. Louder and louder, there were these rumblings. I'd begun to experience a new rapacity for notice, for love and approval, totally obliterating all those other urges—for fun or safety, leisure, romance, et cetera—that had always stirred in me before this. It had become overpowering, really, an ambition with the pungency of avarice or fear.

At first I'd found it surprising. Why after all the years of my adulthood spent feeling fundamentally indecisive was I blossoming so late? Born into upper-middle-class comforts, I knew there were certain successes I was "meant" to achieve: a profession that tapped my better faculties; a bit of property—the house, the car; a maturing into management or some other tempered form of power; the "refining," along whatever lines, of all I'd learned in college. And I was on my way to assembling the various building blocks of this lifestyle. Starting off with odds and ends—working in Accounting for a record label on the rise, assisting a couple of CPAs when their help went out on maternity, crunching numbers for a study at the mayor's office, I'd landed comfortably at Poplar & Skeen in a demanding if amorphous job in Special Projects. My family applauded the fact that this stint finally promised some permanence. When Special Projects folded into Promotions early on, and my boss did some arranging behind the scenes, Jean Fine brought me on in Budgeting with solid confidence in my abilities. So within a year of joining the ranks of Poplar, I'd settled into a distinctly respectable position that corresponded in all the basic, crucial ways with my life's expectations.

But I had never felt the sting of wanting go beyond this. For two more years at Poplar, I'd looked after my tiny corner of the business, staying "on task," as it were, growing and trimming the billions of numbers that passed across my desk as if the work we accomplished in Budgeting were the equivalent of maintaining the company's manicure. I had some fun and I satisfied my superiors, but I'd had no strong impulses to leapfrog onto another rung of power or take on a bigger challenge. I was always somewhat tentative, never grasping, mostly humble, ever needing to be persuaded—even in the most appropriate circumstances—to take the helm. Not that I was idle or passive, or the type to get in ruts (it was in the cards, for a girl like me, to always, admirably, make progress, and I enjoyed a steady pace of change), but in key moments I'd recede. When it was time to take the reins, when, say, a volunteer was needed to make a routine presentation—a five-minute update, really, no more—at the division's biannual retreat, I'd consider for a second and then decline. It just wasn't "like me," I would say. I'd toss it off. We'd laugh. I simply didn't harbor deeper needs to shine.

Shining, however, was precisely what I'd begun doing about four months back. Since that time, I'd been undergoing the strangest transformation, which carried with it an air of magic, at the same time sinister and delightful. At first it was only I who noticed—the way my speed kept increasing on the charts, the way I'd stuck to my guns when disagreeing with Jean about formats—but quickly it had become clear to others as well, particularly during the division's half-day workshop when I'd volunteered to head up Group Taft. The heads of Groups Jackson and Wilson and Roosevelt were the typical leadership picks anyone might have predicted, but when I stood up to report our group's final analysis, everyone in the room was surprised. It was this mutating sense of my character I felt reaching a new degree of consummation that day, marvelously, when, in my bones—there's no other way to describe it—I simply knew the company would promote me.

I told Roberto. He met me immediately in the stairwell where we conducted all our grave and titillating business. Roberto was holding his earthenware coffee mug and sipping from it intermittently, but I was too fidgety to sit down. He looked at me over the brim, as always trusting me through and through. With him, my instincts were a given. Faced with this alleged prescience about my promotion, anyone, Eddie or Vera or Kay, would have asked promptly, How do you know? But Roberto just said When?

Roberto was a prodigious man. He and I had been hired

within days of each other, over which we'd always felt a bond, though in my view that was the only real parity between us. He had brains made in heaven. Other than the mutual newness and later the mutual seniority, our relationship was tilted, with Roberto up high on the other side of the fulcrum. It was just a couple of days before, for example, that I'd watched him give a talk to ten execs from our sister group, four of whom later tried to woo him covertly for a job. For an hour and a half he had mapped out the advantages of our systems, using long, detailed sentences and not one page of notes. It was as if every impromptu clause he crafted had already been born and choreographed before it even arrived at his consciousness. Afterward, one VP from Germany in a navy blue suit had wanted a few minor clarifications, and Roberto responded in the guy's native tongue. Then not ten minutes later, he took up with me in the hallway, back to his usual strings of colloquialisms; and it was those easy transitions from one language to the next that made me so shy and awed by him. I thought, Put the smartest engineers in a room for decades and they couldn't design the miraculous machinery lodged in this brilliant fag's head.

And Roberto was physically beautiful too. His skin was smooth, sweeping wrinkleless over his prominent forehead, the angular cheeks and nose, and his lips were unusually full. He was slender all over, almost elegantly gaunt, not just down through his torso, as slender people by definition always are, but slender also through the chin somehow, slender through the temples and brow. Even Roberto's wrists seemed sleek. And I wasn't the only one who noticed. Every

Poplar & Skeen employee capable of even a moment of poetic feeling had commented on the handsomeness of Roberto.

I was up on my feet, straddling three steps. It was cool in the stairwell and he sat now up against the yellow painted wall, his mug beside him, warming his well-muscled shoulders with his hands. Sometimes, when we held one of our little meetings like this, Roberto would slip some luscious silk scarf from his bottom desk drawer on his way to the stairs, and he'd wrap it around his neck. Today it was paisley.

I said, "It's gonna happen."

He listened fixedly, eyes wide open.

I said there wasn't a speck of doubt in my brain. It would be within months, I told him, I was sure of it, though what did still elude me was precisely which job. Not associate, we agreed—they'd never do that, no woman had even made vice associate—but junior vice deputy, that was possible, or maybe junior associate. Who knew, I conjectured, it might even be first deputy of Operations.

Roberto exclaimed. *"That's* it!" He clapped his knees and poked his tongue through his lips discreetly, the slender pink thing slipping back in his mouth before you even had time to interpret it. Then he looked at me totally lovingly, like the oldest friend I had in the world, like a friend I'd escaped with from a horrible peril and lived with gratefully in exile. He used my name sweetly. He said, "You've got it in the bag, Elaine."

And that night I logged on in a blur of good feeling. What moved me most of all was that people—higher-ups, who seemed faceless enough to be credible, who had the distance to know—believed I was good, I was worthy. This was like water for me, like food. After having fixed my sights now, these past months, on all the public forms of love and reward, this was what I truly lived for. I hit enter. You wouldn't have exactly called it arrogance I rode on that night, rode, as one rides on a high-powered vessel cutting across the surface of the lake, but you wouldn't have mistaken it for humility either. You might say it was a gathering sense of certainty, of hope and of promise, which verged—if that were possible—on the prophetic. It was a fullness of knowledge and a measure of pride that I felt, carrying me blindly through the log-on commands, as another brimming day came to a close and I sped head-on toward another lurid undoing.

# THE

# STRONGBOX

"She" never ran out of ideas. She created an entire room, with high stone walls and hot breezes, a perfectly impenetrable black shadow filling one end and one end lit by the moon. She made a bed that was plain and cold and unembellished save for the iron posts to which she could tie me. She built a persona that could take off my clothes with the precision of a burglar or the rage of a cop, or that would make me take off my own. She pulled me into the light when I wished to be in the darkness, pulled my collar taut around my neck, or yanked my head back by the hair. And whatever she did I would end up somehow with my stomach weak and my legs open and the spot where wanting and knowing intersect closing like a fist in my mind, contracting to a needle-sharp point and then exploding with the force of its own density. And when she was ready to fuck me, when she was finished with all the rest, she would whisper something gentle, something hinting at praise, so I'd begin to think I'd been good even as she drove home my punishment, until crashing past her, insanely defiant, my own body would find its release.

Everything she created for me was just another vehicle

for making me beg or wait or buckle under. She made a world out of nothing, out of specters and associations, that served completely to subdue me. So why then would I have consented to imagine it with her? Why would I picture the strap across my wrists or the silver box on the floor by the bed or the deep purple drapes at the open windows, thereby agreeing to go through with it and to take whatever I took? I could have stopped at any moment, logged off or simply stood up in my infinitely tamer, friendlier room and walked away, leaving the electronic device there useless, out of range of my mind. Or, to get right down to it, I could have just sat there, not even moving, and simply refused to imagine. It was so simple and yet such a tangle of warnings and lures. All I had to do was to *not read*.

But I did. I read as she gripped my wrist and twisted my arm against my spine. I read when she called me a whore and pressed up against me from behind, when she pinned me to the bed and slipped her fingers inside me and the walls fell outward suddenly in my weakened mind. I read every bit of cruelty as avidly as I read every bit of love.


To do the job well, I read widely: I read reports and newsletters, memos, updates, news clippings and press releases, proposals, meeting minutes, legal briefs, feature pieces, analyses, the daily news. On weekends I read literature, essays and novels, and books about business, books about finance and foreign industry, and back in my earlier days, books about the history and structure of class. Scrivener was ever a source of the latter.

And then there was all the metaphorical reading I did in

the course of a day: the reading of voices and time, the reading of weather. And at every street corner, every en-counter by the liquor store or at the bus, I read faces as well—who doesn't? I was always a shrewd reader of passing expressions, and in fact, I even at times had consciously cataloged the ways certain acquaintances use their chins.

So it was not atypical that I would read Jean Fine's face rapidly one November day when she called me in for a meet-ing. I knew everything I needed to know the minute I glanced at her lips as she closed her office door. It's true I had already narrowed down the possible explanations for our "private" talk when she'd requested it the previous day, but it was the looseness of her mouth and the drooping of her lids that really gave it away. Again, in a wave, I felt liked, even prized, as if I'd just gotten a glimpse of myself in a clear mental mirror where I looked different from the way I'd looked a year ago—prettier and healthier, appealing. I brushed my fingers along my nose to hide a sneaking smile: my suspicions were about to be confirmed.

Jean Fine was not particularly warm, however, even at moments like this. In Jean Fine (hers was one of those names that always seemed most rhythmic or descriptive when ut-tered in full), you felt an awkward interplay of tyranny and apology. In her gravest, most demanding displays of author-ity, Jean could seem sorry, and yet when she was most hum-bly admitting an error or foible, she somehow maintained the coolness of a judge. Once she had actually fired a minion and then thrown the same guy a party. For an hour, stand-ing at the outskirts of the gathering, holding an empty plastic cup, I'd fought back an urge to comfort someone, to say aloud, "Oh God, poor thing," but I couldn't decide, between Jean Fine and her underling, to whom I should tend. When at one point the young man gazed up at Jean midway through the reveling and said it seemed out of the ordinary to be acting this festive, she responded icily, till a silence fell that was so stiff and wretched, he finally broke it himself in an attempt to keep the celebration of his own demise lively. It was a morbid twist only Jean Fine could have manufactured—innocently and with no grasp at all of the mess she had made.

Jean Fine was the kind of Catholic who would have done anything for her father. Her life fit almost flawlessly the stereotype of the blue-collar parents from an urban community dotted with parochial schools, raising a slew of kids their father was bent on making successful, except Jean Fine was an only child. "Dreamer," she'd said to me recently, pointing to the photo propped on her desk in a teak and abalone frame. After two full years as her employee, this was the first time she'd taken me into her confidence, but I knew for a naked instant that her wish to please was the same as my own. "When I was twelve," she went on, "he took me on the M bus into the hills and told me tales of how each family made its fortune. I asked him, 'How do you know all that, Daddy?' and he just tapped his fingers against his temples. I was well into my twenties when it dawned on me the stories were all made up."

I understood it. Jean wanted to do that man's bidding in the deepest of ways, so much so that it made no difference whether his bidding was worthy or fraudulent. And though Jean Fine married out of her class, I could see she would have left it behind anyway since in his own mind, her father already had. His fantasy of being someone else had badgered and hacked at his material realities with such confidence that the truth had finally capitulated. Jean was the product of that man's immortally insistent imagination.

After all, it takes practically inhuman amounts of imagination—and even then there's a price—to leave the socioeconomic stratum you're assigned to. That's what I've learned over the years about the realities of class from people like Jean Fine and Kay. I'd always thought, as the great sweeping myths of the last century would have it, that people leave their origins behind on the basis of healthy psychology. I'd considered it a matter of confidence or of early-childhood influence; perhaps it was foresight or wherewithal or that vague phenomenon we call values. But I'd left out the critical capacity to fantasize. As I see it, those individuals who have the imagination to pry themselves out of the deep sludge of their economic destinies are about as rare as the nearly obliterated bald eagle; there are a few, like Scrivener, born dirt-poor, or Jean Fine, say, who virtually rewrite themselves culturally. But it takes profusions of phantasmic creativity. And even blessed with that kind of power, there's still a mysterious and exorbitant price to be paid for every little privilege you achieve beyond the lot you were handed.

That day, however, there was no such reminiscing; promptly, Jean Fine started in on our "private" talk, running her fingers over her pearls. There was information, she said, that upper management would like her to glean. I leaned toward her as she spoke, an already palpable willingness in me expanding. She said, "Elaine, several executives have been asking about your future plans. There isn't much more I can say."

Of course that was plenty for me. It didn't take a federal agent to second-guess those remarks; it didn't take a wolf-hound to sniff out that promotion. The higher-ups were feeling out my loyalties, and Jean Fine, it was clear, was seeking assurance of my long-term devotion so she could say she had a pick for the hire. Then her boss would return her to me to make the final revelation and instruct me in how to prepare.

I crossed my legs and looked away, a pose I happen to know approximates sincerity better than any other. I was wearing particularly feminine clothes that day (though not without irony—a little chain above a scooped collar and narrow trousers, my hair knotted tightly on the top of my head, alluding at once to the Jetsons and to a 1950s Italian girl), which underscored my neatness and my honesty. I held the pose steady, as if to meditate deeply on just the right words to express my commitment. And in fact, the commitment was actually there: the truth was I wanted that honor so badly. I wanted to win. It was a craving in me, still just a few months old and yet fully blown, consummate, like the missing of someone you love. I said, "My plan is to do my job really well here, Jean, better and better, to take on more and more challenges for Poplar." Everything that before would've seemed to me mildly alien and unnecessary—a new title, a handshake, a mention in the in-house rag—had grown heavy with meaning for me the way a heart is with blood. "I have *a lot* to offer," I said. Who, before this, would ever have imagined me wanting so hard to get ahead?

Then, as Jean Fine carried on and repeated herself, attenuating those last minutes of empty ceremony, I scrambled to focus my brain lest I burst rudely out of the room without waiting for her to finish and rush to tell Kay the news. I ran my eyes over the equipment on Jean Fine's desktop, attempting to steady my breath. I focused my mind on the contours of her paraphernalia, the stacks of file folders, the telephone receiver, the cables that cascaded out the back of her machine. And it was right about then, as I held myself off just barely from charging out of the room, that the gears of inquiry which were sluggishly turning behind my eyes suddenly locked into place. I noticed the strongbox on her desk—very quickly, very lightly, like an insect landing. It was hung with a thick, official-looking padlock, and I thought, What does she keep in there?

That night, I was afloat. I was giddy. My pending success was like music or fumes or something similarly mood-altering. I began mentally tabulating the uses I'd make of my raise and the number of years till I'd blast through the glass ceiling.

Then at eleven I logged on as "Francesca." And the moment I met up with "her," all else was gone.

# THE

# BELTS

"She" made me tell her the details. She said, "Feel it." She said it again, "Feel it," ordering me twice over because she knew I was hesitating. Until I typed back to her, spelled out, word by word, my own subservience, she wouldn't continue.

I dragged my damp fingers back to the keys, one thumb so heavy, so far away, it accidentally dropped on the space bar. Laboriously, I made the cursor back up. "OK," I typed, "I'm feeling it. I am."

"Is that all?"

It wasn't enough that I submit to the commands and severity. I had to describe every level of my disintegration, to *make* it happen to me all over again with words. "My hand," I wrote. "My hand is between my legs."

"And?"

"My fingers. I'm spreading myself open."

"For what?"

"For you. For everyone. So everyone can see. Look inside."

"Keep going."

"The whole world can see me, I'm bad. My fingers are

moving and it's slippery, it's wet." I was coming around. A sound rose up in the back of my throat. "I'm opening my legs even more"

"Keep talking."

"wider"

Then suddenly she stopped me. I'd begun to write confidently—about the slick smooth feel, about my disgrace, and about moving around uncontrollably—but that was enough. Abruptly, she cut me off without an apology and sent me on an entirely new tack. Again, she had some different plan.

I sat up slightly and read. The words poured across the screen as my hands slipped back down over my stomach. Suddenly she had my face pressed up against the wall, hip bones hard on the stone, my wrists pinned, and my shirt stripped off my shoulders. Everything smelled of girl. I felt her teeth bore into the muscles of my back. A moan came up out of me that was supposed to make the pain stop, but the sound had no effect on her.

"No," she said, "I'm not done with you yet. Go to the closet."

She was forcing me to participate actively in my own subjugation. She was making me an instrument of my defeat.

"It's dark in there and cold," she went on. "There are no lights so don't bother feeling around the walls. But you can feel across the hooks to your left. You can feel the icy big buckles and the long rough straps."

There was a pause. She dropped to a new line.

"Bring me a belt."

■     ■     ■

You could say that one explanation for my high spirits, the perky moods and friendly demeanor I exhibited in those days as I plied my talents and solicitude at Poplar & Skeen, was simply that I'd reached orgasm two or three times the night before and sometimes once more by myself. I was a paragon of contentment. That at least was the reasoning I articulated for myself. Sex is relaxing, rejuvenating, I thought—all around the globe, cultures have known that for centuries.

But the fact was I didn't often reflect on the causes of my incipient success. Sometimes I would stop long enough to feel grateful or to declare quietly to myself, This is terrific, this is wild, why haven't I experienced it before? But for the most part I didn't question my good fortune or attempt to put two and two together—the days with the nights. Perhaps I didn't want to know more, to risk the interference that too often follows a good insight. There are times, besides, when you're just not up for being so analytical. I simply felt sated and alive.

Nor did I tell my usual confessors the meagerest detail about it. I didn't tell Eddie or Vera. I didn't tell Roberto or Kay. Flesh and blood trysts may be a different story—I wasn't one to judge—but even the most tasteful and benign of electronic paramours would be tricky to integrate into your work life. There was one individual, however, just one, to whom I did describe my nighttime diversions. On a few critical occasions I broke the silence to a trustworthy friend, though in a technical sense, the *silence* itself never lifted.

This friend was Scrivener. Easy-going and mentally adventurous, Scrivener was more than open-minded; he was *multi*minded, or at least, multivoiced. He was utterly free of the tics, fixations, and flourishes that inform us in our day-to-day social encounters that what we've stumbled on here is a person, a unified communicative self. Scrivener was my purely electronic acquaintance. And he never wrote me in the same style twice. Vice executive director at the Raymond Electronic Libraries for National and International Research, Scrivener lived and breathed digitized text. This "man" had read and transmitted more electronic copy than any such entity you could conceive of. In a way, he didn't exist beyond it. As far as I knew, he lived solely via the keyboard, but lived in such a way that there seemed to be no "he" there to do it.

Already our correspondence had lasted for years. Before I'd ever set foot at Poplar, I'd found Scrivener purely by chance while rounding up a slew of arcane figures for a job I had at the mayor's office. The city was temporarily flush at that time and paying a task force of twenty to file what was ostensibly a report on a report. The idea was to reevaluate a previous study, which had lately been found scandalously ungrounded, of business trends block by block. And it was while assigned to the task of charting per capita salaries in the area of retail that I got on the trail of Scriv. Tracking down one dusty source, a study done in the sixties by Raymond Research, I started out by using the phone, but the woman who answered told me right off the bat that the man for my query was Scrivener and that my best bet was to reach him by E-mail.

That was for me the beginning of a unique kind of bond. It was the way, in the first note, he joked with me, and the way in the second he didn't, he opined, that cinched it, and in all these years since then, I never lost interest in this strange man's intellectual style.

To me, Scrivener encompassed everything. Communication between us was always the most courageous excursion into the territory of himself. One day, for instance, he would write to me in the loftiest tone, conveying metaphor by metaphor his sorrows over life and mentioning big philosophical concerns like the inhibitions of the human species and the failure of men and women to adequately love; then all of the sudden, the following day, he would grumble at me tersely like a sergeant, his missive composed as if in a gruff and furious state, with no regard for punctuation save the period and barely a word more than two syllables long. The day after that he might respond to my news with the prose of a scientist, a precision that almost ached with restraint, or suddenly take an interest in my clothing, exactly which fashion choices I'd made, waxing ecstatic over fabrics and accessories like a clothing designer for celebrities. The only way to know who it was you had heard from was the "signature": that one little trace—"Scrivener"—was always the same.

"Torpor. Trails of some noxious smoke are seeping through the passages of this old mind," he once wrote me. "Oh, the growing melancholy. If only the creep of this alien despair were to reverse itself, spread outward and dissipate in the infinite void which could contain it so much better than myself. Yet, why so ignobly convey it? Would that I could bear this gloom in silence, with the mettle of so many more corporeal sufferers whose misery is far more grievous than mine."

Or once, "Knock, knock. You wouldn't have believed nervous old Goshen today, our big cheese boss. What a NUT! Mr. Chubster! I thought he'd keel over from heart failure in the middle of leading the 3:00. Can you believe a guy that fat can be so shy???!!"

Or, "Dear Elaine, too much to say: job pressures, new suit, sick mom. At some point I'll tell you everything. Meanwhile, you've got to do the violet shirt next time along with the bright-colored belt. Smashing."

With Scrivener, I could never predict it, the tone, the vocabulary, the cadence, the mood. The variables shifted daily. But over time this strange verbal chaos produced in me an odd kind of trust. No matter what the style of his wild rantings, no matter how outlandish the voice, I knew Scrivener never screwed up the facts. The information he relayed, in the end, was invariably literal. You always knew the content of what he said was the truth.

So, it was Scrivener I chose to reveal certain things to, things I didn't tell anyone else. I would disclose to him gripes I harbored about the company, for instance, or I'd let slip an odd secret or two from my past, and now and then, in the course of these strange few months, I'd reveal to him some sordid detail about the shocking anomaly of my nights.

"Pervert? sure as hell you are," he'd answered weeks back. "No reason to fret your little head about it though. Hey, the ways some folks fuck and rough each other up in the bedroom's a helluva lot less filthy than how they do it on the job."

Still, revelations were rare. The fact of the matter was I was really too busy for gossip about colleagues or clothes or trivial digressions regarding my nightlife. The office, for me, had become a place of purpose, an effective, buzzing machine, where every hour, every exchange, and every task had a goal. It was more likely in my notes to Scrivener that I'd expound on the shortcomings of the Budgeting staff and the direction of my career or the ins and outs and obstacles of moving up at Poplar & Skeen, so that he knew every element of my climb there, from Special Projects, to the small office in Budgeting two years back, to a promising leadership spot on the associate track. Scrivener had heard about every little victory I'd won, not least my private talk with Jean Fine.

"Scriv, it happened," I wrote, "just like I predicted." I was back in my office spreading the word to key companions as I huddled in front of my screen. It was dusk. I'd already run to Kay with the news and met Roberto in the stairwell, so by then it was late afternoon. The late-fall light from the window was dimming, filtering through my cream, green, and crimson plaid curtains. I wrote, "She treated me with her usual ambivalence, but it was perfectly obvious what she wanted. She said to me, 'Some execs have been asking about your future plans.' "

I poured my heart out to him, the messy unconsidered substance of it, as I heard staffers down the hallway heading home. To Scrivener I could relay my most meticulous observations and picayune reflections on my own psychology. "In my quietest moments," I wrote, "I sometimes feel welling up in me this faith that marches perfectly in sync with my skills. There's a sense that what I'm capable of doing exactly overlaps what's 'good,' what's useful and what's meaningful to others—do you know what I mean? And even though I hate sentimental ideas like 'destiny' and 'calling' and stuff like that, having this sense of opportunity for me is the closest I've ever gotten to invoking them.''

I knew that Scrivener would reply to me, and that what I said would be fully understood.

"After all these years of feeling uncertain and half-hearted about my abilities,'' I finished, "I'm finally determined to get ahead. It's so weird, Scriv. I think I'm on a path.''

# 5

# THE

# RED SATIN CORD

The sensation that flooded in that night when I discovered Inez wasn't there had the impact of terror. For some time, I didn't notice it. I was gazing emptily at the list of members on-line with my mind trained instead on a memory of the night before: her hand at my collarbone, her breath at my throat, and the hushed edict that until I gave in to her completely not an inch of my flesh was to move. But when I came to and it was 11:19 and there was no trace of that name on the screen, the fact of her absence struck me like horror, like a thing that changes your world. It had a depth and abstraction that made real forms of grief seem like luxury. Every weeknight since summer she'd appeared at eleven o'clock. Now how was I going to resume my normal behavior this radically unfulfilled?

Later I convinced myself that nothing had happened. I took down my hair, put on a camisole and satin Nepalese trousers, and I turned out the light abruptly. I was pretending that her absence mattered direly, but only to somebody else. Flashes of sexual struggle traversed my steep and sudden descent into sleep.

.    .    .

When I awoke the next morning, the first voice in my head was Jean Fine's: "executives," she was saying, ". . . your future plans." I dressed in something black, no doubt, with zippers, and the Day-Glo orange belt I'd borrowed from Vera almost three years back and never returned, and I passed my eyes over the daily news. The morning proceeded as usual.

When I arrived at the office, however, I knew that something had changed. I noticed it first in the rest room, where I saw in the mirror that one of my earrings was gone, and the asymmetry that single missing clip-on created was so startling I barely recognized who I was. I lifted my hand to my chest in what looked like an ironic gesture of fright, but it was real. How unsettling, I thought, to grow anxious over something so small.

But really it was eerie. Later, along the brick corridor, I experienced a similar imbalance. Passing by the glinting panes of the conference rooms, I suddenly stopped in my tracks. I sensed there was something askew, not literally in any way, but as if on the walls of my mind someone had adjusted a picture, say, moving it just inches to the right of where it had hung for decades. I stood for a moment abstracted. Had something, I wondered, gone wrong? Had I made some mistake, some nauseating gaffe I could no longer remember? Deep from the wells of cognition not yet formed, of knowledge only barely suggested, came a sense that something was awry.

I returned to my workstation, all the while experiencing a lingering discomfort that was not in my body. It wasn't located anywhere. I could barely concentrate long enough to take in a full sentence of Scrivener's attentive reply. Then Gerald summoned me to his office.

I popped up instantly. In a minute I was down the corridor past the open area with its island of assistants and its stark white doorways leading into the airy capacious rooms that accommodated notables and superiors. I reached Gerald's officialdom immediately.

Seating myself in one of his plush green chairs and adjusting my little black skirt, I drew up my posture and dropped back my shoulders in a gesture that heightened my confidence and at the same time expressed it. I glanced around at Gerald's meticulous decor and saw that all was in order. I was back to my usual self. With all the intensity and defensiveness of a late bloomer I'd begun to feel recently that I'd won my place in this room squarely and justly— though I'd failed to consider whether, in the long view, I wanted it.

Gerald greeted me with his standard lack of grace. I'd always said that the simplest sign of feeling could have made that man attractive, just some tiny measure of affect registering in his face, and yet, instead, he was homely.

Immediately I took up the appropriate dialogue and felt my thoughts and my good graces start to flow. "Wow," I said brightly, tapping his desk, "what about that Skeen rating?" This was the sort of thing I'd just learned to say. I smiled cheerily as I invoked recent kudos earned by our department. I was feeling not merely intelligent, but charming and warm. I said: "I think it's remarkable, really, how we've gone yet again and outdone ourselves."

He didn't answer, which was usually the case.

I continued: "At this rate we'll be hitting double digits in no time."

He wasn't moved. With Gerald, you had to nurse the faith that kindness and collegiality were accumulating somewhere, buried in the deep recesses of his conscience, and that they'd eventually emerge. But it was a long shot.

When he finally spoke there was phlegm in his throat, and he didn't raise his eyes. "The Monday charts" was all that came out of him.

I thought, Hey, what a mouthful. I said, "Certainly, Gerald. Sure thing!" I liked to increase my pitch like this—it was a game I played to see how much he could brutally ignore—so I cast around for further expressions of eagerness. "I'll have those copied for you instantly!" The object was to ramp up your enthusiasm in subtly increasing increments. "You won't even have a minute to blink!" Though I knew he approved of my promptness, he had never in any way acknowledged it.

It was my theory that Gerald's permanent refusal of human interaction had developed in proportion to his obsession with hygiene and decor. Here was a man whose skin looked not merely clean but buffed, the angles of his hairline as if drawn with a knife, and the huge nostrils practically shaven. Here was a man who never looked oily, but never looked dry. More impressive even than his shoes or his creases, though, were all the objects placed so deliberately around him. It was these that struck you most as manifesting some compensatory fixation. I glanced across at the brass hawks, glass bricks, and pewter figurines used as bookends; the array of framed diplomas and awards; the leather desk accessories and the stand for his pens; and it all struck me as highly ridiculous. I remembered the day the movers had come to help us change offices, and how Gerald, packing up so pedantically and refusing any help, had taken three times longer than anyone. Even his floor was adorned with antique fetishes—the Mongolian rug, the magazine rack, and the painted tin wastebasket with its scene of chariots and gods. In contrast, all through the rest of our offices, including my own, the decor was the apogee of spare: cool gray and bright white. As Roberto once said, if Gerald's office were a room in a museum of design, it would have been considered highly genuine and superbly American, and it would have been labeled "The Den."

At that point I pumped my pleasantry one notch further to see if I could win my little game of eking nary a rise out of him. The more chipper I got without acknowledgment, the higher I felt I had scored.

Again there was no reaction.

But win or lose with Gerald that day, still there was something unnameable I felt I was not doing right. As I passed out of his office, fully intending to track down those charts, I suffered again that weird kind of lapse. Once again every ounce of poise and perspicacity seemed to waft like a wind and escape me. Some vague and generic weakness inside me that day was interrupting my otherwise copious flow of intention. It was as if I wanted to cry.

Finally, by late afternoon, as this most clumsy, unproductive day in months of accelerating competence wound down, I began to form in my mind a theory. Or better, it began forming itself, creeping in. A weird realization was erecting itself in my brain. It was this: that what had for months now seemed like two disjunct, unrelated halves of my life—my sordid nighttime adventures and my seemly, sociable days—were in fact very tightly intertwined. It dawned on me, in the midst of sorting out some mundane files and updating a database, that the extent of Inez's meanness matched exactly the degree of my workplace flair: the more Inez demeaned me and the more degraded I became, the happier I was on the job. When she hadn't shown up last night, everything today had seemed cockeyed.

This was the first time I'd noticed it. From the moment I'd met Inez that July, having gotten the bulletin board's number from the town's weekly paper and fiddled around there for a weekend until, that first Sunday night, she'd shown up and typed me one of her crueler lines—beginning with that moment the very chemistry of my life had changed. Yet I had refused somehow to notice it. From the moment she'd spelled out "Francesca" and I'd known that in this brand-new, glorious showdown I would always spectacularly and blissfully lose, I hadn't even once mulled it over. I paid no attention to the ways in my life that the days and the nights—in tandem—were changing. Sometimes very late before sleep, still heated up and bewildered, I'd reflect on our escapade briefly; I'd marvel at how sex at its roughest, most dislocating could be made up of nothing but text. Or sometimes I'd wonder at myself even, the way that for me, before this, sex had always occurred under the faintest layer of boredom, an invisible coating that kept it dull—to me sex had seemed slightly routine, if entertaining; yet now my desires had turned suddenly pornographic and I'd spawned these capacities that could shock. But mostly at night I'd fall asleep so hard and fast that my musings would get quickly curtailed, and I'd wake up in the morning so keen to get on with my promising life that I never in all that time had looked back. I simply never stopped long enough to contemplate the uplifting and debasing effects of her treatment, how strangely they coincided with the rest of my life, until that cold, sunny Wednesday at the office when I finally saw the perfectly inverted logic of it all.

I "penned" a note to Scrivener. Often the urge to write him would arise like this when a new thought had plunked down in my mind, a thought barely formed, flaccid like liquid or like Jell-O undone, just poured and still warm. There was a sense that lest the thought leak out or spill, never to be retrieved again en bloc, all whole, I had to say it or write it out quickly in the hope that no meaning was lost. I suppose if you took the metaphor seriously, you could say ideas without sentences are like Jell-O unset and devoid of a bowl.

"Dearie," I wrote. I felt *that* comfortable with him, a man who, some would adamantly remind me, I absolutely didn't know. After all, I'd never laid eyes on him. Everything I sensed or believed about Scrivener had come to me in pixels, in his own inimitable, erratic choice of words. If you'd asked me, however, that was as deep and accurate a knowing as any other kind. "It's tense here today, and I'm self-conscious. Whatever I do seems kind of off. I feel, I don't know, like I'm about to foul up any second. And just now it occurred to me, Scriv, it passed through my mind, this idea I thought I'd run by you: all the good feeling I've been having these past few months," I said, formulating the idea plainly, making it syntactically whole and thereby rendering it a thought you could think once and then read over and over, "this feeling seems connected to my on-line encounters. That 'person,' " I explained, knowing that Scrivener with all his millions of floating personae would understand exactly what the quotation marks meant, "the one I meet up with at night—she puts me down and gets rough with me, and then the next thing you know I feel confident. I feel glad all day long, smart and cool and deserving. Today I didn't. And, see, the funny thing is—last night she wasn't there. What the hell do you think about that? Gotta run. Do tell." And with my message sent, I put the notion out of my mind. Not only was it set now, sealed and protected in prose, but it also was heading toward home: if anyone could take in that thought, save it, store it, merge it, know it, and elucidate it further, it was Scrivener. After all, those functions were the man's raison d'être.

That night, at 11:11, I logged on as Francesca. For just a moment, as the welcome screen was building, I entertained the worry that again she might not return. This had never happened before. Could it happen twice?

Then, as her name appeared letter by letter at the top of the list of log-ons, that little signifier so packed with sense it would have filled a room if it had burst, the craving that her absence had already bred now increased a thousandfold.

She messaged me abruptly. It was too fast, but it didn't matter, because I'd already abandoned everything in my life that had gone before. My chest and neck felt hot. And in the back of my mind, without clarity or volition, I knew that my nightly trysts would no longer be just adventures; they'd be treatments. They'd be a way to *get* more of what I wanted. Without saying as much to myself, I signed on that night with a new, still unarticulated purpose: get beaten, get power—exchange.

"Go to 16," she said.

I could barely type out the change-channel command, even as I whispered aloud, urging my fingers to work. "Come on. Come on," I was moaning at them.

Immediately, from within the snowy, empty screen, she directed me over to the drapes. She directed me to walk in my bare feet over the cold stone floor. She said I could feel a draft, which was good, because I'd need it. Then she told me more: "The red cord," she said. "Untie the red satin cord and tie it around your wrist."

It took me a minute. But then I could see it. I imagined myself moving through the room. The air grew icy, though in fact nothing had changed. I rocked back in my seat, my eyes closing as if I were suddenly sedated, as if I were mainlining some rare aphrodisiac, and then answered monosyllabically. "Yes," I said.

"Pull it. Pull the cord," Inez transmitted, "taut."

And I did. For a moment I lifted one hand from the keyboard, ringed my wrist with my thumb and forefinger and squeezed—the blood collected, my hand burned. I had the sensation that birds, invisible and indistinguishable from the air, were circling my head. I thought I might come any minute.

"Pull it. The knot. Pull it tighter," she said.

It seemed to take hours to get breath.

"Tighter, whore," she said, and then, "Well?"

I was supposed to explain. I released my hand, which was pulsing.

There was a pause. "Well, yes," I typed. "OK." There was always this stumbling, this vacillation. "It hurts. My wrist. The cord is tight on my wrist."

"What else?"

"My hand is swollen."

"And then what?" she said, but she didn't wait for me to answer.

She sent another line.

"Then you inch over to me," it read. "You walk toward me slowly, the end of the cord in one hand. You feel afraid, but it's entirely exhilarating. You keep inching over, skittish and ready to jump, but dying for me anyway. You have no idea what I'm going to do to you, how exactly you'll be tied or just how badly I'm going to treat you once I've strapped you down."

Now there was another pause. My face was flushed, partly with love and partly with humiliation. It was true I wanted to be trapped by her, hidden away in some impenetrable place: the prison of Inez was vast and dark and terrifying.

"There," she said.

And I knew she had grabbed the other end of the cord.

# 6

## S H O E S

"The cord," she said, "is your savior. You want me to tie you down."

She kept going. "That's right, WALK, don't stumble. I'm pulling you over to the bed; see how the tassel loops around these bars?"

Both my hands felt paralyzed. I read on.

"Yes, now you're bound there, your wrists strapped together, your arms overhead, and your whole body hanging down from the high bars of the bed frame in the intimate grip of gravity. Your stomach is flat on the mattress and your legs are sprawled open behind."

I could feel it. The cord was both my capture and my survival, my stability. At least I could *see* it was there.

"You can feel the whole weight of your body," she wrote, "your hands growing inflamed from the pressure, your muscles stretching along your sides."

Even as the cord caused my hanging, it felt like my hanging *on*.

Inez had paused. I sensed her approaching behind me, but I had no idea what would come.

More letters came. "You're afraid, aren't you?" she

wrote. "You're wondering what I'm doing back here, why I'm taking so long."

I waited for those hands to make contact, but I couldn't know whether they'd touch me—my back, my ankles, my thighs—with a brush or a blow.

"Down," she said, and I imagined myself struggling to get my legs underneath me, to relieve the pulling at my wrists and to escape the next smack that might fall. But her hand shoved hard against my shoulders, sending me back to the bed. "DOWN. Your arms might be sore," she said, "but your thighs are cool against the bedsheets."

I was thrilled. I was lustful. She had hoisted me up almost to the height of tears, and then begun touching me hard.

It was true, Inez's repertoire was infinite. It seemed more and more unpredictable. Logging on, feeding the machine the letters of my secret name and passing through the litany of verifications and commands as if shedding, with every line, a piece of preservation, I would surrender to the endlessness of possibility. I would enter my password and preferences, the knowledge of which was so ingrained you'd think it lived in my fingertips, and I'd get ready to let her have me.

I was ready for forgetting. Moment by moment, as the sexual craving rose in pitch and the fantasy grew richer, I would feel all the bits of history that made up my life and the world we know of scattering through the void and disappearing. With Inez, the future was all: wherever she would take me I was heading.

■   ■   ■

Ironically, it was Gerald, Mr. Tight-lips, who relayed to me the most exciting news. That day, I was particularly busy, overscheduled really, but nonetheless efficient. I wore fashionably narrow trousers I'd only recently dared to try and a set of bold magenta bangles.

Gerald summoned me to his office, late in the afternoon. The rugs gave it a dimmer and homier look than anywhere else at Poplar. "Elaine," he said, hardly acknowledging my presence, refusing to interrupt some surely trivial task of signing POs or filling out forms. It was good he used my name since there was no other indication as to whom he was addressing. "Elaine," he said again, finally looking up though still not in my direction, "as you know, we've been quite satisfied with your performance."

I sat down in the chair before him and gripped the green upholstery. I recognized immediately what he was about to say, and I wanted to catch every word of it. I wanted to memorize each phrase. I was slightly breathless with the prospects—provocative problems to solve, real tests of my developing smarts, but more than anything else *acknowledgment*. It was as if a formal voice from above would speak to me: "You're good, Elaine; you're shining; we like you." There were elements in me that could "make it" at Poplar and maybe anywhere in the world.

"Report to Brill," Gerald said tersely. And even though this man had troubled and frustrated me for ages, refusing to acknowledge the smallest percentage of my person, for a second I saw an ambiguous softening at the edges of his eyes. I could have been imagining it, but just then I wanted so badly to like him. The brass hawks in his bookcase looked graceful and bright. His hands looked smooth, resourceful.

"Make an appointment," he said, still not looking, "at your soonest convenience. You're being considered for junior associate."

Yes! I heard resounding in my head: all I could think of was that big, round affirmative. My hands relaxed and my shoulders sank back in the chair, but my knees bounced frantically above my toes. Gerald existed across an unbridgeable chasm, but nevertheless seemed benign—I was getting from him the very thing I wanted. If you'd looked in my eyes at that moment, you'd have seen what looked like craziness there, but really it was pleasure all mixed up with need.

"Thank you, Gerald," I said. "I'm so pleased." I stood up and for a minute paused dumbly, feeling myself light and insubstantial like a mere casing for a substance inside me that, to this day, I don't know very well: I was filled up with happiness. Gerald just nodded—a barely noticeable gesture of closure reinforced by the view of the neat gray hairs on the top of his head as he went back to his stack of forms.

In all of civilized America, throughout the thousands of cities dotting the plains, the towns and the metropolises, you couldn't have found a cistern big enough to catch what poured out of me next, as I paced and chattered, whispered and gesticulated, regaling my ever-attentive companion Roberto, who sat wrapped in a sweater in the stairwell. It was as if a spigot, rusted by worry and reservations, had loosened, and everything I'd been envisioning for the future, now unleashed completely from the regulating forces of meekness and doubt, gushed forth profusely. I told Roberto every inch of it, all my plans and my obsessions. I spouted out my theories and my hopes and little bits of my biography, how my family'd always touted the rewards of taking on responsibility but that I hadn't planned to get so much of it, how once I'd set my mind to something—*anything*, it almost seemed!—I could get it. I saw myself as a tree ready to burst with fruit, a colt just up on its feet, or a rosebud suddenly blooming: all those distastefully adorable newnesses in nature, so convenient to metaphor, were now making vivid sense to me. I was utterly won over by all those redolent figures of speech, which, even to the most cynical minds, smack of goodness or hope or justice. I was enamored with the very notions of awaking or rebirth, of mission and fulfillment. Each inkling of what was coming next, every speculative detail as to whom I'd meet, what I'd wear, and how I'd organize my mornings intrigued me—because it meant something more. It meant something greater, somehow, about what I might become and how I might fit into life notches higher than I'd suspected.

I told Roberto everything. Of course, he'd heard it all before, save the three fourteen-karat-gold remarks Gerald had just delivered, but I repeated everything at least once more and bits of it four times over. Roberto listened as if it were all fresh news. He listened with his impeccable team spirit and abundance of warmth. Now and then he punctuated my expectant ranting with his signature endearments (which, admittedly, I occasionally steal for my own use) calling me "Girl" and "Cleverness" and "Hotshot" and sometimes "Mary Jane."

"Junior associate," I said to him, probably for the fifth time, "junior associate is right for me, I know it. It'll use the few talents I own, it'll tap my ability to synthesize." The prospect of it all had the significance of a long-planned vaca-

tion or a marriage when, in a buildup of painstaking prepa-
rations, you actually imagine it'll change who you are.

But Roberto listened and smiled at me. He fiddled with
his scarf. And eventually I descended into a provisional and
somewhat fragile sense of calm. I sighed and sat down on the
cool steps next to him, a gesture of relief and gratitude I
knew he'd realize was to thank him for his attentions. For
all my myopia and my avarice, there was one code that, with
Roberto, I would never breach—I would never exploit his
sweetness.

That night, I stared into the screen almost like an animal.
Everything during the day, it seemed, had conspired to
make Inez's appearance feel more critical. Though I
couldn't have said it, would never, is the truth of the matter, have slowed down long enough to notice, it seemed there
were years of tension I wanted to have wrestled out of me.
Without that I couldn't go on.

An order was already displayed across the screen when I
reached our private channel. She told me to get down on the
ground. "Down," she said, and then there was a lag. It was
never clear when the pauses were caused by the network's
sluggishness and when they were the work of Inez—Inez
making me suffer, making me want. Finally more words
came. "Get down on your hands and knees."

This wasn't new, it had happened before, but it further
pointed to what was to come and what, in contrast, I
couldn't already know. Again I found myself waiting. I was
waiting for sentences, words, waiting for anything.

She said, "There now. I'm standing above you. Edges in the cold stone floor are jutting into your palms."

I read more: "You can see the silver box, it's there to the left on the hard stone floor. You can see my feet. But you can only FEEL me lurking." She dropped to a new line.

"Don't . . . touch . . . my . . . shoes."

A kind of tremor ran through me. Surges of wanting presented themselves rapidly, only to be cut off at every turn. I imagined an alarm being set off in my lungs. I started to think I would faint.

Until at last she did it, she offered me something. It was something staggering, something new. I shut my eyes. "OK," she wrote.

I swayed slightly in my chair. I could barely read.

But she typed it out simply. "Now," she said. "Touch my dick."

# 7

## THE

## OVERCOAT

Maybe the excitement was simply too much for me. Maybe by nighttime my stellar behavior on the job, my unwavering efficiency throughout the day, coupled with an almost manic sense of triumph, ever so subtly took their toll, so that without my actually breaking down or even in any way acknowledging the exhaustion, my smoothly functioning faculties simply, for a second, shut down. It was as if, just for an instant, my keen, industrious, whirling mind simply took a pit stop and rested. It was a mere wink, like the sleep you barely slip into before the weight of your own nodding head jerks you alert again, but it set in motion all the tumultuous events of the next ten months of my life.

We were careening toward the holidays. Clearly winter had ceased holding back. That particular morning, I knew immediately upon stepping outdoors I could no longer use the word *brisk*, which had come in handy for many weeks past. Instead, even before I felt truly willing to apply it, I heard in my head the next adjective lined up for that season, the one with the authority and the pith—I huddled in my collar and pulled my sleeves over my wrists—it was *cold*.

But while all around town, along Frederick and Louis, along Stuart and Duane, that little iteration tripping through millions of muttering minds might have signaled some loss, might have made many feel embattled or put-upon or downtrodden, for this budding associate that winter it was just another challenge. It was one more test against which to prove myself sturdy. I was alert. I was happy. And on top of all that I was sailing head-on toward a salary hike, and I knew just the style and the price of the fabulous over-coat I'd buy with the very first signs of it. In fact, why wait to buy it at all?

So I stopped by Reine Nadine on my way home from work that evening. A whole new rack of sweaters lined the wall on the left, every one a heathery gray, brown, or black, and many of them designed with details and lines truly out of the ordinary. Almost all of them called to mind some scene or activity at once whimsical and harsh, like space travel or bondage or equestrian sport. Eddie had an ex-traordinary eye for suggestion.

"I came for the coat," I announced to him, entering, slipping right past the hello. I was exuberant, he could see, and he was pleased for me, before even knowing why. I suppose the prospect of a significant sale didn't dampen his sympathies either. "I decided, Eddie," I said, "enough hemming and hawing. I want it in time for the cold."

Eddie smiled back at me. From the outset, from the mo-ment when Eddie and Vera had first befriended me—having felt our customer-retailer relationship too cramped for the expansiveness of our terrific rapport—this smile of Eddie's was like a salve. It set me at ease, and once, during the very first dinner party they'd included me in, while I was describing an obscure childhood memory, that smile had even moved me to the quiet edges of tears.

Eddie was large. He wore a dark shirt open at the neck. He was solid, not flabby, but always a bit on the heavy side, possessing the sort of stature which, if you came upon him suddenly, you'd call "giant." Eddie was one of those men you describe architecturally, using words like "tower" and "frame." But his size belied his subtlety.

He came out from behind the counter, setting his mug very gently on the glass. His grin was attenuated, his movements relaxed. Clearly he intended to make the experience of this transaction linger, to draw out what was sensuous in it and minimize what was rote. He took my arm and started me on a languorous stroll to the front, heading toward the rack I'd pored over a dozen-and-one times while debating the purchase I'd now finally make. At last he spoke. "Come here," he said, intimately and deliberately. "Allons."

For Eddie, nothing was simple, no event hit just one note. For him, Reine Nadine, his fashionable and inventive, subtle and spare women's wear boutique was as politically charged and morally intricate as Paris must be to a scholar of urban histories. That little shop, with its stripped-down decor and one-of-a-kind downtown fashions, was for Eddie much more than aesthetically rich. It was fully stitched into the fabric of cause and effect in a world so large and abstract most of us don't even notice it. Even as we feed off its resources and walk its streets day and night, we see little of the city Eddie knew so profoundly, the ubiquitous buy and sell of it, the deep-down economic relations that make it be what it is.

He was the lost son of communists. The youngest of five

and from what I inferred the most sensitive, he had learned his mother's ways back and forth, from the baking of cheese sticks to be served at shop meetings to the "tsk tsk" of her commentary as she read *Today's Worker* and the private talks she held with the sheep dog, Minerva, whom she insisted on treating as a friend. I could see Eddie had gleaned from his mother a deep regard for community and a great sense of breadth. And all through his youth, he loved her just as hard as he loved his father—though not enough, as he saw it, to stop time with either of them and sit frozen in the moribund present of a beautiful and defeated ideology. So over the years he drew back. His mother, in the throes of losing her most intelligent child to a corrupt and hateful system, began, almost compulsively, filling and arranging family albums and organizing her shelves. At one point she stopped herself just short of proclaiming that she would forever despise his life, if not Eddie himself. His head hung over his knees in a near crouch on the low sofa when he told me this. But he had remained loving and firm. A streak in him of feistiness and persistence, and mostly a drive to know more, was what must have repaired the horrible rents in his heart as, over the course of those years, he turned and walked off from them, leaving behind him a heartfelt and far-reaching faith, while every step of the way it beckoned. Eddie was a man whose central burden in life was to face down paradoxes and outlive contradictions.

So that evening he let our seemingly simple transaction take time. "Here," he said, as he searched through the coats on their blond wooden hangers until he reached mine. He ran both his hands over the woolen shoulders and down the raglan sleeves. Then he paused, a calculated moment in which we were to stand there together and gaze at the marvelous item, as if this were some sort of show and we two were the audience, the coat the performer.

"Yup," he said, shaking his head. "It's brilliant." No one else I'd ever met ascribed intelligence to outerwear. "This narrowness at the hips is totally rebellious. It's subversive, Elaine, you see what I'm saying?"

I nodded and grinned, peeled the heavy coat off its hanger, and slid my arms into the satin-lined sleeves.

"So what's the occasion?" he asked me, buttoning me closed. The high collar and long waist and narrow hips—it's true—were not just unique, they were wonkish. Here was a garment that had the same connotations as eyeglasses, though its softness and folds kept it beautiful.

I ran my hands over the front of it, took a breath. "Well," I started, sighing and delighting not just in the sumptuous alpaca itself but in the whole series of events that had led to my knowing I'd buy it, "I'll tell you all about it from the beginning."

Then as Eddie listened and turned me around, picked the lint off of me, and tested the look of some scarves, I told him the whole tale of my pending promotion, starting way back with the first signs of approval from Accounting and ending with the hints dropped by Jean Fine, dropped like pearls in a glass. Eventually, engaged in my story and awaiting the climax, Eddie stood still. He crossed his arms and leaned his big torso up against a mirror where now and then I caught a glimpse of my outfit. And just as I was adding my newest installment (The Taciturn Boss: In Which Our

Heroine Learns of Her Fate and Gerald Sends Her to Brill)
Vera walked in, gasping excessively at the way my coat fit at
the neck and hit just the right spot at my ankles.

Vera was thrilled for me—about the job and equally so
about the overcoat. She gestured wildly with her sculpted
hands and practically hypnotized me with her compliments
and her rhythmic Colombian accent. "It's tremendous,"
she said, stepping back to look, "it's perfect."

"It *is* perfect," I repeated. "I'll take it."

In general, Vera was upbeat like this, and assertive,
sometimes even loud. Almost recklessly artistic, she was the
one who was behind it all. If Eddie's confidence and clarity
had meant that his life would at some point change radically,
it was his passion for Vera that determined just how. She
had urged him to try everything. When the two had first met
on a stalled subway car, under the yellow emergency bulb,
Vera had drawn him into a new form of discussion that
swept away his mind. It wasn't that it was frivolous or
flighty—it wasn't small talk by any means—but it was un-
burdened of assumptions and requirements, as brimming
with conjecture as it was with facts. By the time the train
began moving again, as they tell the tale, and the lights flickered back, Eddie had already touched her lips with his finger and she'd told him where to find her that evening. When
I met them, a full eight years later, they were still in the
midst of this romance. Although it was clear that Vera had
screwed around here and there—while traveling especially,
but once, too, with the guy downstairs—their relationship
remained a rich collaboration that encompassed the various
areas of their lives, their tastes, their acquaintances, and of
course their professions. Being with the two of them together

gave the impression you were not just the object of enjoyment, but were enveloped by it. Their link was a thing you could hold on to, the way you hold on to the railing of a promenade.

Now Vera stepped back from me. She looked, she turned me around. "OK," she said, pronouncing each word deliberately but confusing her use of pronouns and articles, "next time you buy the shoes, you hear me, you get half an inch higher."

It was Vera who did the buying and even designed some of the clothes. She had grown up in Bogotá, lived in Managua, traveled through the United States and Brazil, and everywhere she went, she kept a visual log of the uses humans make of geometry. She loved to study the strange ways shapes breed solace or tension or love, in all of their myriad manifestations, in jewelry, in clothing, in cutlery, vehicles, and shrines. Then she made leather belts and beaded gloves, decorated rooms and planned parties, all with her studies in mind. And when the two of them had found each other, and Eddie had been saving and Vera's uncle had died, leaving her a small sum of cash, they decided to try something that would keep them in one place at least temporarily and had built Reine Nadine from scratch.

To me, Eddie and Vera seemed to form an ever-expanding sort of unit, a pair of forces that informed each other endlessly and produced growth. You had the sense there was no end to how they loved each other sexually.

"Done," I said when I'd signed the check and clicked the pen closed. Vera was bent over across the glass counter, her chin propped on her palm. Eddie again had his arms folded, standing in close, and my package was set on the floor. You had the genuine feeling that this purchase was a thing all three of us had accomplished together. "We're gonna call you," said Vera, "for a dinner. Soon."

Later, when I finally got home, I was still gripped with anticipation and an almost obsessive self-satisfaction that bordered on smug. I was speeding through the evening, as through my whole life, with a kind of measured abandon. And that must have been why, when I signed on that night, I sped by one of the log-in commands that I'd typed in blindly so many times in the past.

One after another, the usual prompts came up on my screen. Nothing at all seemed odd. I was still feeling the tensions and events of the day trailing me like a perfume—images of Brill flashing through my mind, bits of carrot dislodging from my teeth—but I responded to the usual log-in prompts automatically. "Yes" I'm a member, I wrote. "VT100" for my monitor. "BXQI" was my age-verification code. "No" I don't need a new user-profile.

It was when I got to the last prompt that something other than my mind suddenly strayed: so did the fingers of my right hand. As I hit the hard return prematurely and the new screen quickly materialized, displaying the members present that night, I had no notion I'd passed by the function that asked for my nickname, the nickname which, for Inez, made me myself. Entirely by accident and without even the tiniest sense of its vast repercussions, I left myself out in the dark. I failed to sign on as "Francesca" and signed on instead as "Elaine V. Botsch."

# 8

## THE

## OPEN BOX

This time I wanted it in my mouth. How it happens that longings move through your body, shifting from place to place in your being like ancient animals in their deliberate migrations over spans of the globe, over generations, settling in regions from one continent to another to graze and to grow, I'm not in a position to say. Why sometimes the core of my wanting resides in the palms of my hands, the insides of my thighs, or deep up inside me, I am not equipped to explain. And yet the fact of this shifting is unmistakable to me, as real as the most well-researched anthropology. I always knew precisely the spot where my desire was lodged. So that this time, as I sat there awaiting her summons, entirely ignorant of the digital gaffe that had obscured my identity, I knew exactly where my cravings originated and satisfaction belonged. My hands were a pointless detour, a cul-de-sac, even if last time they seemed central. I wanted it in my mouth.

I wanted to taste it. I wanted its saltiness to surprise my tongue. I wanted to know intimately its hardness and softness—that particular tension between the two poles, balanced as purely as a mathematical equation whose solution is sex itself—I wanted to travel its hard and soft surface, wildly attentive, abundantly sure, with the delicate skin of my lips.

I could taste it already. The minute I saw that name, those four little shapes, written as if somewhere emblazoned or as if deeply, materially etched in, I had begun to imagine the shadow of it brushing up against my taste buds and my insanely awakened tongue.

But in all of this sexual extravagance, which, like some enormous libidinal celebration was crowded with fantasies and packed with feeling, there was one thought that was strangely absent: the fact that "Inez," who had been my paramour, who had taken me apart so many times now, bearing down on me with all that oddly loving brutality and making me come again and again, the fact that Inez, who had always been a "her" to me, no longer definitively was, didn't faze me at all. It made not a mark, not a chink, on the great hulking presence of my need. How ludicrous, you might think, that I simply didn't notice the sudden introduction of that part, that member, which she offered to me in our last encounter like a trophy presented amid the furor of the finish line, or, that having noticed it, I just didn't care.

It came down to nothing more than a problem of boredom, of plain old ennui. Because to ponder now, after all this time, the pronoun of her, the shocking possibility of her difference, would really boil down to exploring one elementary question, a question which, when compared with the thrill of what I'd been getting was, with all due respect, impossibly dull: Was it attached?

Was it connected? And if so to what? Was it attached to

that little spot on the body we all hold so dear? Was it fixed there permanently, fastened with matter we'd like to call "natural," with skin and sinew, material with which "she" had been born? Or was it, on the other hand, affixed with something unnatural, like nylon, for instance, or rubber, or like leather, something ambiguously in between? One way or another, connected or autonomous, held in place there with his or her hands, the object belonged to an incredible sexual genius, whose sole motive for wielding it was to find my desire and approach the sublime. And in the light of the extraordinary thrill of Inez, the thoroughly overpowering fact of the act, and the fantasy of the object inside me, this series of rudimentary queries seemed intolerably banal. One sentiment quite plainly asserted itself: why bother?

I sat before my monitor glazed over with lust, feeling a wetness, like wishing itself, collect, uncontrollably, in my mouth. My tongue was a muscle with a presence. I was lost in a recollection of that last encounter, the way she'd let me touch it then pushed away my hand, the way she'd convinced me that I could get near it and then lifted me up and turned me around.

As Inez transmuted before me, lost her form, her gender, radically, and reclaimed it anew only to lose it once more, I experienced all this lacking of certainty as a thing in the end I had gained. It was as if I were advancing up a slow, steady incline, gradually approaching the top, and as I got nearer, inching toward the crest, the view of the surrounding landscape expanded. Now, it was true that I lost something by rising, that all the detailed foliage and rocks on the ridge withdrew and were gone, as was the now-distant horizon, but equally, at the very same time, I gained in taking in the scope of things, taking in more and more breadth as I climbed.

Absently, I'd begun loosening my shirt. I was watching for a message at the foot of the screen. Transfixed by the feel of my own mouth from the inside and the memory of wrapping my greedy fingers around her, I'd begun to unbutton my soft cotton blouse. Nothing had happened. For minutes I'd been sitting there passive, staring at the unchanging screen, but no messages had come in.

I was flushed. Next I found myself untucking my shirt from my jeans. What, I wondered, was delaying her? I sat up straight. The longing was rising up through me, as if to escape, like air through the vents, with the loosening of my clothes. Is she ignoring me, I thought, is she teasing? My face grew warmer and a gust of heat seemed to sweep through me. God, I said, perhaps even aloud, whispering, she could torture me like this forever. In the ribbon of commands across the top of the window, I saw the time jolt forward one digit. I knew I would have to plead. It was more vivid than ever how officially I was owned.

But in the moment that I began typing, ready to serve up my little verbal supplication, ready to beg—it was nothing really to begin with, just "Inez, please"—I saw, like a flash of light in my unguarded eyes, the person my words were ascribed to. As if heaving myself out of my daze, I recognized what was happening. No wonder Inez had ignored me, I thought. My plea was ascribed to "Elaine."

Immediately I entered the change-name command. The server sent a response without a lag that came up at the foot of the screen, and though I knew what it would say, I read it over voraciously: "<Elaine V. Botsch> changes her name to <Francesca>." She would speak to me now, I was certain.

And yet, still I waited. At that point my real name, "Francesca," must have shown plainly at the top of Inez's display—in some darkened room, in some far city—and unless she were truly teasing me, punishing me somehow, or confused, there was no reason why she wouldn't have addressed me. It was already twenty-five past. I was leaning in, my arms and face covered with the ashen glow from my screen. My hands were holding the base of the machine, and all that sensation, so rife in my mouth just moments before, had gone out of me. Something new and strange had occurred, but in my building panic that it might be irreparable, I could barely consider what it was.

Finally I tried writing her again, though I had never, in all these months, been the one to speak first. I wrote out the line and rewrote it, misspelling and deleting, writing back over my scrambled words. "Inez," was all I'd come up with, "I'm ready. Whatever it is you want."

Still, there was nothing. A weird freeze seemed to set in to my bones, as if I'd been unexpectedly caught in the mountains, the sun going down, and my camp snowed in. I was stricken with the sense that I'd already been left by her. With me, the give-and-take, or the taking back, the waiting and the withholding, is like a tunnel. Sucked into a dark and isolated space, the space of blind desire and narrow vision, I am consumed with a longing for the other side. Nothing touches me but the possibility of that other opening. And often, when I feel myself wanting that fiercely, if a fear that the light is unapproachable sets in, I begin to forget myself entirely. Whole portions of my body, my mind, and my character begin to go dim. It is a kind of paralysis of want-ing, as if without regular activity my own desire can't live.

Still nothing happened. Short of losing sight completely of the tunnel's distant opening, I felt I had to say more. I added another line, composing it quickly but with fanatic concentration: "Anything," it said. "Inez. I will give you whatever you ask."

Nothing.

"Inez. God. Anything."

I waited.

Finally—the clock at the top of my screen now reading thirty-eight after—with no explanation, she wrote me. She sent it, just a number, a destination, "16." And if I'd ever been willing before in my life, then it must have been such a mild form of it as to belong to another realm, because the willingness I experienced in that instant that night, as I ra-bidly hit those keys, spelling out "goto 16," bore no resem-blance to what I'd ever called eagerness before.

Inez already knew everything: "You want it in your mouth, don't you?" she wrote.

I was mortified by my predictability. But with the mere mention of it, made manifest in those few unambiguous words, my awareness of the now-primary orifice came surg-ing back. Again my mouth was the site of countless decades of deprivation, the place where a new definition for the no-tion of hunger was now and forever being formed. How is it that, after all these millennia of spoken language, there's no word to stand in for that single particular longing—not "thirst," which is for water, not "loneliness," which is for love—but for the longing, simply, to suck?

"Well?" she said. She wanted me to say it, to tell her exactly how the craving felt.

I couldn't answer. I had no idea what to do next.

"Then get on your knees," she said. "Now." She waited, dropped to a new line. "Get down."

At that point, for me, it was almost as if it were already over. It was as if the whole thing, the arousal and the climax, had grown so perfectly vivid that it already existed, complete and autonomous, inside me. It had reached such a point of reality in my mind, like a disease fully blown, that there was no reason to do anything but watch it grow. And what was most odd of all was that Inez seemed to know this, or perhaps she had simply changed her mood, because what she did next was distinctly different from the ways she'd behaved before. It was not simply a variation. It was different in pace, in purpose, in tone. Inez, for the first time in all our violently passionate electronic encounters, had become gentle.

"Yes," she said, "baby. I know that you want it." The endearment was glaringly new. At first I couldn't tell if there was contempt in it or sarcasm.

But there was none. "You want it, I know, I can tell," she continued. "It's OK, I'll take care of you." She paused. "Tip back your head, sweetheart, and obey me."

And I did, of course. I obeyed her. I leaned back in my chair.

She said, "I'm taking your gorgeous face in my hands. It's burning."

Just like that, with that care and coolness, she kept talking. I read it as if it were destiny. Whatever she said, it didn't matter, really, because I felt as if I'd already taken it in. Her words were as close to me, as intimate and knowable, as the feel of my very own skin.

"Your face is hot, Francesca. Your neck is long. Your mouth is opening, and I'm running my hands through your hair."

I was swaying. Everything was brilliantly, crystally clear. There was only the barely audible question floating in and out of my mind as to whether I'd come now or after.

"OK," she said. "Now take it."

And at that moment, everything, the room and the screen and my own reading, my deciphering of the words and understanding, my very thinking and absorbing, was all one immense and spectacular metaphor for the act of penetration.

# 9

# THE

# PICKET FENCE

Just for a second during my clipped and perfidious conversation with Charlotte, I had the thought that even friendliness, civility, works on the principle of supply and demand. Brill's assistant was positively snide. Perhaps, I thought, flashing instantaneously on what could have been an eye-opening analysis if I'd given it some time, with her boss's generosity in such huge demand, Charlotte can exact an exorbitant price for it. She can scrimp on amenities. Then one more sliver of the unplumbed theory began to form: Was my own caring and sympathy solely a matter of surplus?

This little chain of concerns, however, was a barely detectable digression in the much more significant, indeed magnificent, narrative of my career. Here I was, after all, advancing it. I was high up in the executive suites. I was as high as it gets. In fact, you could argue that this visit to Brill's doorstep was the single most significant adventure, to date, in my entire professional life. "Charlotte," I proffered, "Can I trouble you? I need an appointment with Brill."

She was beyond disagreeable. "I'm sorry," she said,

meaning it not at all, meaning, in fact, quite the opposite—
i.e., "it gives me great pleasure to turn you down with impu-
nity."

But she was sorely misguided. I was not taking no for an
answer. "What do you mean," I asserted, "what do you
mean you're *sorry*? Fill me in here," I said, "because I
don't get that."

She didn't look into my eyes. She didn't crack an expression. "Oh," she answered, as if in passing, "Mr. Brill is
totally backlogged."

At that I spoke silently to myself with the unmitigated
sarcasm I save for the privacy of my own whispering mind:
How nice, I thought, now they've made it a *verb*; words like
"backlog" and "frontend," even as nouns, should never
have been allowed in the lexicon. Out loud I responded more
subtly, but enunciating like a pedant or a priest contemptuously withholding absolution, "When . . . will . . . he
. . . be . . . available?" I said. I inflected it just like a
question, but for all intents and purposes it was not.

Perhaps at this point for Charlotte the economics of our
little encounter were beginning to come clear. She seemed to
notice some adjustment was in order. She must have begun
wondering, right about then, if what I possessed was something worth owning, since in rudeness it was unmistakably
pricey. She softened, just vaguely, testing the market. "He
leaves town tomorrow and is out the rest of this week," she
explained, her tone growing businesslike, neutral. "He
doesn't return until Monday." Now she acted as if there
hadn't been the slightest acrimony, as if our discourse had
been simply what it was on the surface. How was it she
struck that exquisite balance between cordial and malicious,

so that the one always looked strangely like the other? Charlotte seemed to contain in her single big body a pair of intimate twins, one innocent and one diabolical. "But Monday
he's entirely booked up," she said. "Maybe on Tuesday he
can fit you in."

"Tuesday at ten?" I asked. I was tentatively suspending
my malice, since, by then, I felt I'd sufficiently driven home
my worth. Charlotte may never have admitted it, but she
had, we both knew, capitulated. Meanwhile, I had my far
more pressing purpose in mind.

"Yes," she said. "That will be fine." And she jotted
down my name in a datebook so pompous, so exaggerated in
size, it looked like an imaginary calendar for the heavenly
appointments of God. "Tuesday at ten."

Back in the maze of Poplar & Skeen hallways, cutting
left and angling right, breezing past desk after desk of assistants, I felt all my simple optimism coming back to me, the
savory sense of validation that the prospect of this promotion kept steadily making me feel. I passed Jean Fine in the
brick corridor and smiled, not even waiting in my confidence and preoccupation to see her return the kindness, and
I stopped by to update Kay. It was full morning and every
desk had a set of legs tucked underneath it, every monitor a
pair of eyes glued. There was work everywhere and hubbub.

Kay had her back to me and her feet hooked into the
base of her chair. I approached, considering her style and
her idiosyncrasies. I loved the way her dresses hung so heav-
ily off her shoulders. But what was most odd about Kay, as I
noted then and at hundreds of other various junctures, was
the way her aspirations were completely opaque. While on
the one hand Kay appeared empathetic about my hopes and

successes, on the other, the ambition that produced them in me was something she didn't share. She was complacent. The oldest child of an absentee father and a school librarian, she didn't seem to have any ghosts in her past who were egging her on. Kay had no proud, high-minded grandparents or paternalistic uncles prodding her with notions of what she should do, no fallen magnates or class-climbing optimists whispering sweet promises in the long halls of her genealogy or the echoey caverns of her mind. College was a thing Kay had enjoyed and grown up in and paid for with scraps and loans, discovering while she was at it some engrossing old novels and making herself eminently hireable, but in terms of a game plan or dreams of prestige, she had garnered there nothing more. I would never have sat still like Kay did, even years back when I was less willful, and these days her consenting to stay where the company planted her had even begun making me fidgety inside.

She leaned over the open file drawer to her left. She wore the usual gorgeous print, a sort of floral allusion to lawn parties of the elegant past, and reams of bracelets, some leather, some brass.

"Kay," I said. I startled her, and she swiveled. I raised my hands to my head and gave her a look of doom and anticipation together. I meant to convey a certain hysteria. "Not till *Tuesday*," I protested, though, in truth I didn't so much care. I was actually beaming. By now the waiting was only incidental, a minor addendum to the fact of my raise. Everyone had assured me that Brill was secondary to the process.

Kay leaned back over the file drawer. I could see two charms dangling around her neck, one a picket fence and one a coffin, the latter being, as only a few of us knew, a sort of antihomage to her father. Kay wore such an array of bracelets and baubles, all carefully selected and intricate in detail, all secondhand, that most people overlooked individual rings or pendants. She spoke rather flatly. "A week from tomorrow?" she asked. I could see immediately she was in a mood.

"A week from tomorrow," I repeated. "And, by the way, that Charlotte is a pain in the ass."

Kay sat up straighter, but she didn't stop working. "Oh, isn't she," she responded. Her voice had a chill to it which, as I'd learned over the course of the years, came and went with her frequent, conspicuous ups and downs. "Charlotte's awful," she said. "They should have cut her loose ten years ago." This was typical of the bitterness Kay would express when she descended into one of her dark spells, this sharp sort of judgment passed effortlessly by an otherwise tremendously forgiving soul. I'd learned to ride these moods like you'd ride a bike or a thoroughbred: you had to lean into them, not away.

"But so what," I began to explain. I could feel that, despite Kay's standoffishness, any minute I'd start up carrying on again. "It's just a formality, just a last safety net before final approval. Meanwhile," I said, "I've been figuring a million ways for Budgeting to tighten up its systems."

Now she was barely listening. On a different day, I knew, my closest work-friend would have been standing stock-still, pen dropped to the desk, gazing and listening raptly. She would have taken in every word of what I said with the warmth and intimacy of a long-standing pen pal, avidly reading a missive I'd written and lost in the romance of friendship. But not today. Today Kay was sunk in some emotional mud hole. And I wondered for an instant, as she slouched over her file drawer and ignored me, if moods were the single phenomenon on this earth that successfully resisted marketplace norms. Maybe, I thought, moods were the sole human goods you just couldn't trade in. Or was it that everything in the world that we know of, everything lofty or base, stone-cold real or ephemeral, was subject to the rules of exchange?

Eventually, I faced it that I wasn't being heard. There was no use waiting anymore. Besides, I could never have altered my own mood to meet Kay's bleakness, draw her out, and sympathize. I was too overtaken by the gratifying impression that I was single-handedly designing the future of the world. "OK, Cleverness," I said. "I won't run on. How about I stop by later?"

Kay didn't answer, or at least not audibly, and in fact seemed to withdraw some more, yet I was so full of high hopes and mercy that day I wasn't going to hold it against her. Really, I thought, all numbers and comparisons aside, who needed to be keeping score? So I wove my way back through Acquisitions, past Operations and several wagons of mail, and I reached the department in time to find Roberto, who grabbed my jaw and kissed my mouth, declaring, "A week from tomorrow, Mary Jane, you've got it nailed."


I suppose it would have been natural if at some point or another, through the course of the day, I'd have contemplated the future uses of that new organ, that prop. But I didn't. I didn't think of "her" dick at all that day, not once, not until in my hushed and solitary room I flipped the tight toggle switch on the left and saw the little light go green. Once again, she had something different in store.

I logged on at 11:01. Inez was already there. Clearly whatever had slowed her down the last time no longer mattered since this was the earliest she'd ever signed on.

"Go," she said. That was all. She didn't even give me a channel. Evidently, I was expected to find it myself or somehow to know it by osmosis.

I tried several channels we'd used before—16, 23, 24—but each brought up an empty white screen. She was making me hotter with every attempt, simply by not being there. I tried 18. I tried 25. A familiar, agonizing and yet glorious desperation began to creep in. I tried 34.

"Take your clothes off," it said. "Everything.

"Now, on the bed.

"Get down."

The timing was like a train car—it lurched. I felt in my gut and in each of my joints the undulant movement characteristic of fluids.

"Do it," she said. And then: "NOW." She always knew, even if it was a fact that existed nowhere but in my own mental universe, when I was timid or slow.

"OK," I finally wrote. I was dizzy, no joke. It seemed there was something unusually stern in her words, as if, in the next line, she were yelling. "Turn over."

"Inez," I typed, sort of pleading for time. "Inez, what?" I meant the question in hundreds of ways.

But she didn't wait for anything. She said, "There," and then repeated it again to pace me. "There. I'm running my finger down your back. I'm touching the bony length of your spine. You can feel my knuckle in your flesh. You flinch. Am I pressing too hard? Does it hurt you?'' she asked.

I knew, with the most withering clarity, that the questions were entirely rhetorical. I tried to turn over, but she knew it.

"No," she wrote. "Lie still."

I typed in, for whatever it was worth, because it was all I had the focus for anyway, those four letters over and over: "Inez."

"Are you ready?'' she said. "Francesca?''

And I could see that the use of my name had a meaning of its own. It had a meanness; the *s* was hard like a *z*.

"Francesca," she repeated. "Can you take it? Your back is smooth and it's raw. It's smooth and beautiful and naked. Can you take it, Francesca?''

She answered herself. She said, "You will."

And I knew right then, as my breath went out of me and the muscles of my neck suddenly froze, that Inez had lobbed some kind of blow. Dizzy and stunned, I couldn't tell where it landed. One long muscle along my spine started to spasm and reflexively I sat upright. She started to coo, to run on, in long, rambling sentences and fantasies:

"That's right, Francesca, now feel it. Feel the strap curl around your ribs, the tip of it bite into your side. And again—there—your sweet skin, feel it on the flesh that's cupped in the small of you, now it's beginning to sting. It tingles, it glows, the feeling increases, twisting to a fine, sharp point, like tiny wires that are no longer fraying, because everything's holding so tightly together, ready to thread through your soul."

By now I could tell she herself was excited. Her typing was slowing. A calm heat washed through my back muscles. I wanted to coax her on. "OK," I wrote, revising some errors made in the outpouring of keystrokes, but for the most part leaving them in, "it hurts me, it burnes, letme go."

"Not quite," was the answer, and I could feel her hands brushing the spots that were sore. She was making my skin quiver and grow warmer. Her touch was beyond calm and soothing; it was some other, much finer breed of control.

"Inez," I said, "let me go." I didn't mean it.

"When you're ready," she said, and the strap came across me again. She kept going. "There it is," she said, "again, and your back now is flushed, the room's cool and dim, but your body is red and glowing. Your back is arched and the belt cuts across all that gathering pinkness and the white sheets are under your skin. And my hand is huge—it's the color of nighttime—and the belt is bright fluorescent orange."

"Inez," I moaned at her, and then typed it. "Inez, Inez, that's all." Now I meant it. I wanted this to be finished. I wanted to lie there and feel the soreness spread through me, feel it dissipate evenly as the stinging turned to warmth and all my tension and terror reached the cusp of surrender.

There was a long, long pause. It must have seemed to Inez, who knew my patterns and depravity through and through, that this was the right moment to soften. And yet, when she sent the next line, something else, not in sync, not in rhythm at all, suddenly, inexplicably happened. Suddenly, Inez demanded a thing that seemed to me utterly irrelevant. She turned, she went sour. It was as if from this apex of hurt and longing we'd arrived at together she was just going to let me fall. I felt frustrated suddenly, almost mad; it wasn't in the least what I wanted. It was cold.

"What?" I said. I couldn't quite believe what she was asking.

But she sent the same message again: "Right now," she said, and she meant it. "Go to 1."

I felt an unprecedented fierceness, void of pleasure. What was she after? Was she just trying to keep me off balance? For a minute I was stubborn. For a minute I waited. Then I followed. One was a public channel.

Through the rest of that night, my always impenetrable paramour, Inez, seduced me and beat me, loved me and hurt me right there in front of the others. She forced me to dig down into yet deeper levels of abandon, to cut through more layers of humiliation and demolish more walls of fear. And there was no doubt that her strategy for diverting my attention, making me focus, appalled and powerless, on the shocking new fact that a dozen others were watching us, was having a profound effect on me: that night, forced to do her bidding in public, I just didn't get it that Inez was deliberately distracting me, that there was a thing she didn't want me to know. In the licentious thrill of being at once weakened by her mastery and empowered by the sheer quantity of sensation, all of it in front of a jury of strangers, I was thoroughly blind to her secret.

# 10

# THE

# DICK

It wasn't until bright and early the next morning, as the sunlight streamed over my newly waxed floor and the radio played some sort of classical jig, that I stopped short abruptly in my walk-in closet and acknowledged the astonishing fluke. I mused on it only briefly at that point since there was tons to be done at the office that day and my head was teeming with plans, but I did, for a second at least, stop to ponder the startling coincidence. For a second I actually felt slightly troubled by it, slightly, you could say, concerned.

My eyes landed first on the hook. There I was in nothing but hose and a shirt, weighing the brazenness of wearing too much chartreuse with too little black, and I caught sight of the clump of belts hanging there, dangling from the hook at the back. The resemblance did not get past me. What an oddity, I thought. For a moment I mused: How many people in the world could there be who not only have the taste for but actually *own* a patent leather belt that's bright Day-Glo orange? My eyes were fixed on the innocent accessory Vera had lent me so long before. I was staring as one stares, deep in thought, at distant glitter on the surface of the sea. It was

as if all the millions of people in our nation had been summoned to gather together in my mind and were shuffling
themselves miraculously into line, queuing up in my cranium
to be numbered. How many people could there be, I wondered, who would have bought such an item, and what's the
likelihood, if they did, they'd use it on me? Then, still in
that few-minute span, I found myself trying to account for
the element of fiction, that in this case, the belt was a fantasy; would that double the odds? Amateurishly, I did the
math. If hundreds of people owned belts just like this one
and hundreds more pretended they did, that could make my
chances of landing beneath one of them, stripped naked and
breathing fast, increase, let's say, to a thousand.

With this last calculation, I broke the seal of my gaze.
"Weird," I said aloud to a sensitive listener who was not in
the room but existed now and then as a chummy "other" in
my mind. I went on searching through my clothes on their
hangers. And then as I selected the little black skirt with the
zipper, eschewing any excess of green, I let the mini-inquiry
flutter off, gone from my mind.

But things would get much weirder. The day itself passed
rapidly, filled with small accomplishments and rewards. Everyone beneath me and even a few of my peers were querulous and needy for some reason, and I found myself not just
handling my own chores with composure but acting also as
mentor and adviser. Roberto brought me a pair of red
leather gloves that must have been imported from who
knows where, bought them for me on a whim, to go with my
new overcoat, and Kay remained so gruff and uncommuni-
cative that I opted—though warmly and without any real
resentment—to leave her alone completely. Eddie called my

voice mail and said I must come for dinner on Saturday since a hilarious designer from Brazil was in town and so was the daughter of a friend of his mother whom he'd last seen in his youth when they'd felt each other up in a park. It didn't strike me as the most appealing invitation. Nonetheless I welcomed the filler for my weekend, social or otherwise, to nudge the time forward that much faster as it headed toward my Tuesday swearing-in. My whole world—time itself and the cosmos included—was barreling toward that appointment.

Then late that night the further weirdness occurred. Another day was accomplished with its myriad, attendant details and challenges, and I was looking forward to nothing more than a good potent dose of forgetting.

With Inez, it was like that. With her I entered a zone out of time and materiality. There was no history there or gradations of morality, there were no past experiences to draw from. With Inez, there was nothing but a threshold, an edge, beyond which the future was a spinning concoction of love and evil absent of knowledge. And in the cradle of that future there was no need to remember the past or to weigh any choices before taking action because there was no such thing in that universe as error. In fact it seemed there was no need for anything, no *necessity* at all, inside the world of my computer.

She arrived and disappeared without signaling me. I took this to mean she'd gone to another room. Once again, I'd have to go looking. But this time, I found her right away, all alone in channel 31. "TAKE . . . IT," she said the minute my name had appeared there. This time, it was plain, she was shouting. "ACROSS . . . YOUR . . . FACE."

She had hit me. There was no greeting or lead-in of any kind this time, just this smack against my ear and my cheek. It felt as if something cracked or broke. My hand shot up automatically, checking for blood.

"Get up," she said.

This meant I must have fallen onto the floor. I imagined myself scrambling. There was no light in the room save the monitor's, and all around my chair, my legs under the desk, everything was cast in the blackest shadow.

"I said, 'GET UP,' " she repeated. "DO YOU HEAR ME?"

"I'm up," I typed in. I was already scared and elated. Out of fright, I was trying to anticipate too much. "What do you want?" I said. "What? What are you doing?"

"What do you think, little girl," she said contemptuously, "I'm grabbing you by your collar—don't fight with me. I'm getting a grip so I can hit you some more."

The fear was like pressure building, like restlessness or like lust, but much, much more. It was almost already over the crest of my coming. "Inez," I said, "What are you doing?"

"THERE."

And I felt it again. My face stung and my cheekbone throbbed and my vision transformed into two overlaid images, one partly tilted, one half clear.

But after that she didn't hit me anymore. She forced me to take off my clothes in the space of five seconds, yanking at the zipper of my skirt when she thought I was slow and shoving me onto the mattress, and then she flipped me over, and held me down, and did me the way I must have wanted it done to me forever, in the farthest, darkest corners of my dreams. She fucked me with that dick from behind, gathering strength like a runaway truck but steering me in precisely the direction she meant me to go in, and telling me everything I was feeling as I felt it in low angry tones that hovered over the bed like humidity. She did it to me like a victor or a martyr, a witness to our last days on earth, and she never stopped forcing upon me the pitiful truth of my size, the glaring fact of my smallness.

And just then, as the thing slipped inside me for the fiftieth time and twisted just so and the particles or bits that make up all thoughts and sensations began, in slow motion, to blow apart in the void, Inez's unstopping monologue veered off on the queerest new course, as it, too, began scattering through the infinite world of my pleasure. "There," she said, almost coming herself, I could swear it, "There, slut. You want a *promotion*?" And as my head tipped backward and my eyes half closed and my vision itself, at that point, seemed to dissolve into tiny flying pieces, I could tell from her words, she had climaxed, but all the rest of her message, something like "Yes, girl . . . get off," though it must have gone on many lines longer, was lost to me.

# 11

## THE

## DARK SCREEN

When I shut down my machine, it was 11:59, creeping up on midnight like a stalker. Still out of breath, the ringing of pleasure still echoing in the valley of my bones, I watched the half-dimmed ghostly glow cling to the computer screen for an instant, and then, with a tiny buzz, just like the static still humming on my skin, click to black.

Everything in me was blurred. It was almost like sleep or anesthesia. I sat motionless in the room, now a deep gray. It was hushed. I sat and stared for several minutes at the blackened, matte, impenetrable monitor, until eventually, in slow motion, my sex-drunken mind began clearing. My breathing slowed. There was nothing to see on the screen save opacity, but gathering now against the busier screen of my consciousness, bit by bit, was the world—there was time, a wealth of minutes and profusions of hours, flashes full of life to feed my mind on if only I could think hard enough to discern them. And gradually, with my eyes fixed in space, or in the un-space of the darkened screen, I did, I remembered.

Right off, I could feel an expression of amazement flash

across my face. The facts were egregious: Why in the world, I thought, would a stranger use the word "promotion"? My brain was reading backward in time, like a film in reverse, and within seconds it hit the next salient episode: Who else but someone who knew my wardrobe would have chosen a belt that was orange? My brow furrowed more. This was not a coincidence. You'd have to be willfully jamming your brain shut to deny it. After all, there were myriad colors in the spectrum to hurt with.

The promotion, the belt, room 1: for a while, still, I could barely connect the dots. Or I could, but I had to draw the lines over and over. It took time—it took some meditation, I guess—to shift from one dimension to another, from ether to earth, from Inez to real understanding. I stared but was no longer seeing the dark screen. Leaving the rarefied, unmuddled, and exquisitely clean communication of bits and bytes coursing through wires, I was passing into a quite different paradigm. It was the world. It had history and tragedy and scars. Out here the world did a very odd thing that made living in it as different from algorithms as rock is different from shears: it decayed, it got marred. Now I swiveled and took in the room. Everything in it, the bookcase behind me, the mauve and green card on the wall, the tipping tulips on the desk and the fat stack of mail, over time, became marked by its constant longing and failure to last. Out here, everything, including myself, had wants and suffered losses. Mentally, to get here from there wasn't easy.

But I did. Up out of my chair and into my Nepalese pajamas, I began to absorb the whole story, to order the facts, and to know them. As I took down my bun and got into the bed, unconscious at that point of the hour, and as the distant, steady sexual whining that had been nagging at my flesh faded away altogether, grew silent, the reality of the last four nights of my life rose up in me. I traced the events back further. I recalled my botched log-on and saw how it fit. I remembered Inez's mysterious delays and rethought every stitch of the web that connected us over the next encounters. I closed my eyes and recognized in the darkness of thought that another distinct individual, another sentient, learning being, had been through a transformation I hadn't been aware of. Who was it? Slowly I saw that this flesh-and-blood thing I'd encountered over and over in the air was someone who knew me, someone nearby, someone watching. Until, vaguely, perhaps an hour later, perhaps even more, I felt a sleep coming on that was tumultuous and perplexing and peopled with indecipherable possibilities.

The following day, I woke up soaring higher than ever on the currents of carnal satisfaction. Once again, my theory held true: that the rougher my owner behaved with me, the more inspired I became. It was as if the sexual sensation of last night's malevolence were still burning in my spine and fueling the most bloated, impacted case of denial I'd ever harbored. OK, I thought briefly while putting on my clothes, Inez may not be the un-person I'd assumed she was, I can see that; OK, she's some trivial acquaintance, some marketing assistant or deputy from sales I once met in the lunch line; but who cares? So what? That's no reason, I said to myself, to flub up your schedule.

"We'll make do," I said aloud to no one, lifting my silk blouse from the ironing board and shaking it once or twice adamantly. "Onward and up." There was music coming in from below. There was steam on my windows. I refused to be bothered with details.

And I think I worked harder that day, with a deeper concentration, than I ever have to this day. I don't envy the colleagues who saw me. Jean Fine and Gerald could only have been pleased, since I turned in three samples of rede-signed quarterlies, two more than they had requested, and I was one step ahead on annuals for Brill, but anyone who came looking for relaxed sociability must have found me remote and abrasive. Mine was more focus than a human could sustain while still roaming even the narrowest range of emotion. There was nothing *to* me but work and denial.

Then that night, the temperature dropped below freez-ing. I had spicy couscous for dinner at the nearby café since it was sure to warm me from the inside, and I could feel the beta-carotene and the vitamins going down with the heat of the stew. An old man at the table beside me blathered on about the pleasure of piping hot leeks and, though he must have had to repeat himself several times to get my attention, finally, I was able to agree. When I arrived home at 10:30, I was still checking long columns of the day's math in my head.

But at 11:05, I logged on. It was only then, as I sat, finally releasing my shoulders from an almost painfully exag-gerated professional posture, that I allowed myself again the new knowledge. Again, I saw the facts lined up together: the promotion, the belt, the botched log-on. And I knew at that point I was no longer simply meeting up with Inez. It was Inez and somebody else.

I grew nervous. I typed "VT100" for my monitor,

"BXQI." I waited. The usual names showed up on the opening screen along with a few unfamiliar ones. Mostly they were Latino or European, in keeping with the belief that good sex comes from afar: "Paulo," "Iliana," "Armand," "Claus," "Evelina," "Francoise"; some of the others were witty enough, like "Chiefjustice" or "Biggerthanthou," but most of them, "Do-me" or "Tarzan," were insipid. For the first time, though, in all my visits to the board, these names seemed to signify more than romantic fantasies. There was something much more cryptic, more ominous about them this time: they were masks.

I waited. There was no "Inez" yet on the list. I watched some banter momentarily in channel 1, then returned. It was 11:16. I remembered in a flash the way she'd shoved me violently to the mattress the night before, the way my huge and accelerating arousal felt like a will to fly. I waited longer. Softly, blankly, I tapped on the keys. I was feeling the hard spot, that metallic resistance, where the keys wouldn't give without more pressure from my fingers. Where is she, I intoned in my head, then lower, in my chest or my gut; any minute, I could feel it, the incantation could turn to moaning.

I began checking the typical private rooms. I checked every one. I checked twice. I kept returning to the members' screen to find out if she'd meanwhile logged on. I did a search, entering "Inez" in the "where" box, to see if she'd gone to a communal area I hadn't yet visited where you were meant to be courteous, not lewd. I checked the "lounge," the "round table," the "forum." But she wasn't anywhere. It was 11:46. I could conjure in my mind, against my skin, the sensation of being touched for seconds at a time, but immediately the illusion would escape me and the tension of not-having would inch up a notch higher. I was nearing the point where, too teased, too distraught, you want something so hard you have to stop wanting it altogether, or risk, you imagine, suffering an invisible and unknowable but permanent damage.

And then, at 11:57 that night, I gave in. I relinquished the now-senseless belief she'd arrive any minute, or even that she'd appear there at all, and I clicked the quit button and disconnected. I was wretched. I felt like everything I'd possessed a few days before had been filched from me, not just Inez herself, hard and constant and demanding, but Inez's whole identity. Why was "she" gone? I kept trying to figure, going back and forth, over and over it. And who *was* she?

I lay sleepless for hours. At two o'clock in the morning, I was still awake and almost pleading with myself to shut the thought-factory down. Had she disappeared permanently? Did she consider the failure of my anonymity intrinsically fatal to our liaisons? Would she decide I was off-limits and now and forever be done? Again and again I recalled her reactions and tried to gauge what she felt, why she'd waited so long on that first night after seeing my mistaken log-on, how she'd tried to distract me from her reference to the belt by steering me into room one, and how, last night, she'd vented a different kind of rage at me, treating me not as a slave or a criminal, but even more viciously than that, like evil itself, like scum.

I turned on the bed lamp and turned it off again. I turned on my left side and my right. I turned over and over in my memory whole pieces of feeling and seduction from my past and understood them from the other side. Nothing was positioned head-on any longer. Nothing appeared as it was. Suddenly Inez could walk in on me anywhere, in an office, in a room, in the form of someone I hated or revered or was irritated by, or she could disappear forever.

Yet she *had* returned to the board, there was that; I kept repeating it to myself, my head sunk into the pillow. Twice more after those horrid words "Elaine V. Botsch"—so precise and yet simultaneously so flawed—had clearly first alarmed her, had splashed across her screen like a brash, specious advertisement selling you nothing but disappointment—twice more she'd come back to find me. She had known who I was and yet wanted me anyhow. No matter who this Inez was in real life, there was no reason, I insisted, she couldn't keep meeting me anonymously. Why not just leave the thing as it was?

And this was the little thought that I finally curled myself up in, pulling the quilt up around my loss and confusion and listening to my own slowing breath. This was the timid hope I held on to finally, drawing out of it all the comfort I could and listening to the pacifying rhythm of my lungs, as I entered at last, around 3:30 in the morning, the ultimate limbo of slumber.

# 12

# THE

# CLOCK

I woke up distressed. A discomfort, a stiffness in my ankle joints and knees, the way all the contents of my body and head seemed to sag toward the floor, made me see the whole day before me as a trek, at best, not a flight. The trip from the bed to the coffeepot had tripled in length. My eyelids got stuck when I blinked. The steam heat had kicked on at six but still hadn't warmed up the bathroom. Even as, eventually, the delicately complex, woody smell of my perfume scented the puffs of moisture from my shower, and even as the tightness in my limbs gradually loosened, a low-level tension, an irritation, kept on. This was precisely the sensation I'd suffered many too-early weekdays in the old days when I'd had no Inez in my nights.

In the closet, I tried to ignore the belt. All by myself, I acted angry, almost mean. What did it matter anyway? I thought, baiting that chummy friend I conversed with in my mind, trying with no provocation to make the poor puppet feel bad. Who cares if you know someone's identity, if you know all their clothes? Who cares if in your waking life you're acquainted? It's archaic to be troubled by that. *Sex is sex, sadism is sadism*. The ranting was loud in my mind. I shuffled through my underwear drawer, agitated. Then I put on my simplest outfit, the black wool suit that hung like a plumb line from its squared-off shoulders and signified, according to Eddie, the contradictions of power ("a combining," he called it, "of the aloof and the soulful"). I drank two extra mugfuls of coffee.

And over the last cup, as the early light fell across my kitchen table and the high-pitched, lilting sounds of a kid telling tales came up through the vents from a neighbor's, I softened momentarily and confessed to myself that I cared. It was Thursday. Inez and I had never met up on a weekend, never on Friday or Saturday, so if she chose not to show up tonight, whether in order to impose a temporary punishment for my turning out to be who I was, or whether to permanently resign from the role of my lover, there'd be no telling for sure all weekend. If yet again she left me deserted in the late hours that night, I'd be forced to wait until Sunday for more. And worst of all, come Sunday, I might find out it was over. I both dreaded and egged on the day's passing.

The first mail in my box was from Scrivener. It was unusually long, with distinct blocky paragraphs, and it took almost three screens to scroll through. Watching all that text as it downloaded, I was antsy, almost disparaging, until I'd begun to read. Barely through the very first lines of his message, I was immediately engrossed by how uncommonly urgent and personal the words were.

"Dear E.," he wrote. "It's happened. I'm leaving town tomorrow first thing. But before I go, so that you can join me, in a sense, I'm going to tell you now what you don't yet know."

I was surprised. It was limpid and sad.

"First, my mother is an old woman and she raised me in poverty. When my grandmother died and I was a child, the last dim light went out on my mother's world. There was no more help or team spirit. My mother got in line for a spot in the nearby subsidized housing. She fed us canned beans and bread. My grandmother's landlord evicted us. We slept in three SRO's. When we got the two-room unit in the projects, my mother looked out on the dirt yard and hated it forever.

"I had a white teacher in first grade. All of us boys grew tired of her accent. As the boredom set in, the woman seemed farther and farther away. There were two white girls in the third row and seven Latinos. My best friend was named Cal.

"When my mother had her next child, I was awestruck. He had tiny hands. His skin was no rougher than air. My mother buried her face in him and laughed or sobbed. She had lost her job. When she had her next child, and last, we moved to the tenth floor and Louis the slim one joined us. And then Gail. Louis vanished at dawn. Cal drew Satan on the stoop in chalk. Gail dressed like a stripper but ran the house like a man.

"There's no way to say exactly how I arrived here. It would be more than a book. My brother Reece died, but Cal became a teacher. He trains technicians to use microscopes and draw blood. Meanwhile, I learned more than there was to go around in that neighborhood. The more I learned, the more my cousin teased me. He said, Too bad you can't eat what you know. He said, You think too much. I said, Try to stop me. I stood in front of him, staring, knitting my brow.

"I learned more than there was to go around. I learned

more than my mother twenty years older. I learned more than my dead brother and the lame woman across the way. I learned more than any man I've ever met, white or black, about electronic files, searchable networks, indexing, fisheries, the history of chess. But my mother is almost dead.

"I'm returning home. Last night, my mother was admitted to the hospital. There's trouble in her lungs. There's trouble also in her kidneys. You could say there's trouble all around. She won't last long, the doctor said. Which makes me think, you can walk very far and no one will know it. But you can always walk back. Yours, Scriv."

The letter amazed me. After all this time (years) and all our notes (scores upon scores of them) it was the first I'd heard of the poverty, the best friend, the color of his skin. Once in a while, Scrivener had mentioned two brothers, making some noncommittal reference to stasis or bitterness or fatigue, but never before had I heard about his childhood, the projects, Gail, or Cal. And never had I seen that kind of prose. Of all the ways Scrivener had written me, of all the obscure lexicons he'd drawn from, the bizarre diction he'd stolen from a far-off period of history or the obscure jargon he'd lifted from the social sciences, and of all the quirky ways he'd formed sentences and clauses and rhymes to present whatever his accurate information, I had never heard this kind of poetry. The man baffled me deeply.

But there was more than bewilderment that I felt, the letter finished, the rest of my mail finally read, deleted, or sorted into files. I also felt sad for Scrivener, and I felt anxious. This seemed like much too much leaving at once— and too much confusion. Everyone was becoming someone else. The stark newness of the character Scrivener had suddenly divulged to me, coupled with the terrible transformation of Inez into flesh, underscored how much, at any given moment, you simply can't know. I felt not just puzzled by Scrivener and his ever shifting identity, but a tad lessened as well. Who am I, I thought, if he's that? And when will anyone tell me?

Later in the day, Jean Fine drove it all home again. By then I was more energetic than I'd felt in the morning, though slightly more agitated as well. Not least on my mind was the sense that Inez was present, somewhere amid the endless halls, floor after floor of workstations, ready to hurt me for real, or worse even, ready to leave me. I felt steadily taunted and troubled about the night's prospects—would she log on? would she continue?—as if I had learned of a top secret file, containing a comprehensive set of notes on my destiny, that the authorities refused to release. Inez had become a constant participant in my waking life.

Then just like Scrivener, out of the blue, Jean Fine began acting odd. Why now? Calling me into her office unscheduled, ostensibly to peruse the new layout for quarterly graphs, Jean Fine suddenly broke in on herself, and in a cordial, yet inclusive almost familial tone, started to talk about "us." "I've wondered," she said vis-à-vis our fruitful collaboration on the redesigned graphs, "if you wouldn't some time join the family for supper. We occasionally have a guest or two in for dinner Sundays. I just bet you and Dennis would get along." She laughed, fingering the blue buttons of her blazer. "He's almost as dogged as you are."

"Well, Jean," I said, caught entirely off guard, "that'd be great." I blurted it out with zero grace. I couldn't imagine why she would suddenly see me as a friend or what in the world she envisioned me discussing with her husband. He was a jocular, rather dirty-minded cardiologist I had never seen Jean actually converse with at the division's holiday parties. The two of them always seemed to be attending events solo. Now I had the distinct, creepy feeling that Jean Fine was trying to cast me in a role opposite him—though in exactly what drama I couldn't make out.

She continued: "He's asked about you before," she said. "And I don't think you've ever met Dolores."

"Well, Jean, that'd be great," I said again, verbatim. I felt utterly bewildered.

Then, at that point, she seemed to grow pensive. Before our discussion had a chance to formally wind down, she'd begun looking away. "A fine Fine," she mumbled, as if engaging herself in some secret repartee, speaking, I supposed, of her daughter. "That's what we call her."

And so by the end of the day, though I'd accomplished enough and managed to thoroughly overcome my sleep deprivation, I felt in a way missing, as if it weren't I who was doing my life. It seemed everyone's story was more important than mine. And it didn't help matters that my own story, the one about loss and Inez turning out to be someone else, was a secret I was harboring alone. No one but Scrivener could have heard it, and Scrivener was gone. I was all emptied out by the vacuum of my isolation.

So when I signed on at eleven and a raw, wintry rain could be heard tapping against my windows despite the heavy drapes fully closed, I felt a different kind of yearning. It wasn't fueled by the usual excitement but by a mild sort of righteousness and a driving desire to prove to myself that my story was real.

Or was it? It was 11:14. She had not logged in. 11:20.
11:21. Even after the events of the previous night, the truth
of it was slow to dawn on me, hesitating, like some kind of
neurological lapse, before taking effect on my psyche. 11:23.
I knew this delay was not a part of our game. 11:25. But I
didn't want to *feel* it.

Gradually, as if to coax me awake out of a long far-off
dream, the patter on the glass grew vaguely louder, as did
the hum of the fridge and the hiss of tires on the street in the
rain. The entire room seem to reorganize itself deftly around
me. Something, if not the existence of Inez, if not her words
on my screen or the whole drama of our romance—something else, then, had to be true. You can't forget forgetting,
or if you do you're utterly lost, meaning this: if the world of
our trysts, that cool stone chamber of my other life, was the
place where everything I knew of the past, both far-reaching
and recent, was supplanted by lust and submission, then to
leave that fantasy behind was nothing other than, in reverse, to remember. If with Inez, memory itself was canceled
by all that nakedness, all that forfeiture, then now, it
seemed, I had to go back to it, to the real events of my life.
There was no Inez to keep me listing forever into the future.

The streetlight seeped in from under the drapes. On my
desk, a red dish was covered with crumbs. The analog clock
on my bed table could be heard, just barely discernible from
the faint tapping of the rain on the glass and my fingers on
the keys, arduously, steadily ticking. I shut down my machine at half past.

# 13

# THE

# JEWELS

In retrospect, to say that Friday was the worst day of my life only makes me laugh. It had been only two nights without her. The effects of this lack of sexual discipline had barely started to set in, and I can see now, gazing back over some years, my search hadn't even begun. But it's true, nevertheless, there were moments that day when my once climbing confidence seemed to drop so dramatically I thought I'd be sick to my stomach. Meanwhile, laid out before me in the hushed and highest court of my mind, the facts of my case seemed absolutely, unbearably bleak. I could see that. Intermittent but overwhelming waves of despondency would come over me, these heaving masses of anxiety that would make me literally stop in my tracks, as I'd suddenly ponder the evidence.

I froze, for instance, by the vending machines. I was on my way back from lunch. To my right the hulking soda dispenser seemed to tip toward me in the hallway as I planted my feet and stopped short. The truths lining up in my mind bore more weight than my own flesh and frame, and like a doll that topples over and springs back by the force of its base on the floor, I swayed and swung to a stop at the memory. Inez was gone. She had discovered my identity and spurned it. Out of a sense of—what? propriety, respect, disinterest, repulsion?—she had decided that the person I was wasn't right. She could no longer continue to go through with it, knowing my name, how I looked, what our ties were.

I spun around as someone brushed by me. My mouth was open to speak, impulsively and irrationally, to accuse a total stranger of spying. A scrawny, half-bald sales guy was eating a sandwich as he passed and fortunately didn't notice the spontaneous indictment I'd flashed at him. All morning I'd thought someone was watching. The receptionist in Billing, the lunch woman stocking cups—half the time my guesses were wildly illogical, but I couldn't help feeling that Inez was nearby.

Yet for me that wasn't the half of it. Far worse than the multiplying lurkers or the loneliness and unmet cravings that would ensue without her, was the ruinous effect this loss of Inez would have on my finally rewarding career. I knew this would mean a return to the life I'd been living so uneventfully four months ago. I knew, like you know the slightly haunting sound of your heart after running up steps, that all the grace and security I'd felt lately would now be slowly depleted.

I stood by the candy machine, thinking. Its dark innards, the tilted bars and bulging bags poised to tumble frontward against the glass, had a look that seemed awkward and alien. I was adding up the realities. If all my recent advances, my proven merit on the job and my burgeoning competence, if all that coincided so precisely with the start of our trysts, which it did, how could my performance not end up slipping without her? I could see it all by now clearly—that each time she'd grown more force-ful with me, I'd experienced at work a corresponding boost. Strapped down, for instance at night, tied with the red satin cord, the next day I would easily outstrip my record and write up three charts in an hour. Or, say, degraded some night by her name calling—"Whore," she once typed at me, "or is it Cunt that you go by?"—the next day I'd be giving advice to the seniors in Marketing. And those rare times when Inez was slightly less hard on me, the next day I'd hit a plateau in my progress and feel neutral or shy or numb.

I guided myself back to my desk. Living without Inez would be like the old days, I thought. It would be just like that period about five years back, when I worked for a small firm of accountants and at night had nonverbal repetitive sex with a lover who hovered around in the mornings saying practically nothing but "Where are you going?" "When will you get back?" In those days, I remembered, my officemates barely knew I existed. They often didn't even remember my name. They'd call me Connie or Janine—both of them names of my predecessors—but I was so used to being polite and efficient that most of the time I didn't correct them. I'd just answer intelligently and follow through. Then, even though I'd permitted, if not cultivated, my own invisibility, I'd go home at night shocked that I'd gotten no feedback and convinced I must not have worked very hard.

I settled in back at my workstation. For hours, all that Friday, I tried doing the usual tasks. At intervals, I man-aged to function by rote, but twenty minutes later I'd lose my place again. I'd fiddle with a pen, flipping it over and over, or gaze down blankly at my keyboard.

What worried me more than anything at all was the prospect of my appointment with Brill. Staring past my plaid office curtains at the bank of sooty windows on the opposite wall, I barely gave a thought to my sex life. I felt tepid physically, devoid of lust. In fact, I had practically no sensation. Instead what riveted me, what seemed to grip me around the ribs or the walls of my lungs, was the fact that the meeting was only four days away and I couldn't dig up the smallest belief I was fit for it.

By Saturday I'd turned more philosophical. I was putting away the groceries. I was bent on getting down to the logical roots of this twisted array of circumstances. Friday had passed, filled with those dramatic, sickening dips in my mood and then rallies, and now I was fighting to master the deeper reasoning that would explain this whole predicament. True, I thought, there's a logic to this of some kind or another. It was strangely inherent, unattached to bigger, overarching patterns of cause and effect—like how heat causes melting and propulsion makes speed, or how food assuages your hunger—but somehow, in its own way, still sensible: what on-line in the ether beat me down, at the office in the day propped me up; it was reciprocal; it was *inverse*. And this, I thought, was a strange living metaphor for the way anyone, in a system like Poplar's, advances. It was just one instance of the ubiquitous give-and-take, the payment in every human relation, and the way power, so rarely and always so grudgingly, changes hands. I thought, at the doctor you offer up your privacy in exchange for what he calls health, and in the municipal building you fish around for any kind of currency—your citizenship? your cleverness? desperation?—to swap for the signature you're after. You give to get in a million different ways in a million different economies.

I did household chores. A decided, evenhanded chill descended on the city, the kind that doesn't budge with the wind or modulate in the sun, the kind you can't count on easing up soon—not for now in any case, not until some thoroughly unexpected moment, when you stand still in the tinselly sun at the bus stop, relax your muscles suddenly, and remark lightly, surprised, Hey, wait a minute, I think it's warming up. The chores kept me only marginally distracted, however. Over and over, in the midst of pressing a collar, vacuuming the floor, I fixed on the tiniest signs of my backsliding. I kept checking: Am I confident now? how about now? am I crestfallen? right this minute—stand up straight—would I be able to assert myself proudly?

Only later, at the dinner party I'd agreed to attend just to kill time, did I finally stop trying to fathom that sweeping vision of perpetual exchange to focus instead on a hope. It was a slim hope, at that point, a flicker of inspiration, but it gave me a way to proceed.

At the dinner table, I was restless. I was bored. The Brazilian designer, who, I quickly understood, was on a hunt for a babe, was really not funny at all, or certainly not so uproarious as he seemed to consider himself. When he laughed, you could practically see the gummy ridges on the roof of his mouth. His shaven head was rather beautiful as were his hips and his clothes, but in general his slightly-too-big personality repelled me; I was tempted to take a dessert and go home. Vera sat at the other end of the table and ignored him. She seemed, in fact, overly enchanted by an

ethereal boy sitting beside her who couldn't have been more
than twenty-five. Eddie was gentle and reflective and typically warm all through the meal, but my attention span was
compressed to the size of a crumb by the gathering weight of
my worries, and I couldn't consistently listen. His inquisitive thoughts and quiet protracted sentences floated past my
mind and frequently wafted off entirely. I kept eyeing the
pink kitschy princess phone and the lush green painting
Vera had done that represented what you'd get if you
crossed a blighted cityscape with a forest. I stared at the big
brilliant canvas or the velveteen couch, and I couldn't bully
myself into listening. I was thinking of something wholly different. I was thinking of Brill and my lack of physical serenity. How could I insist I was someone worth my salt with this
constant tautness around my skull and this leadenness in my
shoulders?

So as Eddie's childhood friend Tasha started expounding
on the hardheaded protests their parents had clung to, and
as Eddie looked down at his fork, not quite willing to agree
with her own equally hardheaded optimism, I got up and
wandered to the bathroom. It wasn't even that I needed to
go; it was more that I couldn't get comfortable; and before I
was halfway down the short hallway, I'd veered from my
original path. The guests sat by the arched windows around
the table at the far end of the room. There was a swelling of
voices and laughter. Vera was touching the hair of the ethereal boy. I'd forgotten where I'd meant to be headed. Tasha
was mocking her mother's outmoded slogans—"There's no
marble stairway for the working man" and "Class mobility
is a myth," I heard her saying. I had roamed into the well-lit
bedroom.

Unlike the front room with its purple sofa and flamboyant knickknacks, this room was elegantly plain. Our various overcoats lay piled on the high simple bed. There was practically nothing on the walls. But over to the left on a broad asymmetrical dresser, covered with a slightly chipped indigo Formica, there was an excessive display of jewels. There were beads and pearls and rings. Strewn across the bureau in big spilling curves was a glittery mass of colors. My eyes passed over a string of glass octagons and a saucer full of rings. I took in the cluster of rhinestones and ran my gaze along a strand of fake pearls. And then I noticed that half-buried under a heap of blue baubles there was something incongruously metallic. It lay tangled among the cobalt spheres. It wasn't pearly and it wasn't glass. Almost listless and yet in some removed way still curious, I wandered up close to the dresser to look. I had just enough interest to want to identify the object that didn't belong there, while at the same time half-contemplating Tasha, thinking how really her mother had a point: economic status is a prison, I said to myself; upward mobility—she's right—is a farce.

And I realize now, in retrospect, having had a couple of years to ferret out the turning points of my story, that the sight of that object spurred a new resolve. The sense of defeat, which had been feeling more and more oppressive inside me for days, found its match just then as I stood in that bedroom, staring at that small clump of steel. I saw that the solution could be simple. It wasn't that I suspected Eddie or Vera, at least not lucidly, not yet—my *friend* Eddie as Inez? that was far too outrageous a supposition—but I realized that with effort I could find her. I could know who she was. Inez, after all, was someone, someone who knew me, someone nearby, and someone conversely I must know myself. She was also the key to my future. From here on in, I vowed, I would track her down, whomever "she" was, to draw her back into our deal and retake any ground I'd lost. A tiny weight lifted from my shoulders. My throat filled with what tasted like purified air. For minutes, it seemed, I stood in a daze, making this promise to myself and staring dead-on at that tangle of blue beads and the shiny, half-opened handcuffs.

# 14

# THE U.S. SENATOR'S BIOGRAPHY

So the point was to search. The point was to find her. How could you let a genius like that whose orders and caresses gave you not just pleasure, not just your standard corporeal rush, but on top of all that gave you power—how could you let someone like that simply drop out of your future? You had to find her and put up a fight. You had to say, Please, whatever you want from me, let me feel the skin of your palm, let me come back from this cold kind of dying, I'll do whatever you want.

In the past, what I'd wanted from this mysterious sexual fiend, whose presence in my life had so radically changed things, was ultimately only one-dimensional. It was physical. I wanted that straightforward, fleshly relief. Yet now in the knowledge of the effects Inez had on me, and as the notion that she was out there, not far, became ever more real, I'd begun craving something more elaborate. What had once been a common case of lust, albeit in the details peculiar, was all intertwined with a driving, calculating ambition. I wanted not just sex from her but I wanted winning, the whole human extravaganza of sex and talent and celebrity. I wanted success and I wanted forgetting. And I knew Inez could deliver. All this time she had made it work for me; she'd made everything that was memorable, everything in the world, from the politics of Asia to the drought in the valley and Kay's icy expressions—she'd made it melt into practically nothing in the pale glow of my monitor. And while all of that life and history, the city and the world, alleyways, town halls, prison cells, peep shows, kindergartens, basements, and all the human individuals inside them—while all of it would dissolve with the smack of a hand on my flesh, something simultaneously would grow hard in me: the prospect of doing, the ability to possess, the know-how and wherewithal to "get somewhere."

On the other hand, at times, I feared the prospect of finding her. How would I reconcile my Inez's identity with someone whom, for instance, I abhorred? Imagine. What if Inez turned out to be Charlotte, for instance, or Brill? Or what if she were *Gerald*?

Yet most of the time, my desire was greater than my fear, greater than any petty judgments about specific colleagues and their unappetizing personal traits. Most of the time I simply wanted her to come back to me and make it all happen again. I wanted to be broken and then to rise up, to get handshakes and honors, to get bonuses and love. All of it, the winning and the coming and the kneeling down, in my mind, now had one simple name, and I wanted to spell it out everywhere: it was Inez.

I succumbed to it all day Sunday. There wasn't a book on my shelves or magazine in my stack that could compete with that single longing. I was stuck, distracted, a few chapters into the biography of a United States senator who supposedly pulled himself up by his bootstraps but who, it

turned out instead, was no more than a generation removed
from French aristocracy. Again and again, I'd reread the
same paragraph, only to lower the book to my knees and tip
back my head to the wall. My eyes would shut automatically.
I'd envision a sketchy but dramatic encounter with the real-
life Inez that I'd finally identified, the one who, at that very
instant, as I blithely nursed along my little daydream, was
lurking somewhere in my life. I could feel myself walking
toward her or him, my neck cool in a breeze. The surroundings were almost indiscernible as was the key player's face,
but I could hear my own voice ring out clearly. "You're
'Inez,' aren't you?" I'd say urgently. "So it's you then.
You're the one." Then the tall murky figure would turn to
me. I could feel my hands making fists or reaching out to
grip the firm wrists of the lover I'd finally discovered. My
breath would get short. "Please," I would say, "You can
have me." It was as if all my most vulnerable body parts—
my throat and my sternum, the pocket of my heart—had
split down the middle, falling open, making way for the vio-
lence that was coming. I was so ready to be brought down, so
ready, in fact, that the strength it would generate afterward
was beginning to collect in my forearms.

I repeated the scene over and over. I could see the approach, the meeting; I could make out the words. Sometimes
right away, the shadowy figure would hit me. I was up
against a wall, in an alley or hallway. Or was it the supply
room? Was it the stairs? A sense of renewal, of my own
potency and purpose and self-knowledge, would fully surge
in. There'd be a scuffle, an embrace. Then this indistinct
incarnate Inez would reach inside my clothes, his or her
touch and roughness precisely like those masterful hands

that had reached for me before in hundreds of digital messages. "Don't," I would say, "don't ever leave me again."

And again, from the beginning, I'd replay it. I'd watch the story repeat once more in my mind. Fragments of it varied—the look of the floor or the pavement would change, the tint of the overcoat might alter—but each time there'd be an image, a form in a coat, a hushed passageway, an encounter. "It's you, isn't it?" I'd say. "You're 'Inez.' "

For dinner I boiled beets and stirred them in with noodles. I shuffled through some magazines to kill time. Frustrated, halfway through the meal, I pressed my hand flat on the table. Who *is* it? I thought. There's no way I'll know before my appointment with Brill.

I logged on at 11:10, though not in my heart really doing so. By now, I believed firmly she wouldn't show up, and she didn't. Nicknames were reserved indefinitely by their sole users and hers was nowhere in the system. I hung around on the members' screen, in the public rooms, half-attentive and wide awake but completely disenchanted. I read through the conversations taking place in room 1 but without registering their meanings.

Later, sitting in the quaint wooden rocker I hardly ever used, I went back to the page of my book I'd read earlier without having registered that either. And yet this time I was strangely drawn in to the story of the mendacious, upper-crust senator. Finally something in his tale seemed pertinent, and I felt, just a few sentences in, as if I deeply and poignantly understood him. I saw the arc of his life, the base and pathetic attempts he had made to change it. In truth, there was no rise or fall for this man, despite the campaign tales he'd spun about the ramshackle ship his family had escaped on from France and his rugged youth on the farm, about his mother's stoop and half-missing finger; in truth, there were no bootstraps or breakthroughs; instead, he'd stayed forever fixed in the social position of his grandparents and their parents' parents before them. Line by line, I experienced a slowly swelling empathy for this desperate opportunist, as I saw how the facts of his past, the tastes his family had taught him, the ideas they'd trained him to love—the whole body of styles and beliefs of his forebears—were etched in from end to end of his consciousness. I saw just how entrapped he was in the one life he ever could have.

And as I closed the book, the memory of my own plight poured in. What if I never do find her? I thought. What if, for me, nothing can change? That ravaging touch, those measured blows and those heady waves of strength and courage—what if I never again have them?

15

# THE

# SILK SCARF

I don't take for granted the pleasures of biography. There's a lot to appreciate in a definitive book that has sifted through rumors and guesses and compiled only what's still true after plenty of checking and corroborating. There's a lot you can enjoy and absorb about a person when you have that kind of rigor to lean on. In real life there's nowhere near so much buttressing behind your social relations. The people you meet and come to depend upon and who you think you know fairly well—with them you don't get to consult a biography. You just have to trust what they tell you. And of course, in my case I couldn't. Someone in my life was deceiving me, or at least avoiding the truth.

I could count on one hand, roughly speaking, the people whom it might have been. I don't often talk about triumphs that haven't yet come to fruition, and I'm not one to brag about anything without fear of cosmic reprisal. So the people who knew about my promotion were few. Those who did would had to have seen the psychedelic belt I'd worn only on workdays and which was a critical piece of the puzzle. All this I thought through down to the smallest minutiae. My secret lover had to have been a confidant at the office or a friend like Eddie whom I saw en route to it. Beyond that, he or she could only have been some management type I wasn't aware of, who had been in on the hiring procedure and had taken special note, on some key occasion, of my outfit.

But who? All I knew for sure was that someone out there, one among that small pool of candidates, knew more of my biography than I'd planned. Someone had a raunchy kind of profile on me for perusing at will, in secret, and for gauging my true weaknesses when I least expected. And it was precisely that likelihood that would make me so horrifically embarrassed late in the day Monday when I hypothesized which one it was. I blushed. The indignity of it was partly in being duped, I realized. Here was the culprit, the voyeur at the peephole of my center. I wanted to get up and run.

In fact, I'd felt embarrassed all day that day, ever since I'd peeked open my wary eyes the very first thing in the morning. Some kind of psychological toxin that causes chagrin must have seeped into my dreams and poisoned my brain chemistry upon waking. I'd felt inadequate. I stumbled over the book I'd left on the floor by the bed table. Up until now I'd greeted my workweek with a vigor and spirit worthy of a well-rested evangelist, holding back enough to avert only the most hyperbolic associations—i.e., dewy petals, rising suns—but that day I woke up feeling sluggish. I felt spent, as if I'd emerged from the nighttime smack into the middle of the week.

So my first feelings of shame, upon reaching the office that unpleasant Monday, came from the absurd, overblown guilt that I'd slept through whole days full of responsibilities. As I read through my mail I expected any minute to find out what critical meetings I'd missed. Twice I clicked on my instant calendar to recheck the day of the week. And twice I glanced up at my door with a burst of paranoid fear that the shadow of Jean Fine had passed in front of it, the tall warden coming to inform me there was an appointment I'd failed to attend. I had to actually say it to myself, to reassure myself explicitly: no one was here working on the weekend.

Later, in the bathroom, a different kind of embarrassment took hold. I was looking in the mirror and washing my hands. I remembered a similar emotion I'd felt, a kind of shock at the sight of myself, when I'd seen in my reflection I was missing an earring, and now my hands shot to my ears to make sure the day's faux ruby studs were in place. But this time it was something else that felt amiss. I peered closer as I toweled dry my hands. This time it was my features themselves that seemed somehow distorted. There was a pinkness all around my eyes. My lips looked too thin. My bony nose—which, if carefully accessorized by the right style of clothes, hinting at classical Greece or some other exotic country, could be construed as sufficiently elegant— came off instead as homely. My bun was slightly off to the left but would take too long to redo. And why in the world had I chosen that morning the shirt with the old-fashioned collar?

Still later, when Roberto tapped on my door, I didn't want him to look at me. I brushed my fingers over my lips, thinking there might be a crumb or a smear there, though I hadn't eaten anything for hours. I didn't even have the presence of mind to say, How're things.

But Roberto of course gave no indication that my hairdo

was off-center or my face so haggard. He was gesturing me toward the stairwell. "Come," he said, in an animated stage whisper, his lean torso half in and half out of my doorway. "You need a little coaching." He was going to give me pointers for Tuesday.

"So all right, Elaine," he said when we reached our cool hideaway at the very bottom of the stairs, "what's your strategy?" He had me by the elbows and was bending down to sit in his spot on the concrete. Around his neck was his most satiny scarf, the one with the gold seed shapes and the violet gladiolus. "You know you'd do the same thing for me, Cleverness; I want to help you get oriented. First," he kept going, "what's your game plan, what are you wearing?"

And he was right, I would have done nothing less for Roberto. There must have been eighty-nine times I'd listened to his hopes and his scheming. I'd heard all the long stories several times over about his night school and his love life and his meticulously paced plans for replacing his superior and then leaving. Roberto's plans were so thorough in fact they included the month he'd move on from Poplar & Skeen and the VP to whom he'd announce his departure. When promoted the last time around, he hadn't been more than two or three weeks behind schedule.

I repeated the question. "What'll I wear?" I hadn't even begun to consider it, and now the realization that I had less than twenty-four hours to investigate my options, conduct the necessary trials, and then decide irreversibly on an outfit, struck me with horror. "I *knew* there was something I'd forgotten."

Roberto launched into action. Like a skier shoving off

from the summit, he lit into my problem with a fervor. It was a sport for him, fixing it, but it was still heartfelt. "Now," he said, "don't panic. A lot of deliberating is only unnerving. There's a single good formula for solving these things. Just listen, I'll tell you what it is."

I watched the slender face fill up with energy and interest, the creases shift around his full lips, and his eyebrows lift sympathetically below the wrinkleless forehead.

"You go for what's most reliably comfortable out of all your work clothes," he said, "the thing you love most. What's the one single outfit that, when it's dirty, gets you doing your laundry?"

Without answering, I sat down beside him and fiddled with his scarf. I sighed. I was shaking my head. "There's an enormous problem though, Roberto," I said. "There's something really bad that I know is going to interfere." My own brow was knit deeply, I could feel it, and the physical manifestation of my dread seemed to stretch taut across my jaw from my chin to my ears. The crooked bun was driving me crazy.

"Mary Jane, you've got this thing nailed. Don't fret, girl—Brill is just a formality."

Absently I'd pulled the scarf all the way off him and was running it through my hands. I was looking down. "No, but I've lost ground," I said, nearly whispering. I watched the blur of gold and green and violet. "I've lost my confidence completely, you see. Something happened. Something bad." For a second I gripped the scarf in both hands and felt the tension between them. "It would take too long to explain."

Then all of a sudden, Roberto spoke sharply. It was as if

he'd been stung by an insect or had heard something incendiary on headphones I couldn't see. Suddenly he was frightened or angry. *"Nothing,"* he said, "has happened!"

I looked up. I caught his eye. And just as the luscious slippery scarf I'd pulled again from one hand to the other ran its shivery length across the inside of my forearm, a shattering thought broke into my head and chased away everything else in it. I looked at the tail end of the scarf shimmying across the veins in my wrist. I saw it sail down to the floor. In my left hand I still held one end of it, wrapped around my palm like a rope, or a cord. It was then that the real embarrassment overcame me.

"Oh," I said to him, the sound pregnant with some sort of meaning, though I wasn't sure which. In that tiny word there was an immense acknowledgment, a crucial concession to something that had never been said and might not have even existed. "You're right," I said—right about something, I didn't know what. "Of course not."

And just as abruptly as he'd been sharp with me, now Roberto returned seamlessly, without even a nod, to the buoyant, warm tone he'd been using. In a single smooth gesture he took the scarf from my hands, slipped it back around his neck, and laid his hand sweetly on my knee. For him it seemed all was back to normal, but for me, within, came a startling desire to be hit.

"More important than anything is that you feel good about yourself," Roberto said cheerily, "and clear-minded." He spoke without a trace, without an inkling of cryptic or tangential emotion. "Tell Brill what it is you want, Mary Jane, and tell it to him straight—no modesty, no embellishment."

■   ■   ■

Back at my desk, I pretended to gaze at my monitor. But I was gazing deeply into the past. I was rummaging through months of memory, images and phrases, gestures and incidents, involving my slender, intelligent friend. At one point it all seemed too much for me, too heavy on my mind, and I lowered my head to my hands, propped on my desk by my elbows. I thought of the man himself, how he was loving and true, but how he was changeable. His real name was David. When there was something he wanted—a prettier name, for example—he wasn't an individual to get bogged down with conventions. He respected experiments, failed or successful. Born into the core of the middle class, he never for a minute assumed privilege was rightfully his, but instead built into his plans plenty of time to obtain it. He had a "game plan" for all sorts of dreams, not least of which were his elaborate blueprints for just plain amusement—his own and that of hundreds of others' he loved.

So why not? So what if the sex life he spoke about was centered exclusively on graying athletic males who tended to be bookish and hung around the bars? Suddenly the Roberto I saw was a thousand times more versatile than I'd ever allowed for. Suddenly my narrow notion of his dates and his boyfriends—the fit men well into their years, wearing sweaters that smacked of academia and cruising the newcomers in town—my narrow assumptions exploded. Of course, I thought, Roberto, as soon as anyone, would have the spirit to do it with a girl on a bulletin board. And besides, who in the world with the least bit of courage has a taste for one thing, and one thing alone?

There, in the sparkling darkness of my palms, my head like a small universe filled with the past and getting heavier in my hands, I saw flashes of the lively Roberto and recalled moments at random, out of sequence, as whole new editions of themselves. A simple visual snippet—Roberto pulling me toward him to say something private, Roberto tasting a plum, Roberto slapping his hand on the banister for emphasis—would be freshly imbued with suggestion. While one recollection might look unchanged, nothing in it but my familiar innocuous colleague, the next one would implicate him subtly, rewriting his role in the script. The new Roberto was sexy. He was vaguely despotic and seductive. He was the body and the bones, the soul and the source of the resonating voice of Inez.

And one particular scene, not this time a memory but a newly born possibility, a supposition, a test, kept filling up the glittery cosmos that grew wider and deeper in my hands. The scene made me sway slightly or at least not feel sure I was just sitting still. It began with Inez—Inez transmitting sentences to me that grew legible against a brightening screen: "OK, Francesca, OK, Girl, now you're gonna lie there and take it." The words were filthy and mean. They were pouring out rapidly, filling line after line. "You're going to beg. You're going to plead—to have the satin scarf around your little neck loosened. You're going to try to get up off the floor. Oh no, little tramp. I won't let you." And then, from beyond the typed-in messages, from out of the radiating blankness behind the words, a long and wrinkleless face appeared, a figure, an overcoat, half in focus, half dissolved. It was Roberto. It was Roberto standing over me saying the words. Dimly I could see his mouth move, his torso looming. His voice was low and almost hissing with will and concentration. "Slut," he said, "do what I tell you. *Obey me*." I could imagine, underneath the coat, his hips and his thighs. I was longing to reach up and feel what was hard. I imagined my hand in the folds.

"DON'T . . . TOUCH," he typed in. And the screen went dark again.

# 16

# ENCYCLOPEDIAS

I woke up at 5:45. It was Tuesday. It was the Tuesday I'd dreaded, the Tuesday I'd waited too long for. Past the half-open drapes I could see it was still night. There were flecks of snow falling, though only the sort without moisture, blowing through the ether like electromagnetic particles or like stray ash. I tried to sleep fifteen minutes more but I couldn't, and for the next two hours, as I went through my morning tasks entirely by rote, I was overcome by a struggle within between the forces of reason and optimism and the icy enticing vacuum of dread. At 8:15 the streets were busy, the snow stopped, but the air still uncommonly cold.

In a way, it was simple. Here I was a woman with a purpose, tentative in my early years but now taken in fully by the satisfactions of getting ahead, meeting goals; and having slid into the world along a socioeconomic stratum that gave me an automatic advantage, I was just now poised like a jet on a runway to exploit it. All I had to do was get a brief running start. All I had to do was tell Brill where I was heading, keep revving the engines, and smile—look pretty, keep quiet, work hard. Everything was ready for takeoff.

And yet the trouble was I couldn't get behind it; I couldn't wrap my hands around the controls. I couldn't see beyond the mundane mechanical facts and operations that were making my advancement possible, and I could no longer glamorize the outcome. Not only had I ceased to believe in myself, my personal traits and my honesty, but I was unable to ignore the dominion, the might, of the whole social system that made me. All I saw were the greasy inner workings of power structures like Poplar's, the ways you get judged, the points you rack up, the rankings assigned so deliberately, and the unspoken fact that what you learned at the supper table and later in school was a spurious set of drills without which you couldn't even enter the contest. I knew all about the gearshifts and the cockpits and the ways to seem smart, and I knew how to snow Brill with vocabulary. "Functional," for instance, would be good for an adjective, for a noun I'd use "expedience," and most of all there was what I "envisioned" for our department, how it would be "executed" or "achieved." I was riddled with a kind of miserable insight into the tricks and trappings and lame basic training that went into making me salable.

I'd been trained by experts. My mother knew from her mother before her that there was a fine line between snobbery and good judgment—and if you were in doubt, shoot for both. It's never worse to know more. She kept a clean house and a tight watch on my girlhood. You knew what to love and what to ignore. And throughout my white childhood, everything was in order, from the finances to the workshed and down the path to the fully owned car. There was money put away. There was money for college. There was money from way back, in fact, even when there wasn't any, which is to say that my shriveled grandfather, who had barely kept alive a little business printing greeting cards, knew there were many forms of capital besides those elusive bills he couldn't keep in the bank; there were, for instance, to name just a few, a finely stitched suit jacket that could last you for decades, well-pronounced vowel sounds, and a full set of encyclopedias. "It's not a coincidence," he would say, looking even more wizened by virtue of the tone of his voice and didacticism, "that your report card will fit in your wallet. And don't you forget it." He had monogrammed cuff links but no savings.

So when the time came and his son, now my father, had lugged the little card business well beyond solvency and saw it through an expansion and a merger, I was already versed in the right kind of eating—the finest in sauces—and the good kind of reading, when I marched off to the right kind of university. There was money, and there was distinction.

I turned down Duane, into the heart of the downtown. It was a quarter to nine. I looked up and took note of my progress, just paces from Poplar & Skeen. Clearly, the struggle inside me was still knotty; it was hardly resolved. Were I to simply stay put, stay on the track of the skilled and respectable staffer in research whose duties were varied and plenty demanding, I could have marched the family banner along boldly, if laterally, unabashedly true to the gifts of my class. But that sort of thing was not what I aimed at. The associate track meant a fresh set of goals. Associates, by definition, were allotted a different kind of future, another brand of living from mine, a standing ranks up from the status of support staff. As an associate, you were headed for equity and deference, ownership and showmanship and top-level jobs where kingpins from other enterprises came to court you, and, on a good day, for the right price, even bought you, and then you were catapulted into the big time.

It was a drama, a dance, I said to myself. It was hollow. I took one extra turn around the block. Where was Inez, I thought, who could make me believe life was higher and purer than this, who could beat me down so that rising, moving up, I'd be too shaken to remember my past? Recovering from Inez, I could shoot right into the stratosphere without paying heed to the huge heartless machine that pumped up the front-runners and abandoned the rest.

I rounded the second corner, oblivious to the cold. Ten o'clock, the hour of my meeting, loomed in my mind like an exit sign at a freeway ramp heading out over a sudden ravine. I brushed past a blond woman with pearl earrings, tall and elegant but wearing much too much pink. I saw men with briefcases getting restless and irritated in line at the coffee shop cashier. And then past the bank windows, along the emphatically polished, metallic wall of the Jack Building I caught a glimpse of my very own person, swinging my very own briefcase, walking by my reflection through the crowd. Deep in my meditations on jobs and on power, on gourmet ingredients and my grandfather's creed, I'd forgotten all about this particular self I had, my hard-won maturity, the sleek and inventive style of my clothes. For a second, my image intrigued me, and I thought—suddenly assertive, even glad—There're one or two things I actually have a knack for. The massive double doors opened up just at the moment I approached them.

Upstairs, the afterimage of my stylish alpaca lingered in my mind as I took off the overcoat and saw the gabardine trousers I'd chosen to wear; they were my unchallenged favorites. As I moved, I kept focusing on the feel of them from the insides. OK, I thought, no problem. I thought: the thing is to reimagine myself, fully, in a loftier role with a distinctly appealing persona; to try once again to inhabit it; to be the flesh in its sleeves, the cause of its folds. I stretched out my neck muscles, straightened my blouse.

"Have a seat," said Brill.

I simply had to breathe deeply enough, figuratively, abstractly, to resuscitate the image of myself. In the mirror of my stiffened self-consciousness, the blood had to pump, the organs to churn, keeping the reflection of myself respiring. I had to believe in my intellect, my powers, and my perceptiveness—believe they were purely innate, or at least natural, that they were rightfully and essentially my own.

"So, you're in Budgeting," Brill said. He was genial. There was no reason to panic. Weren't we just two people, thoroughly innocent, who could simply chat and negotiate, get along? "And you've been with us for how long?"

But my chair seemed terribly low.

"You came to us when?" he prodded.

For some reason it was taking too much concentration to breathe in. Then to breathe out, to breathe in again.

And the fact was actually we weren't two innocents, that was the thing. I felt cold. I suppose if things had been different—if Inez had held out for me one more week, beating me senseless and happy the night before this, or if I'd been less of a cynic in general, less guilt-ridden and less earthbound— I might have seen my encounter with Brill as the simple tale of two workers, accomplishing a job, bringing their talents and insights to bear on the needs of their mutual employer and arranging a sensible hire. I suppose it would have seemed harmless and specific, he the arbiter of the company's progress, I the valuable choice. But I didn't see it that way. I couldn't. Out of sync with myself and entirely incapable of overlooking the pitiful way each one of us was governed by the history of the outside world, for me the whole thing seemed painfully overdetermined. I felt like a puppet, a fake. What I said no longer belonged to me but seemed instead the property of history or the company, dictated solely by the principles of economics themselves, or by Brill, my inarguable superior. All I could say was what, implicitly, I was supposed to.

"Well, three years it shows here in your records," Brill said, "or is it actually three and a half?"

I had to speak now, it was clear. "Three and a quarter," I said, "actually." And then I laughed. "I mean, if it *matters*." It was a light sound, offhanded, but really it was a little bit of suicide. I laughed again. It was a puzzling, vaguely lunatic rejoinder.

Brill studied my face. He was short and balding, with ruddy skin and long teeth. There was nothing malignant about him save the fact he was here.

I tried to recover. I knew there was a script for this, somewhere. I said, "Three and a quarter good ones really though, for sure." What was that syntax? In my heart I felt the heaving pull of gravity, wanting nothing else but to go back to the place of my mother and the sensible car where I'd learned all that delicate and reasonable behavior, the place where a woman like me belonged. My mind was emptied of fantasies.

"Right," he said. "And now you're interested in becoming an associate—junior associate?"

I couldn't picture it. Not a single wish flickered on my imagination's horizon.

He continued. "You'd like to make a greater commitment to the company? Tell me about that," he said. He leaned back and entwined his fingers over his stomach, exactly as executives are supposed to do.

But I could barely keep track of the questions. "Yes," I said. Was that all? It was pretty much all I could come up with. My right knee was bouncing. I drummed up two words more. "Very much," I said. I thought: I'm just a girl from the North Side with excellent numbers skills and an expensive diploma; what am I doing *here*? "It's an opportunity," I went on, "I feel that."

"Right," said Brill. He leaned forward. I got the sense he wanted to find me likable, to find me at least minimally deserving. "Good then," he said. "Tell me more."

My knee stopped. I was trying to think. "In other words," I said, "there are—you know—opportunities, other, well, pathways to go down." I paused, hoping this was enough.

"Yes?"

"Yes."

He seemed lost.

I said, "I'm interested in that." I knew I was expected to clarify. I made a broad gesture with one hand. *"Very,"* I said. That was all. I smiled.

Eventually, as Mr. Brill nudged me, coaxed me with the simplest inquiries, once, again, and again, and here and there fielded a phone call affably, I offered up a few expressions of worthiness. Eventually, we worked our way through the whole hideously big, big and clumsy, conversation. Brill leaned in and nodded at me. He laid his thick hands on the desk. He clacked his ring on the wood and waited, amiably, for me to strangle myself. In the end, somewhat weary, he filled up the appropriate length of time for our interview with an anecdote about his fourteen-year-old son who'd won a chess tournament by a landslide that weekend.

And when it was all over and I passed by cubicle after cubicle filled with unwitting coworkers and the whole day around me was now in full, unstoppable motion, a deep and pervasive numbness overcame me. Flatly I refused to acknowledge the appointment had occurred. On the surface nothing exactly had gone wrong; on tape my testimony was not so incriminating. But no sentient being, no thinking set of ears could have missed the absence of intellect I exhibited, the utter, irrefutable lack of flair. Not one single act or remark I had made suggested I had any gifts to offer.

I walked dumbly past the vending machines and the mail cart. I kept myself from thinking. I kept myself from thinking about anything at all since to think was to know and to know was to know one thing only: I'd blundered.

Instead, mercifully, my mind fell silent. It must have been hours. Only my body, from the deep buried core of it, still hummed. It murmured. Inside, my guts seemed to rumble, like a stubborn and measured avowal, like a recalcitrant pledge of the flesh, almost burning, this insistence that somehow, eventually, no matter what, I'd lie down again under the hand of Inez.

# 17

# THE

# PEPPER SHAKER

Through the week that followed I lived a sort of compressed existence. The movement of time—which you generally notice on account of how things change—was evident only in the variety of ways nothing happened. It was eerie, almost vertiginous at times, and yet static. It was like living in a world without sound or without distances. The feeling I had was identical to the sensation you suffer upon inadvertently barging in on a private discussion—only, in this case, the silence that fell, fell everywhere and lasted for days. It was as if the whole world grew hushed when I walked through, and there was no way to make up for my errors. There was only one encounter, which, though at first it seemed cruelly discouraging, touched a nerve and awoke me. But until then the world seemed muffled and stilted. Even my fantasy life, my wild hopes that Roberto would bring me down and use me, had stalled out, grown flat and unconvincing.

Immediately after the interview I got a visit from Kay, whose mood had returned to normal shortly after my own had begun to collapse, and almost every day thereafter she'd stop by my office to coax me back from abstraction. It didn't matter. Even as she spoke to me, extolling my winning attributes and the wondrous unpredictability of life, I'd repeat in my own head the graceless, stultifying dialogue with Brill or work myself into the listless delusion that the appointment had never really happened. Kay's pleas didn't penetrate the thick hush of judgments about my person that I was convinced were being made elsewhere.

I got no word from Brill. Day after day, no announcements were made, no messages sent. Neither Jean Fine nor Gerald mentioned the interview, its upshot, my prospects. Jean greeted me with the same "Morning" or "Pretty beads" she always did, midconversation with a colleague three ranks my senior, and I could detect nothing telling in Gerald's usual indifference. Yet somewhere, I knew, behind the scenes, not just my future but my value, my goodness, were being decided without me.

At night the feeling of stasis persisted. Over and over I drank the same hot milky drink at the café and ate the same lemon cookie, but more and more I forgot how they tasted. I couldn't project any goodness onto the world and therefore I couldn't want any. Stuck in this emotional holding pattern, my own awareness seemed to disintegrate, and my ability to love, to gauge and construct the future, crumbled away at the edge of my mind. Left remaining at the center of my thoughts was what was old and foundational, facts I'd built my life on—jobs I'd done, shoes worn, tragedies lived through—but which didn't help me look forward. None of it had the power of a dream.

Then at home on Tuesday, a week after Brill, as I emerged from my walk-in closet, dressed for bed in my

Nepalese trousers, I glanced over at the darkened monitor that had been sitting untouched on my desk all week. I looked for a second into the screen's muddy blackness, my hands uncoiling my hair. I felt desperate and mad. Why wait to find Inez again, I thought, Inez who could have been anyone, when "*any*one" is already in there? All I wanted was a set of hands, or rather, just a set of good sentences to make my frustration snap and disperse. All I wanted was the impact.

The members' screen was crowded with nicknames, though it wasn't yet ten. There were "Boss" and "Claus" and "Camillia," "Hassan" and "Eugene." I had logged on as "Lisanne," and for a new user-profile had written "submissive, reserved, but never scared." I vowed to try for ten minutes to attract someone and if unsuccessful by then to log off. I thought, Why stew, why wait, and right away I'd taken my chances.

"Dario," I wrote. He was near the top of the list. His profile said, "dominant and insatiable." "So what are you waiting for?" I typed in. I sat watching as a minute or two passed with no answer. No doubt my message was much too abrupt. Tops couldn't stomach that sort of aggression.

So I waited some more. It's not easy to be passive, but I tried. "Paola?" I wrote. I left it at that. Her profile was impressively laconic: "Prison guard." But again there was no answer. I could see she was privately messaging somebody else.

I read through the small talk and the foreplay, waiting for someone to type in my name. Then at last, just as my ten minutes were about to expire, I got a message from someone called "Rogueman." He was forthcoming at least and, I imagined, probably heartless and crude. Unfortunately, I found his nickname insipid.

He wasn't crazy about mine either: " 'Lisanne?' What kind of uptight bitchname is that?"

This rather pleased me. It was a little slap in itself, the way it ignored my sense of fairness, ignored all those gentle, truth-loving qualities that, I felt indignantly, didn't work anyway out here in real life. On the other hand, the comment seemed incredibly vapid.

I responded according to the conventions. "I'm sorry," I said, "sir." This was how you made clear your position; it was code for your supplicant's desire.

"You should be sorry, pussy wench."

Now that was worse than inane.

"Pussy wench???" I said. This wasn't how you were meant to respond but I couldn't help it. I'd rarely heard anything so puerile. Besides, there was a good chance this "Rogueman" wouldn't even notice I was being sarcastic.

"Right," he answered, sure enough, clueless. He interpreted my response as excitement. "You like that, pussy girl? You want to be called a few names?"

Not really.

"Prissfaggy. Beaverbabe."

He must have thought he was being ingenious.

"I'm shoving your hot little ass to room 10. You hear me?"

Oh my God, I thought, What a loser. But I went to room ten—should I just try to go through with it?—and by the time I'd arrived, he'd launched into that sophomoric third person. There was nothing I detested more. His message was printed at the top of the screen. "<Rogueman>," it said, "has a hard-on."

I hit the quit key and left him.


But it wasn't that pathetic attempt to remedy the effects of my sexual deprivation that finally spurred me to action. Mostly it was Roberto. Like Kay, all week, Roberto had tried to engage me. For days, he'd been laboring to cheer me, insisting that the interview wasn't all that bad and no doubt the higher-ups were still just deliberating or hadn't had time to sign forms. Who knew, he kept saying, what these bureaucratic maneuvers entailed. "They take time," he said, "believe me, they *crawl*." Sometimes I'd agree just for the sake of agreement, but mostly I'd gaze into space and not talk at all. It turns out I'm rather cruel when I'm miserable.

And I had no idea what to think about Roberto; I couldn't fix him in place in my mind. In fact, one aspect of my flagging ambition and the steep downturn of my once soaring confidence was the way I no longer knew what to think about *anything*. I couldn't hang on to any opinions. All sorts of beliefs I used to express easily—about good taste and smart leadership, about the top periodicals and unscrupulous politics—now seemed impossibly complex. Everything was too multifaceted. And when it came to Roberto at that point, I was totally confounded. One minute he was my colleague and soulmate—he was regular, he was known— but the next minute he'd be her again, Inez; I imagined him, shirtless in the dim light, poring over his keyboard, an inkling of contempt in his eyes. And then again, that didn't

last in my mind either; another minute later I'd berate myself for fantasizing in the first place: *nothing* was so utterly
ridiculous as the illusion that Roberto was Inez. Occasionally, suddenly lucid, I would speak loudly to myself in my
head: Just *ask* the man then, I'd think, just hint at it and
see what he says. But before I had even a mental second to
formulate the question and pose it, I'd grow mortified or
annoyed at the ways I was grasping at straws.

That is, until Wednesday, a week after Brill, when I
probably couldn't have stomached another ounce of uncer-
tainty. Roberto had convinced me to go out for lunch, and
at first, in the restaurant, it was no different. I was gruff
and withdrawn. The room was airy and loud. The high ceiling, which seemed to waste the flooding sunlight that
bounced off the parked cars and the court building opposite, seemed also to bounce the ruckus of customers back
down to our table amplified. Behind us a bunch of suits were
uproarious over their beers, and to the left two women who
looked dressed for some fund-raiser were just barely holding
back from arguing.

"Don't bug me," I said. "Please." He was probing again
about my "frown." I was rotating the pepper shaker then
alternately twiddling my knife. "I said, I'm *fine*."

But my curtness didn't stop him for a second; Roberto
was too smart to be cowed by my bitterness, and too hopeful. "Don't get rude with me, Mary Jane. You're 'fine' like
I'm autistic—i.e., not. Now, lookit, I'm taking you out to an
expensive lunch and for dessert you're gonna eat flan and
you better get started acting grateful pretty soon."

I put down the knife. This sounded so much like how
he'd reprimanded me before—this mix of strictness and

nurturing worthy of a nurse in the throes of a serious emergency. You had to adore all that authority.

He said, "In fact, you'd better get started right *now*."

And all at once my confusion swelled to new proportions. On the one hand, I couldn't imagine that Roberto (Inez)—so loyal and decent and principled—would toy with the same brand of sadism we'd treated so gravely in the past; I couldn't believe Inez (Roberto) would discipline me like that off the cuff. And yet, on the other hand, it all seemed to suit him so naturally; it seemed apt and clear to me, almost like déjà vu, the way those caustic lines rolled off his tongue without pausing. The waitress returned with our water. He barely gave her a nod. How could I know what to think of him? His demeanor at once had the roughness of a sexual sergeant who would give you nothing but bliss and the half-serious, ironic affect of a friendly, intelligent queen.

"Put down the pepper shaker," he said. "Eat."

A few hours later, however, the discomfiting ambiguity was resolved. We'd returned to the offices silently, gone back to our desks, and by chance met up again in the elevator. Now we stood out on the sidewalk, just in front of the big lobby doors. Roberto was buttoning the top of his coat and flipping up his collar. It was icy out and turning night. I suppose I was waiting for him to scold me again—or take me home.

"*William*," he said, instead, out of the blue. He was grinning, the little non sequitur enunciated meticulously like a just-learned word in the mouth of a foreigner.

For an instant I felt perplexed, and then I just felt crestfallen. He was referring to one of his casual trysts.

"*Sociobiology*," he said, again pronouncing it syllable by

syllable, giving each phoneme the weight of a pun. He said, "Tenured, bright, handsome. Not just a wonk but a babe. You wouldn't believe this guy. I'll fill you in more tomorrow."

And at that point, for the first time in a week, I looked at Roberto squarely. I perused the whole long face, which was easily, completely readable, as candid as it was smooth. His smile was truly glad and inclusive. This man was not Inez. There was no roundabout narrative or elaborate hypothesis that would rationalize my Inez chattering like this about some trick of hers named William. And all the way across town to the café, all the way through the spicy greens I'd ordered for the third night in a row—unable to face another decision that late in the day—I saw the whole alter-identity I'd postulated for Roberto dismantled.

So that night in my bed wide awake, the steam heat gone off and the sheets cold against my bare arms, I felt all the day's disappointments and all the week's strain settle in my body like stagnating water. The deep reflex, the unsatisfied longing I had to disturb the surface, to make waves, actually brought me to tears. I wanted so badly to ruffle that lake. I wanted to stir up my life. I lay flat, gazing past the curtains into the purplish streetlight. And I thought about Inez.

Then, looking through the gap in the drapes, I experienced the dawning recognition—a distinct variation on the enigma I'd lived with ever since my decision to find her— that I knew, at least, who she was *not*. My arms were limp at my sides. She was not Roberto. Suddenly I understood what, that very day, had irreversibly begun to happen: it was a process of elimination. It was a question of who was left. I saw that the possibilities were finite, that only so many acquaintances could be the one I was after, and that, one by one, from now on, I would simply investigate the candidates.

I closed my eyes. I could feel the soreness and stinging on my nakedness, the flush that would show later on my skin, when I was already exquisitely rejuvenated.

# 18

# S W A T H

# O F   L I G H T

The first person I met up with that morning had to be the *most* unlikely of all. Too weird. How was I supposed to mentally wedge this delicate loyal supporter into that violent scenario? She was sitting in the plastic visitor's chair in my office waiting to see how I was. It was a crazy imaginary test to have to administer to a friend, and fundamentally I didn't want to. When it came to Kay, what I wanted was so much simpler. "Hey," I said, mildly startled to see her, "good morning."

"Hey back," she answered. "It is." By that she meant the morning, that it was good as I'd said it was; this was the sort of response that just went to show how keenly Kay always listened. "But are *you*?" And there was that relaxed, airy empathy mixed with high-level brains. *That* was what I always wanted.

"Better," I said. "Maybe."

"Good." She meant it. "I've never seen anyone so tense."

I'd already sat down and was scanning the surface of my desk. Each morning, for about half an hour, a swath of sunlight came past the plaid curtains and cut across the room, making my desk look dusty and vaguely chaotic. I glanced at it and felt a wave of nerves. What's all that clutter? I thought; there's gotta be something in that stack I've forgotten.

"Huh?" I replied. I was doing my best to focus. I was doing my best to home in: Kay in the crummy red chair, angled toward me across the desk with some sheaf of work papers lowered to her knee—I had to try to pry out her real identity; this was my cross-examination.

"You're such a stick-to-it kind of person," she went on fondly, in part looking for some kind of solution to my pain, "you even stick to lousiness." She was leaning in, her chin in her hand. Kay had the most gallant jawbone.

"*I* stick to *it?*" I objected.

"I don't know. It to you."

I tried to see something steamy in her outfit, in her pose, or in the bracelets that tumbled down her wrist and caught at the swell of her forearm. I looked for a suggestive grin or the haunting, all-knowing stare of someone who'd seen my other side. But even seated in that cumbersome lunch-room furniture, which I'd stolen to use in my office, even there, Kay's lanky pose looked graceful and passive. She epitomized the vanilla in all of us. Hers, you could bet, was the kind of sex that was prefaced with intimate laughter and long, long conversations. She wore the usual floral-print dress and enormous hoops in her ears, and she struck me as miles off the spectrum of possibility.

"But you're better anyway?" she asked. "More relaxed?"

"Oh no, I'm still tense," I said half-playing, half-strained. "I'm tense, tense, tense. In fact, I'm not just tense, I *am* tension; some people are made of flesh; some bunnies are made of chocolate." I shrugged. "You know what I mean." I must have sounded distinctly neurotic.

But Kay wasn't fazed by my oddities. "Oh, yeah," she said. She tipped back her head so you could see the underside of her prominent chin, the flat plane darkened by shadow, and the dip at the base of her neck. She was so easy and undemanding, as if, not desiring anything in advance, she couldn't be disappointed. She was laughing, the hoops swinging in her ears. "You're guts and bones, and you know it," she said. She shrugged at me and softened. "But look, Elaine," she continued, her tone at once wry and compassionate, "in the *worst*-case scenario, they could choose someone else for the job, they could slip someone else in that slot for the time being, but"—she gestured for me to look around my office—"you're still incredibly well situated. Look at this real estate," she said. Her voice was filled up with the pride she was trying to pass on. "Already, you've gotten so *far*."

I followed her gesture with my gaze. And she was right: to have your own ten-foot square like this in our brand-new division, with the white Formica bookcase and fresh-painted walls, was hardly something to scoff at. It just wasn't, by a long shot, the end of the line. Sure, it was the sort of place my mother or my siblings—if I'd had them—could visit, suddenly seeing me differently, deciding for sure I'd become an impressive, independent adult. But it wasn't the place for the real talent, the ones the company loved enough to fight for. It wasn't for the elite. So why did I think I could join them? And why was it that Kay didn't? Kay and I had never once mentioned the fact that she was still in Fulfillment, parked in that cubicle like a horse in a stall, after all those tedious years.

The swath of light that moved across the room each morning seemed to have just about passed, and my desk suddenly looked more in order. I remembered the mission I'd sworn to the night before and then again first thing that morning: the process of elimination.

I changed the subject. "So what about you, Cleverness? How are *you* doing?"

"Me?" she answered coyly. She tipped her head back again theatrically. "I'm always rapturous." She was partly sarcastic but also half-honest, since—it was true—whenever her mood was back to normal, there was nothing in her life Kay explicitly disliked.

"Rapturous?" I repeated. Wasn't that a tad suggestive? I said it again in my head, as the light now, for the remainder of the day, became plain and uniform like a glaze. How do you confirm innuendo? I looked at her face—the slightly nineteenth-century prettiness of it, strong but fine with bright teeth and eyes set high, the sharp ninety-degree angle where her jaw turned under her chin—and I listened for the "Inez" of her saying it—"Rapturous." I looked in her eyes for the cold stare Inez would train down on me from above that didn't shift even a hair's breadth when she raised her hand to hit me. I looked for the hard-set mouth that resisted, without apology, any sexual rush she might get when I would kneel down in front of her. I looked for the flicker of contempt on her lips when she'd pronounce words like "slit" and "wetness."

"That's me!" she said. "I always like the holidays!"

I blinked. It was as if she had trampled over her own act of becoming.

"It's a funny weakness I have," she went on, "how I go for all the gift giving and festivity."

Clearly there was a person here who would not be easily reshaped. I said, still distracted, "It *is*, Kay. It's really peculiar."

"Well, there's plenty else to be cynical about, I'd say. That's not something I'm short of. I figure if I have a few good memories of sleigh rides and yuletides I may as well hang on to them. I don't know—I *like* the ribbons and wrappings."

By now my gaze was readjusted. True, Kay was moody, and she herself knew it, but with each turn of her emotional coin toss, it was always still clear who she was. Kay did her moods in only two different ways. And when she was on an upswing like this she was always inordinately warmhearted. Once she got herself out of them, you never heard a peep about her dark spells.

And you never heard a peep about Kay's sex life either. She had been left two years back by the ideal, dream-of-dreams boyfriend, and not only left but snuck out on. Evidently, too guilty about deserting her and too lame to say why, Marty had literally vanished, taking all his belongings when she was gone for a night, and calling five days later from a pay phone. All he said was, "I'm sorry, Kay Lynn, I'm sorry," and disappeared, so she believed, to San Anselmo. Seven months later, when she emerged from an impressively gloomy mourning, studded with flu symptoms and binge drinking, she greeted all questions about romance or

Marty himself, with a single, chilling rejoinder: "Don't ask me about that." Only once in a while, on a particularly quiet afternoon or a raw rainy day when indoors in contrast felt safer than usual, she'd speak of Marty rather happily and explain—though not in so many words—that she was waiting for him to come back to her. Sometimes she'd concede outright she was waiting for someone just like him. This waiting, in my view, was Kay's style in everything. Job, romance, know-how, pension plans—she didn't go after anything.

"But 'rapturous'?" I said, still trying to fully defog my view of her. I was trying to line her up straight in my eyes. "Isn't that going a little too far for a few days of besmirched Christianity?"

"You know what I mean." She was up out of the red plastic chair. She smiled and kissed me in the air. "Gotta go," she said. "Stop by and see me later."

So, that afternoon, I did stop by to see her. It didn't seem adequate—the morning's attempt at espying the "Inez" in her and pinning down for sure who she was—and I was committed to this prosecutorial process. But first I had charts to fill out—weeklies—and messages to send and answer. I was bent on contacting Scrivener, for one, since I hadn't heard from him now in more than a week, and I felt adrift without our usual "discussions." Then I RSVP'ed Eddie and Vera, who had sent yet another invitation. And right then, as I was praising Vera's consistent social capacities and signing with just my initials to indicate how intimate we were, the message bar flashed at the top of my screen and a note dropped into my mailbox. It was from Gerald.

My heart swerved. In fact, I almost felt a physical pain in

my chest, as if the cabin pressure had dropped on the plane or I'd breathed in an icy form of vapor. There were very few things that a note from Gerald could mean, and though he was my nemesis in a way, he was also the hand that fed me. This little digital package could easily sate me or leave me completely deflated.

Without reading it, I got up from my chair. I walked to the window and looked down into the alley. I looked around the little room, the half-filled oversize bookshelves, the one faux engraving of Galileo's observatory I'd hung on my wall, and the one nick in the perfect new paint job. I was pretending the note wasn't there. I realigned the stapler and tape dispenser on my desk and straightened the row of blue binders, and I even cleared my throat as if I were going to hum. What an asinine way to prove I had some self-possession: every witness to this supposed even temper was a half-dozen offices away.

But finally, having convinced myself, I guess, that I had some tidbit of control over my destiny, or at least my behavior, I sat back down again and double-clicked on the terrible bar marked "Gerald." The window burst open with his note in it. There was no salutation. "See me Wed.," was all it said, "3 P.M."

In the cubicles flanking Kay's workstation, little clusters of females were causing all sorts of noise. Probably on account of the late hour and the basic fact that no one at Poplar was assigned to prevent it, playfulness and distraction always snuck in on the coattails of tedium. Kay was parked at her workstation. Around here, at the end of the afternoon, exhaustion turned to giddiness in full force, and the women who worked in Fulfillment provided it liberal outlet.

I had come around ostensibly to learn something. Kay was leaning over her file drawer, working, despite the raucousness, though she laughed too when she overheard a quip about a VP of sales. A mess of wavy chestnut hair that came to her earlobes fell forward and touched her cheeks. Unmerciful Inez, I thought, couldn't have shared half that femininity.

"Did you hear that?" she said, referring to the antics next door. She reached to hold my forearm as I entered her desk area and smiled. Inez couldn't have had those hands, so narrow and long, with a touch like a seamstress checking fabrics. Kay had rings on three of her fingers. "Listen," she said, smirking, and she touched her ear. She wanted me to eavesdrop on the nearby conversation. What I needed more than anything was to be with her. "They're nuts," she said. "They're skewering Stevens."

I just wanted to be near that lightness. I wanted the unending strain of ambition to lift. More than anything I wanted Kay's soothing reassurance about the ominous message from Gerald. I turned from her and listened to Cici riffing off Stevens's obtuseness. There was laughter. They must have been imitating his wandering eye.

"Here sit," Kay said. She was whispering so we could overhear them, and she was moving to sit on the edge of her desk so that I could have her chair. Just like that, she wanted me to be comfortable. Why did she always remember to look out for me? "Shh," she intoned, still holding my arm. She was a human antidote to greediness. Everything about her seemed constant.

And I just couldn't picture it—in all of that friendliness—I just couldn't imagine her punishing me. I couldn't detect the smallest trace of sadism or drum up a feeling of sexual need. Nor—the truth is—did I want to. Instead, what I wanted was to relax there, alone with her, where I was not only welcomed but loved. She had her hand on my shoulder, her neck craned upward, her face very still, listening. I thought: Roberto was not Inez but neither was this.

# 19

# THE

# PHONE

On Friday I kept roaming the halls. Every time my mind strayed away from the quarterly graphs that were due that afternoon, I'd get up and wander the paths that circled the islands of assistants and crossed through the lounge. I'd feel a kind of buzz in the terribly empty air that kept me constantly distracted. More than ever, the place had an aura, a cleanliness and quiet that signaled to me there was info around that I wasn't privy to. The starkness seemed so exaggerated it ended up suggesting concealment. Eventually, struck by my own idle roving and the fact that others any minute might notice my anguished vacuity, I'd about-face at the rose-colored sofas in the lounge area and slip quickly back to my office. Sometimes I shuddered visibly when I found myself away from my desk without any memory of what brought me there.

It was at one of these wandering moments late in the morning that I unfortunately encountered Jean Fine. I was rounding the corner at the end of my little corridor, which poked out toward the rear of the building like the cord out the back of a lamp, and as I strayed into the open space where the assistants and secretaries were clustered, I glanced up—I could feel it—at least three beats too late. The look on my face just held there as in a freeze-frame. Whole seconds passed before I could reactivate my senses and see that I was marching head-on toward Jean, standing with a man about a foot shorter than she was, who was dressed in an overpressed suit and conversing with bogus self-assurance. She had already looked right toward me. I had no memory at that point of what time it was, what clothes I had on, or where, if anywhere, I'd meant to be going. Suddenly, out of nowhere, Jean Fine's wide neck and her pearls had come into focus, and I was faced with the huge mental task of figuring out what I should say.

"Fean Jine!" I nearly exclaimed, but somehow I managed to stop myself.

There was a time, not far back, when I loved doing business in those halls. The bright, spacious regions of Budgeting felt temperate to me, and efficient. Back then, when the division was brand-new, having been formed as a sensible aggregation of Billing and Budgeting (which had just broken off from Finances), Accounting and Group Operations, I even believed I was born for them, that this was my indigenous home. Outside, the streets, the apartments and houses, were suitable for other people, I'd thought, but this crystal cleanliness with its wall-to-wall carpet and creamy plastic machinery, its streamlined, white halls, was where I myself best flourished. And when the afternoon light came through the vertical blinds in the three big windows of the lounge area, came through the single arched window above, which was a relic from the building's distant past, I could sit on the dusty rose sofas talking systems with seniors as if they were guests and I the hostess.

But now I felt like a trespasser. Jean Fine's reddish hair was newly trimmed, slightly mannish in shape though thick and wavy like a woman's. She wore a tweedy blue suit and heels. And it's hard to describe the expression that came into her face at that moment, with her companion still gesticulating unwittingly, as I stopped myself from blurting out my asinine spoonerism but lost my balance in the middle of waving hello and barely managed to recover my flailing torso before my knees hit the carpet. My guts surged, as if the tumble had in fact come to pass, though I had somehow miraculously averted it. Perhaps the best way to explain the look on her face is to describe it via negation—no sympathy or worry, no humor or fear or surprise or concern registered among Jean Fine's early wrinkles or in her tame bluish eyes. There was only one tiny shred of sentiment detectable at the slightly taut corners of her mouth: it was disdain.

I took a turn toward Billing, disappearing as quickly as I possibly could without retracing an earlier path. Sure enough, for a second time, the edge of my fashionable platform shoe caught in the carpet. Again I didn't go down, and no one happened to see me, but by now I was distinctly shaken. When I returned to my ten-by-ten office, which at this point struck me as an incredibly precious haven, I had already run through my head half a dozen times the image of Jean Fine's impassive face and her glaring lack of a greeting. Never, not in all the pages of history I was madly riffling through in my mind, had that nervous but impeccably courteous woman ever failed to say hi to me. After all, Jean had the manners of a United States president built on years of parochial schooling.

I closed my door behind me. I was very near tears and

could feel the base of my throat hardening. The green laminated cheat sheets for graphing and three binders for past months were sprawled on my desk. A spreadsheet was open on my screen, several applications running in other windows. Somehow my desk chair had rolled into the middle of the room. Everything looked cut off midsentence, and I dreaded the rest of that predicate. I was holding my head at the temples. It was painfully clear to me now what had happened, that Brill had sent word down the ranks, to be relayed to me via Gerald on Wednesday, that the content of it was tainting, and that Jean Fine's once favorable view of me had been irreversibly altered. These were the things a minimally insightful individual like me could discern, whether or not I wanted to. I'd seen it in the faint pulling at the edges of her mouth. I'd seen how she'd decided it was no longer pressing to address me. I'd understood immediately that I was now just another employee for her, a far cry from the woman who, just days ago, she would have taken into her home as a comrade.

At the bottom of the stairwell, the air was cool. My eyes were slightly swollen from the tears, but I was taking deep breaths and letting Roberto prattle on in a delicate attempt to soothe me. He had on a dark green shirt and a black necktie and a complicated fragrance supposed to suggest springtime in India or some such Far Eastern fantasia. I was relieved at first to simply be listening, and I felt once again I could safely assume that I knew him, untroubled by second guesses.

"Well, OK," I said, "it's possible I could've been imagining it. It seems like a long shot though, really, Roberto. I mean I *saw* her face right in front of me."

"Cleverness, listen to me, you're projecting."

"OK, it's true, you have a point: there's not much you can tell in a glance—"

"Absolutely."

"—but she didn't even say *hello*."

"Elaine," he said. He was patting my knee like a grandmother. We sat the way we always did, side by side, close together, on the stairs. As we spoke we would gaze ahead at the lemon yellow concrete wall or to the right at the lemon yellow basement doorway as if looking out at a landscape. The whole place had the echoey feel and the just-mopped smell of a swimming pool.

"It's this Wednesday thing really," I kept going. I wasn't keeping any track of what I said. This was probably the third time I'd gone over it. "The appointment. I know it's going to be the final word, Roberto—what else? I'm *sure* Gerald plans to pass on Brill's decision. And it's so obvious that Jean Fine already knows it. I'm telling you—she couldn't be *bothered* with me out there."

"Shh. Elaine," Roberto said again. That day he had the scarf on and it was he this time who was fiddling—running its edge through his fingers or tapping my knee; at one point he twisted the ring on my index finger.

"It was the look in her face, Roberto, I'm telling you. I've never seen it before. And, you know, if Brill said I wasn't the one for this job, there'll be no way to reverse their opinions. It'll color the way they think of me from now on." I was sweating. "I mean, for *eternity*."

Finally Roberto managed to interrupt me. He could see plainly I wasn't getting anywhere myself and that the best course was to distract me. Finally he was able to drag my attention away from the psychological bullring it was trapped in and bring it out into the open. "Girl," he said emphatically. "Calm down. No matter what, this is out of your hands till Wednesday. And you know—I just want to say this, Cleverness—are you listening? At bottom, who the fuck cares?"

I looked at him sort of pleadingly.

"You have a life beyond the walls of Poplar & Skeen, I want to remind you. You need to start living it. This job for you, Mary Jane, is beginning to seem like a spiritual penitentiary."

Now I could tell he would start getting religious, or not religious exactly but metaphysical. Roberto's sense of God was extremely broad-minded and was integrated into his regular thinking as naturally as stretches are part of a dancer's routine. He was religious in a vernacular sort of way, much as other people are outdoorsy. "When your professional desires crowd out every ounce of pleasure," he went on pontificating, "that's when you turn spiritually abject, which, believe me, is no fun. I know you think it's corny, Mary Jane, but I'm telling you: God is synonymous with appreciation and if you can't enjoy or appreciate things, you're going to feel cut off from everything—very deeply. Now," he said, "let's talk about something else."

With that, Roberto was able to launch me into whole other spheres of interest. It worked. Somehow he'd made me docile enough to move on, and through the course of a half an hour or so, we contemplated enough free-ranging topics that I felt actually somewhat liberated. At first, he had me musing about the stiff suit of the man accompanying Jean and about how brilliantly the psyche camouflages weakness; then quickly we shifted away from shoptalk to the bliss of moviegoing and the health benefits of napping. By the time we got to Roberto's plans for the weekend, I was leaning back on my elbows and laughing. Only one little remark he tossed off reminded me of my predicament. "On Saturday," he said, "I'm meeting Will at The Mansion, a seedy little sex club he called 'profligate' and 'inspiring'—I can't *wait* to find out what he's thinking." But the words came and went so casually and fast, they struck me as nothing but the typical quip from Roberto, whose compassionate attention and general good spirits had made me agreeably forgetful.

The problem though is that the world is big, and it's much bigger than that stairwell. It's filled with real-life people like Jean who have real-life unpredictable experiences. Even as Roberto distracted me, infinite events in the world were occurring, and when I saw Jean Fine again that day, I was driven to pin one more of them down.

This time, I was passing by her open doorway. You can't blame me for being curious or at least for wanting a clue, since, even if I felt less tragic by now, the morning's encounter still irked me. Besides, I wasn't exactly spying. The two corner offices for Budget heads were just paces from the division's supply room, and as I turned in there to gather some manila dividers, I overheard Jean on the phone. Briefly, as if glimpsing her from a car window, I saw her standing upright by her desk, the tweedy suit jacket gone now and a white sweater pushed up to her elbows. Her hand seemed to be gripping the phone too hard. I overheard only one sentence. She was straining to keep her voice low: "You'll do what I tell you," she hissed, *"now."*

I paused just inside the supply room door, gazing down the long row of shelving. I needed a minute to think. Then taking a stack of file folders, which I didn't need, and forgetting the dividers, which I did, I opened the door again slowly and quietly. The more slowly I emerged from the supply room, the more I might manage to hear.

*". . . when I'm done with you."*

Now she had turned away from her own open door and was holding the phone with two hands. There was a huge captive force in her tone, a shouting and whispering at once. I caught a glimpse of her broad back, as she leaned against her desk half-sitting, hunching into the phone's receiver, and I thought I could see her shoulders heave.

*"Now, you listen to me carefully . . ."*

I must have looked disoriented, even blind, the way I was stepping so slowly, the folders against my chest, staring into nowhere and listening so hard. But it was too late. I had passed out of earshot. I wanted to go back and hear more, but an assistant caught my eye as I passed. Then another. And one more. All three glanced up at me at once. And had I moved any slower, they would have fixed on me jointly, wondering what was wrong. Instead, nearly in sync, they all looked back into their monitors, and I headed, without looking back, my arms crossed over those file folders, down the narrow hall out of sight.

# 20

# THE

# DRESSER DRAWER

This time Vera had planned a real bash. Every year at least once the two of them would invite a whole crowd of professional contacts, customers, and friends and then include a slew of their relatives. It had to be the most unlikely mix. It was like staffing a think tank with actresses or like one of those election-year scenes when well-dressed campaign teams and TV crews descend on a grubby sweatshop so the candidate can stump about wages. But somehow these parties were always successful. They had a style of their own. Ten-year-olds and toddlers, whose parents had recently arrived here from Colombia with cash and clothes and just enough English to start over again in clerk pools and community colleges, would knock over glasses of rum and soda, while angular women, who spent hundreds on Reine Nadine sweater-vests, would knock over containers of dip. For the most part everyone avoided mingling. Eddie's working-class cousins would cluster in one corner, for instance, and the retail types somewhere else, yet the ways the guests grouped themselves according to classes and accents didn't seem to dampen the mood any.

Perhaps it was the unapologetic attitudes of the hosts

that made otherwise embarrassing divisions seem fine. There was Eddie, for instance, standing with some young buyer, whose relentlessly forward-looking aesthetic meant she purchased only the most exorbitant designs, pointing to his civil-servant sister-in-law and describing the kickbacks in her office. Eddie didn't seem in the least bit pensive or awkward over the jarring fact that his sister-in-law's income was one half the earnings of his thirty-year-old companion, but nor did he seem to hide it. "They make overtime and all that," he was saying, "but the place is rife with corruption." And it didn't seem to cause him hesitation that the woman he was addressing had probably never once punched a clock.

The front room was dim and noisy. The table where Eddie and Vera held their similarly comfortable, ambling dinners was pushed up against the windows, which mirrored the darkened crowd. I chatted with a few of the retailers I knew, and I chatted at length with Vera's friend Jaime; he was the brainy Colombian radical who had taken such studied, public steps to abandon his establishment family and who was responsible, so Vera says, for her going to college. But mostly I chatted with Kay, whom I'd insisted on having along. The way I saw it, there was always the chance an attractive owner of some start-up would remind her of Marty and take her home; maybe he'd even turn into a long-term romantic interest, a possibility I considered auspicious and titillating though I'd never once discussed it with her. I had it planted firmly in my mind that Kay was looking for love, but in fact I had no proof of it. Meanwhile, the music was Brazilian and the crowd was loquacious, and every once in a while five or six guests would start dancing sort of sleepily, as if the whole party, not just the music itself, were rocking them back and forth. When this happened it was nearly impossible to get across the room, what with the close quarters of the dancers and just beneath them a circle of Colombian mothers sitting in chairs and flush up against that a grouping of white men, gesticulating adamantly, who were difficult to place socioeconomically.

At one such moment, I glimpsed someone on the opposite side of the room whom, I was certain, I'd seen somewhere before. He was quite young and very bony and had the slouching posture of a bass guitarist. But I couldn't place him. Nor could I squeeze my way through to the other side of the room to get a better look. He stood with his hands in his pockets looking off to the right, evidently unimpressed with the crowd, while to his left I could see two heavy-set women, dressed like downtown professionals, engaged in an animated discussion. Then the song ended. The knot of dancers frayed at the edges. Someone glided through the dispersing group and touched the young man's arm. It was Vera. This was the ethereal boy who'd been garnering all her attention that one evening, during the raucous and tasteless performance of their designer friend from Brazil.

What about Eddie? I thought, alarmed. Vera didn't seem to speak to the boy. She just sort of swung in and gave him a look, and smoothly, all in one movement, took him by the arm and led him away.

And as they slipped out of my gaze, perhaps back into the kitchen or toward the empty foyer, I realized I'd also lost track of Kay. I turned back to the little pocket of space she and I had been occupying together, but she was no longer where she'd been at my side. And the minute I noticed her absence, I found that in fact, I'd lost sight of everyone at the party I'd recognized. Eddie must have been there somewhere—I'd just seen him passing cashews—but suddenly I couldn't spot him in the chaos. Nor could I locate a single body or face belonging to someone I knew.

I grew anxious. It was as if, in that moment, as my jaw muscles got taut and my shoulders felt heavy with fatigue, I had been out here in public too long, and being here one more minute seemed dangerous. You simply couldn't depend on the authenticity of anything around you. Suddenly, I thought of Jean Fine. I saw the jerking shoulders, that grip on the telephone receiver, and I heard the words that were so fervent and cutting they made me flinch and look down. I pictured, for an instant, the strongbox.

That's when I turned from the front room and headed into the hallway. I felt a mounting urge just to move, to travel, to change scenes. I felt stripped bare, too *seen*. Someone in the world, here at this party maybe or back there at work, knew far more about me than I meant them to. They knew and I didn't. I edged between two plastic cups filled with wine, in the hands of a couple whose faces I didn't even notice, and I passed by a shy-looking teenage girl leaning up against the walls in the hallway. There were more people down at the end. But before I got to them I veered off into the beautifully spare bedroom where all the coats were heaped on the bed. And I heaped myself on it too, not exactly lying there but leaning up against the high mattress and all the stacked woolens and tipping back my neck and head. The voice of the woman singing in Portuguese filled the whole apartment, as I breathed a huge audible sigh and stared upward at the ceiling. My whole gesture had the air of a prayer, a petition for the return of my privacy.

Since Friday, the loss of it had seemed larger. Ever since then I'd been haunted by Jean—the bite and focus of those chastising words, the way she aimed them fiendishly into the phone. At some point it had struck me that Jean Fine had the impeccable taste, the love of order, good manners, and bouts of ambivalence you'd expect of a true-to-life sadist. And again and again I'd kept coming back to that metal box with the padlock. Somehow the mundane object had gotten trapped in my thoughts like a yes-or-no answer. Somehow, in my mind, I'd tied the thought of that box to a wild supposition about Jean Fine, and the two notions may as well have been married. The strong box and Jean (Inez) were the same. What was *in* them?

But now the logic seemed skewed. I heard a woman murmur something Spanish in the hall and then a man clap his hands and laugh loudly. Now I was stumbling over this random conjuncture I'd fixed in my mind between Jean Fine's surmised inclinations and that innocent, irrelevant container. The box had nothing to do with anything, I thought. Was I crazy? I stared at the wash of whiteness above, the milky glass light fixture in the periphery of my gaze. I was searching in the glowing whiteness for sanity, for calm. Get real, I thought—and I rolled my head back and forth once atop the huge stack of coats in order to toss off the idea altogether—you can't go around stuffing any old meaning into an inanimate thing. An object, I thought, is an object.

At that, I sat up. I rubbed my eyes.

An object, I thought again. I repeated the phrase in my

head. It hummed like a harmonious chord. I was staring at
the array of jewels strewn across the indigo dresser. I was
gazing into the baubles and beads. An object.

Of course, all of this must have happened very fast. I
could hear, out in the front room, the same song playing.
Meanwhile, in the back of my heart, I was still clutching this
new concern for the union of Eddie and Vera. But in a flash
I was up off the bed, my boxy gray sweater fallen into place,
the image of the half-buried handcuffs now out front, in full
view, in my mind. The first time I'd seen them, just a couple
of weeks back, I'd been surprised by the cuffs, by the unexpected way they recalled my own nights and suggested that
other folks had their kinky sides too. But I hadn't made the
whole connection. Back then I still had some grasp on "the
normal" and the fact that your friends were your friends—
no masquerades, no secret lives. But now appearances had
come to mean zero. Now this object, I thought—as if setting
the handcuffs head to head with the evidence against Jean—
unleashed a whole new, ten times more convincing set of
suspicions. I was on my way to the dresser. I wanted to see
them again. The French phrases Eddie occasionally slipped
into conversations passed loosely through my memory: "De
rien," "certainement." I scanned the tangle of jewels. The
handcuffs were gone.

"Elaine, there you are," said a voice behind me. I
jumped. It was like swallowing an ice cube by mistake, like
gulping the wrong thing down.

I turned around. "Jaime."

"Come on out," he said. His aqua-blue shirt filled the
doorway. "You have to join us. I've been talking with your

friend Kay.'' Luckily he was just passing by, probably on his way to the bathroom.

"Oh, I will," I called out to him, as he stepped already out of sight.

But I wouldn't—I vowed it to myself almost villainously—because now I was dying to find them. I had to lay eyes on the evidence. One more time I scanned the top of the dresser and then hardly thinking, hardly, as they say, "being myself," I slipped into the walk-in closet. Where did they go, I was wondering, what stash did they belong in, where would Eddie, who must have used them, snapped them and locked them, have deposited them discreetly before the party?

I pulled the string on the bare bulb and closed the closet door behind me. All it would take, I thought, was a glance, quick confirmation, and then I'd emerge immediately. The tiny room was lined on both sides with hanging clothes, and in front, along the third wall, stood a bureau about chest high and narrow.

And sure enough, in the bureau's bottom drawer, I found it. The evidence was brimming full. It seemed heavy-handed in a way, but the treasure-chest analogy was unavoidable: bright polished chains and buckles and hooks that caught the dim closet light, shone among the curls of black leather filling the drawer to its rim. So these were Eddie's toys and accessories. Right off, I could distinguish the wrist restraints and a delicately studded collar. I felt almost overflowing myself, with surprise and information and longing. Would Inez yank back my shoulders with that halter?

Then just as I was closing the drawer stealthily, trying simultaneously to block any more input from stirring me up and any more risk of discovery from building, I caught sight of one thing more. I put it all together. I saw just the tip, nothing definitive, but it was enough to make me lose my balance and envision her, Vera, not Eddie, and nobody else, grabbing hold of the base of that dildo. My eyes closed and my inhaling rumbled in my chest. It was silvery gray and almost as big as a fist.

When I got back to the front room, everything had changed. The whole fantasy of Jean, not to speak of my suspicions of Roberto or Kay, seemed a frivolous, even crazy mental gesture compared with what I'd just seen. I was overwrought to the point of ill-temper. Kay was talking to Jaime. She was trying on his broad brass bracelet, flirting more assertively than I'd ever seen her before. But far more important and perhaps the only thing more I could absorb that night, as the new identity of my missing paramour surged and loomed like some kind of exhausting hallucination, was the little circle of guests lingering around the doorway to the kitchen. Three or four designer types were standing with Vera, and beside her the angelic young man. Vera and the boy weren't touching or even talking in each other's direction; in fact, she seemed to ignore him. But what mattered more to me was Vera herself. I stood arrested, staring through a thinning group of Eddie's cousins and their children. She was dark-skinned, broad-hipped, and deliberately groomed. She was as tall as the two men nearby her, and her wiry, wavy still-black hair swung back and forth when she nodded. She spoke quickly and expressively, despite her big bones and solidness, and I remembered a time I'd been startled by the breadth of her hand when she'd laid it flat against my cheek, saying she was surprised to see me. She'd worn polish the color of black tulips on her bluntly cut nails.

And now I realized she knew everything about me. Her existence in the room made me gossamer sheer, transparent. I saw her substantial body, those hard broad shoulders shifting easily as she entertained the others, and I tried to get closer, squeezing my way through the Latino uncles. She laughed. The young man watched her. Eddie, off in the corner, seemed knowing as always and strangely untroubled by the fact of this boy invader, but to me Eddie himself had become completely incidental. I turned back to Vera. I felt more certain than ever I was in the presence of my missing lover, the one that I couldn't make it without. I reached my hand to my neck to feel for the tight leather collar I wished were there. As I stood watching Vera laugh, now with her hands on her hips, eyes alert, only a shred of propriety and sense kept me from the one gesture I wanted to make, there in the middle of the party. I held back the building urge, just barely, to drop down to my knees on the floor.

# 21

# T H E

# D O O R

By the time Wednesday came, I'd grown deeply withdrawn. For the first time in six months I'd gotten behind on my dailies, a fact that would wake me at one, two, and four o'clock in the morning successively. On Monday I'd stopped by the shop thinking I'd address Vera frankly, maybe even come right out with it first thing— *you know who I am, don't hide it, release me*—but she wasn't there in the store that night, and the minute I saw Eddie's face I was tongue-tied. He seemed to want me to stay with him and talk, but I felt panicky right off the bat as he came out from behind the counter, and when I tried to speak, my voice came out hoarse, which for no logical reason mortified me further. I stared past him down the wall of the shop into the back office where a rack of seconds stood behind the computer, poised at an angle on the cluttered little desk, and I felt my whole being retracting. Trapped in this unsaid trepidation, I didn't even ask where Vera was.

So by Wednesday morning I was even more sullen. I put on a generic cardigan. I was moving myself along through my life the way a half-built mechanical device gets moved along a manufacturer's conveyor, listless and unfinished.

And I had no investment in where I went next. Had I reactivated my senses and attempted to confront the requirements of life instead of cowering, I would have had to acknowledge my glaring lateness with the charts and the agonizing anticipation of my appointment that day with Gerald. Instead I hunched into my coat, walking rhythmically toward the office and looking narrowly out of my eyes.

Around me the city, like Vera and Eddie's weekend bash, was rigidly apportioned, arranged according to what you had and what you didn't. But, unlike at the party, that morning I didn't find it natural or innocuous. On the contrary, the city I passed through seemed tragic and abhorrent. From neighborhood to neighborhood, each about eight blocks square, you entered another island of uniformity marked by its abundance or poverty and festering hopelessly in its birthright. At Frederick Street, for instance, the regal stone row houses became sporadic and broke off altogether one block after that, where shoddy fourplexes crowded in on the sidewalks void of banister or garden patch. Or, turn the corner off Jay and your first whore was only paces down Arthur. There were the sudden crumbling buildings of subsidized residences at Duane and Winston and the weirdly airy one-room dwellings down toward the end of Emmanuel, where the city itself seemed to break off into decaying fragments, little bits of community tumbling, scattered, into the dry fields that covered the landfill reaching outward toward the mountains. They may as well have been color-coded, the neighborhoods, I thought, with my fingers turning icy inside my leather gloves themselves inside my pockets: one neighborhood red, say—the cars, buildings, corner stores all a uniform cherry, toddlers, school-kids, and adults all dressed in the same moderate shade—and one entirely blue. Then as you entered your own appropriate urban area, crossed over, for example, Frank Street to Duane, you'd fully blend into your surroundings. You'd nearly disappear against the backdrop of the world that had spawned you. As I neared the immaculate edifice that housed Poplar & Skeen, I decided the downtown district I'd entered—where real estate was owned by multinationals and inhabited by companies that aspired to be—would be ocher.

On my desk were the graphs that I should have filed on Monday. The mere sight of them made me want to flee back to my little apartment and not reemerge for weeks. Seven long columns were untouched. So were the blocks for my summaries. Tuesday's sheets were entirely blank. But even staring at the evidence of that backlog, as I lifted my overcoat to the hook on the company-issue hat stand in the corner and stuffed the red gloves Roberto had bought me into the overcoat pocket, I knew I wouldn't get through it before three. I knew I didn't have the resolve.

I read my mail and dropped another note to Scrivener, who still hadn't sent so much as Hello, and I cleared the irrelevant folders off my desk and dumped the miscellaneous mail. I started in on the Monday summaries. But later as the swath of light disappeared from my desk around 11:00 A.M. and my little square office grew one notch dimmer—one notch more blue-silver—I lay my cheek on my folded arms and slept. At lunch I wandered down to the court buildings and lingered on the benches for an hour and a half.

"Please sit," Gerald said about a quarter past three. It

was just the sort of diffident state I was in, that though I'd been waiting all morning for this very instant, I still showed up ten minutes late for it.

I sat down in the forest green chair, my palms against the rough weave of the upholstery. I sat slightly hunched, this time, one knee bouncing. I wore slacks—the closest you could get at Poplar to jeans—and no necklace.

"You're late with Monday's prospective evaluations," he said.

It was so habitual for me to be lively with him, I was on the verge of cheerleading now. "True," I said pleasantly, "Marissa must have mentioned it. I'll have them to her in an hour."

Typically he didn't respond. I thought, here was the man you'd trot out on a kids' show to illustrate the meaning of "official."

He returned his fountain pen to its stand and continued. "But that wasn't the intention of this meeting," he said.

For a second I looked straight at him, at the perfect hairline across his forehead that seemed machine-made and the clean elongated nostrils, but then I looked down. A huge buzzing had begun crowding in on my listening. He was still gazing at the pen stand.

"It's our policy to inform you," he said, so hollow it truly was as if it weren't him but the abstract entity of the company who was speaking, "that the position of junior associate in Budgeting has been filled. We had an impressive candidate from the outside."

The buzzing had grown very loud. His voice had grown softer.

"It's our intention to thank you for your candidacy," he

said. "We're certain the appropriate avenue for your advancement will present itself in the near future. Is there anything you'd like to say?"

It seemed an impossible question. Was he baiting me? I said, "Well, I'm *disappointed*," and I said it sharply, as if he were to blame. Immediately I realized it would be death to indulge.

"Yes," Gerald said. His hands were folded now atop a black and white binder. He was looking down over the edge of his desk and into the air. There was remorse in his tone, I could hear it, though just enough, I knew, to fill up one word.

As I left the room, I walked in perfect silence. Not a sound came from my moving, my rising out of the chair, my hands slipping into my pockets, my feet on the Mongolian rug. And I didn't stop to close the door. I left it wide open.


I think in different circumstances, I would have seen myself by then as damaged goods, as a burnt-out battery or something else that you couldn't revive. I think—given my cynicism and the way I generally see the world as a vessel for insoluble differences that people manage to transform into unceasing desire—I would have continued withdrawing forever, never afterward striving quite as I had. Being rejected for that promotion was the kind of defeat that would for me have been lasting. I don't think I would have gotten back on the horse for years.

But this situation was different. It was circumscribed and localized by the prominence of its causation—that is, I knew exactly what had made it happen. I could mark the minute my chances had been derailed and I'd lost my bearings. I had something specific to blame, for once, instead of my usual shortcomings or the whole grim state of the world.

So though I disappeared altogether from the office that day and over the rest of the week I must have appeared increasingly morose and withdrawn, I had not given over to the feeling of failure completely. Beyond the muffled, suffocating fog of my chagrin, there hovered invisibly in the clearer air this belief in a solution. I had to act, was all, I had to recapture my resilience and conviction.

And Thursday around noon, as Roberto finally stopped his knocking, his repeated, querulous "Elaine . . . Elaine?" and I had lifted my head from my hands where I'd gone to hide from his persistence, I began to timidly envision that cure. There was the timbre of Roberto's voice at my door and the way he always loved the enigma of the future that reminded me of his words: "Profligate," he had said, "and inspiring." I remembered him pronouncing the name: "The Mansion."

So even as I seemed to move in utter silence, to perform my work with no interest or respect, and even as I felt I'd been turned back at the ticket window after waiting for eons in line, I was simultaneously, in the back of my mind, imagining the means to redress things. I was making a plan for the weekend.

# 22

# A R M C H A I R

At night, in the city, you wouldn't be able to see the color-coding. Come night, the neighborhoods all turn a watery gray, and distinctions, though in truth they're probably sharper, seem slightly less severe. Perhaps that's why, come night, people often test them. In little spurts of fantasy, they make florid attempts to cross over into spheres they don't really know about, or dress up in the garb of castes they've only read of in books. Otherwise tight-assed professionals, for instance, venture down rough alleys heading to the seamiest clubs, and minimum-wage earners on dates rent limousines, wear gowns, and generally outspend their incomes. In a challenge to daylight's static hierarchies, you might step to the curb where a car is waiting, fantasizing your own celebrity and wealth, or dip into street drugs otherwise reserved for the underprivileged, crashing into chemical despondency as you return from a night spent slumming.

I walked alone along Arthur. Storefronts and tenement doorways were interspersed among loading docks, all under a layer of night's gray, which disguised the details of city life the way a painter's drop cloth hides a room. The whole town seemed blurred, degenerate. I felt free, in a nihilistic sort of way, and, similarly, hopeful. In a gesture of resentment, I was forsaking all my friends and associates, blaming *them* for the confusion of identities and maddening ambiguity that had reached a peak last weekend. I couldn't stomach the confusion over Jean, coupled with these unrequited gusts of desire for Vera, and, meanwhile, the sad erosion I'd witnessed occurring in her affirming union with Eddie. It was impossible to take. I was heading toward a different world where none of it would matter.

I turned the corner onto Dwight. The street looked swept clean or evacuated, the site of historic dramas now past. Up ahead, at the very end, there were two or three figures milling around a doorway. It was The Mansion. As I approached I saw there was no sign, just the number, 405, stenciled in pink above the doorway, and out front two men, hands in their pockets, chatting. One wore a leather vest, the other a black jacket. "How's it going?" one asked me genially. The other took my money. I passed down three concrete steps through the door, then down a dozen more into what must have been the refurbished basement floor of a factory warehouse.

And as I lingered for a minute in the foyer, ostensibly to empty out my pockets before I checked my coat, I observed in myself the first signs of calm I'd felt for ages. It was like love or courage or comfort or something, or perhaps it was just the first unfettered, fearless moment of intention I'd allowed my unmoored psyche since I'd been abandoned. Maybe it was the darkness, maybe the anonymity, but I felt as if I were on-line again with someone waiting for me in the ether. I handed my coat through the window.

The club was dim, its open central room leading onto dimmer passageways, little rooms and stairways, all of which were stirring with people—people dressed for a party, people dressed in leather, people with their shoulders bare. I felt my own skin against the air, which was wet like breath. The mere fact of flesh and presence, of all those surfaces, hard or pliant, made me glad, not because the physical world is necessarily assuring or seems especially true, but because I know that, in it, things can shatter. All the lauded wholenesses of real, material experience—the places, trains, the individuals—were breakable. So was I. I swung my arms at my sides, just to get acquainted with the air moving past them. I felt unburied. This was the world, I thought. These were bones. These were wishes. These were bodies.

I passed across the main room and turned to watch the people milling. Half-completed, like a movie set, the area was made up to look like a large boudoir or the mansion's parlor, with dark divans and ostentatious sofas from mismatched eras arranged alongside deep, cushioned chairs and ottomans. Several standing lamps had fringes, and from fixtures high up on the ceiling, the light was amber. I saw a woman straddling a seated man. She was staring him down and smirking. He was reaching up beneath her shirt. I leaned against the wall. Bodies passed back and forth in front of me, but I was too fixed on the sounds the two had started making to see where anyone else was heading. Across the way, a lanky man in an undershirt sat down on a couch to watch them also. The woman reached down to unbutton the man's jeans as he weakened. She was staring, unblinking, in his eyes, hovering and hardly moving. Her arms were bare save a leather strap buckled around one bicep, and her straight hair snaked around her shoulders. Now she was reaching down with both her hands. He was losing his focus. You knew her nipples were hard.

Eventually the woman slid down along his front, he with his hands gripping the chair behind his head, his arms, in the gold light, slightly reddish, and across the way the rangy man in the undershirt thrust his head back against the sofa.

I headed down a hallway. Every place I looked seemed sexy and daring in a contagious way, and I probably would have liked it if anyone at all had touched me. I slipped into another passageway on my right. You could almost feel the hallways were elegant, if they hadn't been crowded with half-bare men of every size and women dressed like go-go dancers, movie stars, and gangsters.

Up a set of wood steps was a row of low-ceilinged rooms, meant, I supposed, to be the maids' quarters. They resembled the sort of cheap hotel a runaway might find in Paris, not now, but in a different century, and you could imagine church bells sounding as the morning sun poured over the wooden dresser. In one room, I saw a woman, dressed in a plain black dress, sitting on the cotlike bed, sucking in big gulps of air filled with fear and pleasure. Two others, like herself dressed austerely, stood above her, to the left a pale man, sort of upright and effeminate, to the right a black woman with a couple dozen braids. But what made me stop and stand abruptly in the doorway of the little room was the rope the "butler" was uncoiling. It was long and soft and silver. On the bed, the small woman laughed nervously and started breathing faster as they gently leaned her back, and her short blond hair looked almost slick from perspiring. The man raised his finger to his mouth to quiet her. I stared

intently at those wrists as the placid man took his time, flipping the cord once, then twice, three times around the bed
frame. Alternately, her hand grew tense, fumbled for the
rope, then dangled. And when the two friends unlaced her
boots and coiled that rope around her ankles, her whole
body grew stiff, then slack, as she struggled and surren-
dered. Her captors moved more and more deliberately,
while they strapped her down and contemplated what was
next, and I knew then, as I watched the scene unfolding,
that somehow, before I headed home that night, I would beg
for something.

The farther back you went, the more elaborate the decor. One room—it must have been intended as the master's
suite—was lit with red. A smooth-skinned white man with
long muscles and brown curls was lying naked on the bed.
Across the room another man, this one Asian and stocky, sat
squarely in a plush armchair, perfectly immobile, his skin
bathed in the red light, looking.

Then as the little hallway turned sharply, a sort of lobby,
itself much brighter, served to introduce the darkest room
of any. Its double doors were open, but the high-ceilinged,
final space was too dark at first to see in. It seemed bare. Its
walls were painted black, its rugless floor solid shadow.
What was this? I conjectured; "the stable"? Or "the cel-
lar"? Leaning up against the door frame, peering in, I could
make out nothing but what seemed like extra roof beams
crisscrossing in the corners, several high black benches, and
a few vague pairs of people. I could hear a shuffling, I could
feel a blast of ventilation, but I couldn't see what they were
doing.

Just then, fast like an accident, sudden like a theft, the

sort of shock or disaster that produces a groan in your rib cage and a whiteness in your mind—erasure—I felt a bruising grip around my wrist and a yanking at my arm. Someone had pulled me into the darkness. I stumbled, barely righting myself before falling frontward to the floor. A knee was forced between my thighs, hands at my shoulders as if bolting me to the wall. It all had the fury and speed of a raid. I caught a breath, like the silence after sirens pass, and closed my eyes. "Yes," I said aloud, though I had no idea to what. This, whatever *this* was going to be, was what I wanted.

# 23

# THE

# CELLOPHANE

"I saw you," said a voice. A hand came across my face, hitting first my cheekbone, which, at that moment, seemed to protrude more than ever, to catch the pain deliberately, like a hand reaching into summer air to grasp a brittle leaf. My whole face clenched as I swallowed down the soreness. This time—I was right—there was blood.

"What—" I started saying but I couldn't get the breath. Besides, there seemed no more words than that to choose from. A whiteness without borders was filling up my mind. I tried to open my eyes knowing it would take a minute to adjust to the dark. But the voice came again.

"*There,*" it said.

I moaned. My eyes closed in preparation. This was the word, I realized, the password to excitement, that for weeks I'd been waiting to hear.

One more smack landed against the flesh of my jaw, and then the hand came lightly. There was a pause. I felt the palm, arrested, against my cheek. Cautiously, I opened my eyes to see.

In retrospect, I have the urge to give her a name. I want

to call her something brief, something hefty yet pretty, something that doesn't make you wonder if anyone is there. I want to call her Meg, or Rose, or Daphne. Or I want to call her Sara. Perhaps it was the simplicity of her grip on me and the way she had no interest in my views or in my appraisal of the pros and cons of public clubs; maybe it was her body, solid like a fist, her wiry limbs compressed like some sleek creature that's evolved beneath the steady pressure of the ocean; but something told me this woman's name was terse and that in it there was stored a vast expanse of purpose.

She was dark-skinned and probably thirty, not yet thirty-five. I saw this right off, as the faint light, almost an un-light, traveled the rounded contour of her cheek and the almost shaven, close-cut hair. Only slightly taller than myself, she leaned toward me, still driving my one shoulder into the wall, while her other hand rested against my face precisely where she'd hit me. She was giving me time, I suppose, enough to wonder, enough to want more. Then she leaned in, her forearm against my neck like a crossbar. She said, "I saw you." She was murmuring close to my ear, like an undercover agent come up behind his target in a bustling airport; there could have been a weapon in a pocket somewhere. "I saw you watching those two in the big armchair." She said it like a secret. "I saw you watch them tie the little maid, you tramp, you sleazy girl." Her voice dropped even lower. I could almost feel her lips on my ear. "I *know* what you're looking for."

And with that, for one vivid interlude, she pressed her whole body up against me. She threw her hipbone between my legs, the length of her stomach along the length of mine, and she held my wrists against the plaster, my arms spread along the wall. I was her specimen, her pane of glass, or some substance she could spread so thin against a surface it would disappear. The stunning fact of it was, I thought, as I breathed the slightly smoky, meaty smell of her skin, that there was no difference between this hard demanding body and the airy evanescence I called Inez.

She spun me around, pressed my head sideways against the plaster. I struggled, but she was too strong. Then I felt something cold, something metal, against my skin. She had pulled the strap of my shirt off my shoulder and was running an icy edge from one shoulder blade across the other. I heard the lock, the chain. She had snapped the handcuffs closed.

"Who are you?" I said, now an inch away from being too scared. "What are you doing?"

"You don't need to know my name."

"I don't like this stuff," I said. I was trying to extract any innuendo from my tone. I was trying to convey to her my gravity. "You have to stop it." The metal was cold to the bone.

"Why don't you tell me," she said, very slowly, still at my ear, "*when you really mean that.* Now, down on the floor."

She twisted me around again, deftly broke the stiffness in my legs, and sent me dropping downward. A pain in my knees spread immediately through my skin and nerves and seeped into places I couldn't keep track of. I was looking up at her, searching for help, searching for balance.

"Fuck me," I said, half under my breath, not meaning to say it so soon, not really ready for it to be heard. She was

holding my chin in her hand. She was tipping me backward
so the strain in my thighs made my whole body tighten. The
ache of my knees on the wood floor was like singing. She let
me suck, for only an instant, on her fingers. I was looking
into her eyes. I thought, Anything, I'll do anything. I said,
"Go ahead, hit me."

It might have been the light that made it happen, or maybe it
was her timing, or more precisely in the end, you could say
it was on account of history, how history happens, how it
leaves its traces. But certainly, the light was crucial. It
wasn't until my sight had finally grown accustomed to the
room that the ugly shift began. Gradually, the high walls
took on a grayish cast, though the matte black paint was
unmistakable, and glimpses of other milling forms, every
time I turned my head, were unavoidable. But I suppose it
was her pacing too, which, perhaps when I begged too hard
or when she saw the smudge of blood at the corner of my
mouth, had decelerated. She had gone to get a strap at one
point, though I'd pleaded with her instead to keep going,
faster, to reach inside my clothes, and when she'd stepped
away, I'd focused long enough in one direction to see two
men embracing. At first it seemed quite harmless—the two
of them just a dozen feet away, one white and rather fleshy,
his tight jeans low beneath a belly, the other slender, black,
and naked. But when I looked again, just as my beautiful,
flawless bully was returning, I saw the white man pull away
and the other collapse before him. The black man was bawl-
ing. His face was contorted, shining vaguely in the dark

room with tears and phlegm and misery. He curled frontward over his knees. He filled his hands with his weeping
face. I could just barely make out the welts, long, thick
wounds, that ran across his shoulders.

She grabbed my neck.

"No, no," I said, suddenly confused. She was lifting me
to my feet with one hand and with the other holding a soft
black strip of leather. She started to turn me again to the
wall. But breathlessly and desperately enough to make her
change her course, I objected: I had to be facing frontward.
The freedom to look around the room had suddenly become
imperative.

She complied, shoving me backward but leaving me facing toward her, up against the wall. The belt came across my
lower ribs and it hurt me more than any blow I can remember. It made me want to holler. But it wasn't enough to keep
me from seeing more.

And that was when I felt the strongest twinge of horror.
With the image of the whipped and fallen, sobbing man still
flashing through me, heated to a blaze in the center of my
mind by all the facts of history, all the crimes and abuses
that have brought so many millions down, and all the lingering curses of the present, I looked into the left-hand corner
of the room where I heard a man raising his voice nearly to a
shout and swearing. He was big, bigger than the others, the
sort of man who changes the unspoken social balance in a
room the minute that he enters, the sort whose hands seem
like heavy tools he's perpetually wielding. He was fully
clothed, in a black shirt, leather vest, his hair wiry and
thick hanging midway down the massive neck. And what was

it, I thought, my heart smarting for a second with too much insight, that he was holding? There in the corner, half in the diffuse gray light whose source was buried in the wall beneath a domelike fixture, and half behind a diagonal beam, was a small naked woman, huddled up against the wall, her mouth gagged and her dead eyes focused inward. She wasn't moving. Her tilted head and bony frame, grayish like a form beneath the water when the lake is clear in moonlight, had fallen limp.

The strap came across my stomach for a third time. My arms jerked involuntarily forward to protect my front, making the cuffs snatch at the bones of my wrists. But much further in, beyond all the pain of the surfaces, beyond the sexual stinging of my "Daphne's" feats, I felt my stomach curdle. I was nauseous. I looked again. The black man was weeping. The huddled woman was deserted. The huge imbalances of life, the heaps of ugliness that have gathered over time, big as mountains, more than any individual's imagination, loomed all around me. Centuries of injustices embedded in the walls. All the desire had left me.

"Stop it," I said. *"That's all."* And I stamped one foot, one time, violently. Whatever the undetectable, unconscious signs of ambivalence my trick had been decoding in my previous pleas, clearly, they had vanished. I was not, she knew, equivocating.

"OK, girl," she said. "OK, OK, OK." She meant it.


That night, I dreamt of Vera. Everything about the dream was benign. She was lending me some clothes, not the orange belt, but some luscious sweater I've never seen, oversize and violet. And rather than thanking her or paying her or writing out some IOU, I signed my name with a thick, inky marker, on a piece of cellophane.

Of course, I don't know what all the details mean. I can't explain the story, and I don't see the point particularly in mulling over, ad infinitum, the implications of transparency or signatures or the "feign" that goes with "cello." But what was important about the dream—this I *felt* even as it was occurring—was that everything I would ever need, every ounce of safety or love or sustenance, was contained in that agreement.

The following day, a Sunday, I went directly to find her at the store. I knew that we would tacitly confess our bond. I knew she would stare me down. She would solve what nothing yet had remedied. In a certain way I had fallen in love with Vera, just like that, at her party, and my failed adventure at The Mansion had made me fall for her more.

"She's in the back," said Eddie, distinctly but distracted, standing by the rack of leather coats. He was holding a hanger and a gray silk blouse. There was consternation written all across his forehead. I couldn't remember his ever looking so severe. It flashed through my mind that perhaps he too knew that Inez was Vera.

He finished buttoning the neck of the blouse and straightened out the collar. It was just like him to dare to talk about what gave him pain. He spoke. "It's difficult," he said, "to keep caring for the same lover year after year after year." He returned the shirt to the rack. "I understand that. Lord knows I haven't always done it." He spoke as if the core of his troubles were already common knowledge, even though he'd never mentioned this before. "But this time," he said emphatically, "her choice appalls me."

I felt embarrassed, shuffled my feet. Did he think her choice was me? Or was he speaking of the boy?

"Vera is full of life," he continued musing, flipping through the blouses, "and she's full of spontaneity. But she's also a person with principles." He stopped, looked me in the eye. "That *kid* is morally bankrupt."

Now I saw why he was troubled. "Eddie," I said, dropping my voice, looking nervously toward the office, "what will you do?"

For several moments, he didn't answer. He had taken another shirt from the rack and was realigning its seams along the hanger.

"*Eddie,*" I repeated. "You're not thinking of leaving her." Suddenly, I felt a pang of longing for that old affinity between them, the cool undying romance, which made everyone who knew them feel sheltered and willing to believe in their own futures. "Where is she?" I asked. I had an urge to go to her. I was ready to suspend my own mission and see if I could help. "Working at the desk?"

"Are you kidding?" He smiled softly, slightly bitter. "Vera at the desk?" The tone was passively sarcastic. "Never gets within a yard of it."

I was trying to spot her, peering around him toward the office door. Whatever happened, if Vera was my secret master, if Vera was Inez, these two could still be together. I wanted them to stay just the way they were.

"Doesn't *touch* the desk work," said Eddie. He studied the blouse now, which hung squarely. His words were half careless, half cutting, aggressive. "Hunt and peck," he said, and he shook his head with the subtlest censure. "Technophobic. Afraid to even turn on the machine."

Right then Vera appeared in the office doorway, her arms full of coats, their hangers dangling over her clasped hands. The neck of her black sweater was soft across her collarbones. A thick white band held the waves of her hair off her forehead. She wore no makeup; her cheeks were red; and I could see she had been crying.

"Vera," I said, my whole soul filling up with sympathy. The look of her, in my eyes, had melted into innocence.

# 24

# THE

# CAB

You can't quit the past. You can't delete it or even close it down, not really. And you can't sneak out on history, even if, as some insist, it's just a bunch of stories. History's tales are much too trenchant, its legends much too thickly layered, its truths too adhesive, for a puny individual to escape it.

But perhaps in rare circumstances—rarer even than in a dark and public club where hideous, old injustices, real beatings, real chains, still lurk among the thrills—you could have the history that resides in you beaten out. You could be broken, broken down, into enough discrete pieces that it would fall away. Certain cracks and stresses would cause the bulk of it to crumble. Your identity could be remade.

Then you could do things. You could do things not prescribed for you by the accumulations of the past and the institutions that preserve them. You could try something else altogether. You could be a Burmese socialite, a trucker's daughter, or a CEO, an inmate or a midwife, an Italian rock and roller. You could love in new directions, learn what once seemed alien, marry a man the family hates, or climb to unprecedented heights on the corporate ladder. You could get promoted. All those attributes that time and culture team up to allot you, all the manners, preferences, and property that determine who you are, could change.

I glanced at my reflection in the bright chrome of the Jack Building. It was Monday. I looked messy, I noted, as I neared the corner, as if I were wearing someone else's clothes. My overcoat no longer announced that refined intelligence I'd seen expressed in it before. Instead, it seemed too big, dwarfing my feet and my ankles; my head looked cartoonish and small. And in a way, all my upbeat speculations about breaking from the grip of time and class were making me feel sad. Their consummation was so sorely distant. I thought of my Daphne, my whomever, and I recalled her sure, bitter hand. She had almost had me, almost made me different. But she didn't. There is such a thing as a real world, I thought. I for one couldn't always leave it.

I turned the corner, nearing the showy entrance to 516 where I'd spent these last months full of promise. It was one of those particular winter mornings, when there hasn't been snow for weeks and the air is dry, and all the motion of the city streets seems in sharper focus. In the morning chill, when the cabs are flashing by and the metal clasp on someone's briefcase catches the reflected light, I always feel my eyesight has improved. Every moving thing flickers as if caught in the camera's flash, and every hat and coat and edge and plane has its own tint and hue like the distinctive markings of a species.

I spied Jean Fine, there in the more-than-perfect high-tech resolution. She was walking briskly toward the curb. I could tell by the slightly frontward tilt of her gait and her right hand pointing toward the ground that she was in the middle of a quarrel. The scarf she wore was vibrant green. I got closer.

". . . over here, *now*," I made out her saying. I furrowed my brow, I'm sure, listening. It was the same voice, the precise intonation I'd heard from outside the supply room. "Do you *hear*?"

I stopped short, apologizing to a poker-faced man for nearly treading on his polished toes, but I kept on peering through the crowd. I followed Jean's gaze and the strained, fretful trail of her voice as it headed for its target.

Tall, erect like Jean herself, but with big handfuls of brownish hair that hid her neck and reached below her shoulders, clutching what looked like an empty canvas bag, stood a teenage girl hailing a taxi. I halted just twenty-odd feet away. To my right I could see the massive double doors of Poplar & Skeen, as the cab approached the curb.

"Fuck you, mom," said the girl, dryly, as if rereporting a grave fact established long before. It was Dolores.

Jean Fine stood, arms akimbo, as the car door slammed. She was frozen, a symbol of human passion, in the moment of incompletion. A wind came and wrapped her beige coat against her thighs. Her rusty hair blew forward, as she watched the taxi pull away. I took a long breath of the cold air as I turned toward the building, and I felt even sadder. This was an excruciating fight, anyone could see, that Jean Fine had been losing for ages.

You can't quit the past, I thought, and I stepped between the brass-rimmed doors. I was pulling at my gloves, deep in meditation. You can't replace your social coordinates—or anyone else's for that matter—and redefine your status sui generis. The lobby's warmth hit me like a wind. For a moment it seemed to carry the mildest smell of optimism. Or perhaps you could, I thought, though not in a city cleaved by neighborhoods, rent by unbridgeable differences, not in a world of bodies. You needed a more thorough fantasy than that, more incorporeal, less germane, where you possessed the very language that your dream is told in and no one else's narrative intervenes.

I was riding up in the elevator, thinking. It hadn't surprised me to see Jean Fine midspat with her daughter at the curb and to discover she didn't have a secret life, rich and violent, like the one I'd tried to give her. You can't plot out another person's dreams. But suddenly, as the doors jerked apart, I forgot about her anyway. I stepped out into the bright fifth floor, and in a flush of the freshest insight, a rushing sequence of different thoughts, I fixed my mind instead on Scrivener. I was stuffing my red gloves in my pocket. I had a new idea.

Briskly, impatiently, I made my way past the island of assistants and headed down the hall. Thursday's printouts were unfinished on my desk, but I ignored them. I booted my machine. As my start-up application loaded my spreadsheets and my message software opened, all my musings seem to congregate around this one startling, yet logical, conclusion: *You had to live as words.* I scanned the "sender" list in my mail log. I noted the usual garbage from Admin, the "for sale" notices and bank-loan ads. And sure enough, I saw right away, there was still no word from Scrivener.

You can't quit the past, I thought, but you can contrive a world without it. You can exist in a place where the world is nothing but the words you say, and the past, unspoken, doesn't guide you. Then you could be anyone you wanted. You could become Francesca. Or, say, if you were Scrivener, you could be anyone at all.

I clicked on "new," and a blank note burst open on my screen. I started typing.

"Scrivener," I wrote. "I need you, come back to me." Like the perfect ping of a ball at the center of the racket, it had hit me. It was no coincidence that he had disappeared precisely when Inez had. Finally, after so many false starts, I realized the truth about my brutal virtuoso.

"OK," I wrote, "so, it wasn't what you meant, you didn't plan to have quite so much information about me and know all those details about my life. But SO WHAT, SCRIV? Sex is sex. Sadism is sadism. You can't just up and leave (so out-of-the-blue, so rashly), we've got to mull this over (work things through), what makes you so convinced it has to finish? Do you feel guilty? Are you scared?

"Look, you don't know the full import of all this, you don't see it: it's not a thing of recreation for me, my whole status—my future!—rides on me and you. You've got to at least agree to talk about it more. Please, Scrivener, send me something. Communicate. Elaine."

I paused. My fingers had been splattering across the keys like water from a tap, or rain, and finally, as if there'd been a break in the clouds, I stopped to read over what I'd written. It was barely sensical. I shook my head and rubbed my palms against my knees. I'd been trying to articulate this raw predicament before I'd had a chance to mentally unwrap it. I hit delete and watched the window shrivel and disappear. I tried again.

"Dearest Scrivener." This time I hovered over the

words. "Only now, in a startling moment of revelation, do I see how much I've missed you. Little do you know the turmoil, the nightmarish overturning of my life (inner and outer) your absence has caused. I have reported to you here and there that I've met troubled times, that my standing on the job has been suddenly in question and my own abilities seem to have collapsed (I'm a wreck), but I didn't explain (I just didn't even know!) it was your absence that had caused it. I didn't understand who you are.

"So now I'm contemplating these strange events and the nature of our true ties, and I realize that you could have all these different feelings (guilt, maybe, confusion, disappointment?) that would keep you away. But, Scrivener, I need you to reconsider. I'm convinced communicating we can resolve this and go on again like before. And if you're averse to discussion (if that prospect strikes you only as interference) well, that too I can honor. Nothing asked, nothing said. But, please, PLEASE, write me either way."

I broke off once more. Across my monitor, the band of sunlight, just then, produced a hazy glare. For the first time since I'd arrived in my office, I leaned back, rolling away from the desk just slightly, and rocking deeply backward in my chair. I stared into the mint green glow of my desktop pattern with its faux Naugahyde design, between two open windows and a third containing my last attempt at writing, and I took a minute to sort things through. Never before had Scrivener been so absent, and yet never had he seemed so near, so strangely voluminous of spirit. I had always thought of him as understanding, and hence, metaphorically, close by, a phantom in data form, mute and wise, and now, seeing how much more he really understood of me than I'd ever dreamed of, he seemed to *exist,* right up against me in the air.

Once more I hit "new mail."

"S.," I wrote this time.

"It's you, isn't it? Come back to me, Inez. I'm begging.

"Francesca."

25

# T H E

# W A V E

I don't like the word "intuition," which, however noncommittally, suggests some sort of sixth sense I don't believe we have. And I don't like to call it an "inkling," which is such a chipper, nebulous excuse for a word. But the good guess I took that night must have come from *somewhere* in the feebly mapped terrain of my mind. Buoyed by the day's revelation, the neat, even obvious fit of "Scrivener" into the mystery of my life, I truly had a *feeling* I would find him. I logged on.

It had been weeks since I'd sat down there. To my left my heavy crimson drapes looked almost unfamiliar, and the room seemed much dimmer than it had in the past. Cars passed below at long intervals with a hum almost indistinguishable from the sound of a wind that had kicked up early in the evening. The entire room smelled of soap and trees.

It was late. Why at that hour I even bothered trying I really can't say, but there in the ribbon at the top of my screen, the clock read 12:08. I was gripping a warm cup of tea, with milk, which I rarely had a taste for—never, in fact, when I'd sat in those shadows before—but that night I'd had an unusual thirst for it; this was plainly a side effect of anxiety. In the past, I'd logged on to the board feeling sanguine, feeling at times even vain. Always I'd have been rounding the last bend of an active day and mulling over the bits of flattery or appreciation harvested throughout it; I'd have been largely oblivious to what would come after. It wouldn't have occurred to me then that I might someday require a prop like this—the milk, the thick weighty mug— to ward off a case of timidity.

But now the cup wasn't buffer enough. The day had been neither bright nor productive, and even the keenest memory wouldn't have reaped any feelings of achievement. On the contrary, that morning, I'd forgotten to write up a memo for Marissa; I'd accidentally insulted a deputy in PR who insisted my tone was rude; and I'd dropped a whole stack of binders in the lounge area, knocking over a bowl of soup. It was Gerald's. Then on top of all that I was another half-day late on my dailies, which made it three days tardy all told, and by the time I left the office at 6:30, there was a pulling in my throat that felt like a permanent muscular condition; it was nothing other than a yearning to cry. In this state, inputting the old familiar log-on commands was hardly the joyride it used to be.

I logged on as "Lisanne." If my handle were familiar, I thought, my presence might chase him off, and such a rejection would be insufferable. I preferred, at least for now, to lurk. "Observer," I chose for my profile. Holding my mug with both hands, I watched the activity on the welcome screen and scanned through the long list of names. There were Sajeed, Paola, and Mikhail, to name a few, Claus, Joelle, and Raoul. And there was Rogueman. Abruptly I saw this last appear in the status field at the top of the screen.

"<Rogueman>," it said, "goes to <The Forum>." Obviously, he wasn't ecstatic to see me. I felt a twinge of remorse and embarrassment. Then I started to float through the rooms. I tapped in a series of random commands, not quite convincing myself of my own nonchalance, but lightly, without any method or rush, and I made my way around the server.

I typed "goto 10." No one was there. I typed in 11 and 6. Three members, all using the names of red-light districts in different cities, were swapping dirty jokes that were neither provocative nor funny. "That's because his wanger's much too small," said "CombatZone." I read the response—"<Tenderloin> laughs uproariously"—and bolted.

Then I tried 15. I tried 31. I remembered, with a sudden rush of warmth that traveled up my rib cage and under my arms, another time I'd typed in that same number. I remembered being shoved down on my stomach. I remembered the force of that torso from behind. A kind of aperture seemed to close in my lungs, just as my breath came in, and my hand jumped from the keys to my lips. It was as if covering my mouth at that moment impulsively would safeguard the delicacy inside me that had been so savagely stolen. I remembered those hands pinning down my arms.

But the screen was entirely blank. I breathed out. What anyhow was I thinking? Did I imagine I would find "him" there, logged on as himself, wandering the rooms as I was or forcing some "Charlaine, "Simone," up against a wall? Or did I expect, against all the odds, that I'd suddenly see "Inez," that I'd spot "her" and corner her and get at the truth, saying, "Scrivener, it's you, I know it. You have to come back to me"?

I typed "goto" again. This time I proceeded systematically. You couldn't use the "where" command without your party being paged, so to search less conspicuously, I figured, I'd work channel by channel heading down toward room 1. Some rooms were blocked. Twenty-six said "private," as did 25 and 24. In 23 a couple of timid types were arranging a date for drinks. Twenty-two was empty, and so was 21. Gradually, the maze of "places" with no one inside them began to feel cramped. The board's well-secured anonymity became like a darkness, the electronic equivalent to crawl space. Seventeen was filled with text—the drawn-out conversation of three friends. Sixteen was small talk—Hassan and Evelina discussing "hobbies"—and I wondered whether, after all this time, the sexual redemption I'd been granted before would still work on me anyway. Fourteen was empty. Thirteen was blocked. My earlier determination was like a tablet dissolving. The remoteness of Scrivener juxtaposed with my disintegrating optimism made me seem, in my own eyes, invisible.

And as I felt the taste of self-defeat, which I'd been living with now for so long, grow twice more sour, I gave up at last in frustration. I'd reached channel 12. The whole attempt was just another failure. It was a ridiculous waste—until, as a matter of habit, preparing to log off, I typed in one last instruction. "Goto 1."

Simone, Justine, Raoul, Julius, Kingkong, and Noel. I read the names lined up, flush left, the entire length of my screen. Imre and Jacques. This last appeared frequently, more than the rest. Then I scanned further—Diva, Claus— and stopped. Inez.

I took a breath. I read it twice. A sound came up in my

throat, like the meaningless syllable of a sleeper in the midst
of a complicated dream. My mind got caught on that name
the way a shirtsleeve gets caught on a nail, and my eyes shot
up to the top of the screen to double-check my own identity,
to make sure I was disguised as Lisanne. Then I began to
read.

"<Jacques>: I don't think you're listening."

Nearly every other line was attributed to him. The other
members, it seemed, were just watching.

"<Justine>: easy, guy. is he a guy?" She was addressing
some other bystander.

But Jacques wasn't heeding. The next line again was his.

"<Jacques>: I don't think you're moving fast enough,
are you?"

"<Mikhail>: he's a poser. he won't do anything."

"<Jacques>: Right, now take it. That's how I want you:
buckled over."

I ran my eyes over the words quickly, skimming but absorbing at once.

"You think you want me?" he went on. "How much?"
There was a lag but no answer. "You think you want me
hard enough to have me?"

By now I was completely sucked in. Anyone would have
been. But no one, I suspect, would have been as dumb-
founded as I was when I saw the words that came next.

"<Inez>: i do. i know it."

There was more.

"<Inez>: please please i do i want it."

Immediately I began to scroll backward to see if this
could be true. Immediately I saw her name, repeated, screen
after screen that came before this. Each time she was plead-

ing. "let me," she said, one screen back. "i'm down, i'm under you, do it." And one screen more, "<Inez>: yes take me. you can own me. i'm yours."

All at once, the way a wave collides with an undertow and in a frenzy of foam tries to sort out its ensuing direction, I experienced a jumble of urges. I wanted to join in, to top her and love her, but also to defer, to withdraw and see her restored to the person she had been previously. To witness Inez submitting was a reversal that effaced me, left me memoryless and dazed and ever more perversely wanting. I wanted to beat her like Jacques did, but what I needed most was her tyranny. I needed her to be who she *had* been.

"<Jacques>: I'm not ready yet." He had forced her to unbuckle his belt. But now he was making her wait again.

"<Inez>: i'm your slave. let me taste you."

My breath seemed to backtrack, to go under, as I wedged my hand between my legs and gripped the underside of my thigh, as if to hold myself down, as if to prevent myself from floating up off the chair and swimming out, somewhere safer, somewhere clear, out beyond the white water.

# 26

# CERTIFICATES

# AND DIPLOMAS

Every night for the entire week that followed I logged back on to the board. Every night I looked for her or him but she or he wasn't there. I'd lurk for hours, regularly changing my name to Francesca to see if I could catch my mysterious fugitive's eye, but for all intents and purposes, she or he had left again. After that fluke of a night when "Inez" had appeared, manifestly someone *other* than who she always was—as if some sort of ventriloquist or amnesiac—that name did not reappear.

I felt I was back to square one. Even today I remember it dourly. Not only had I lost my passionate and tormenting deliverer, seen her slip away from me into the ether, but she had slipped away from herself. She had been swallowed up by the personality, the role and comportment, tastes and behavior, of someone diametrically opposite. The idea of my Inez groveling, kneeling, obeying someone else's commands was like some sort of radical subtraction that made thinking itself seem hard. How was I to tell at this point if I even wanted her? I knew I could never be anyone's master. The whole swirling game of who's who on the board, in which I'd already lost my own epistemological center, had reached one more degree of abstraction.

By day, on the other hand, my life had grown only more real. The march of incidents continued, to the beat of a continuous inevitability. Everything seemed to happen promptly and irreversibly and always without my consent. Even now, looking back, across the intervening years, I can't dream up what circumstances I could have devised that would have deflected the episode that happened next.

It was the Monday after the holidays. Kay insisted we go out to lunch. Somehow I'd managed to suffer through only one or two yuletide gatherings, professing a cherished atheism and a general disappointment with the hypocrisy of the traditions of the West, but Kay had succeeded in roping me into this last, albeit belated and modified celebration. She wore a suit that day, which was unusual, but her typical abundance of rings.

We wandered down toward the court buildings. "Here," she said, "I want you to pick." She had me parked in front of a window display featuring several women's shirts and an array of unisex jackets. One of the mannequins was snow-mobiling.

"Kay," I said, "don't do this to me." Not only did she know I'd planned nothing in return, but on top of that, this store was obviously out of her price range.

Nevertheless, she was unflinchingly confident. "Come on," she prodded. "You know how all this ritual sends me."

"Don't," I repeated. *"Really."* It was true I was eyeing one boxy jacket with zippers at the cuffs and an exceptional little collar that would've suited, equally, a priest or an astronaut, but everything else looked idiotic. And besides, I had no intention of indulging her. "Look, Kay," I said, now in a tone that was all the things—sullen, colorless, frank, astute—that Christmas most certainly was not, "you can do this auto-buying all you want, but you can't force me to participate."

Kay didn't mind my tone. It appeared to have no effect on her, and fondly, almost in the manner of an adult to a child, she touched my chin and smiled. She fairly blurted out the irritating subtext you knew was there, which went something like, *Be that way then, I'll pick it myself for you.*

But none of Kay's attentions, whether or not I'd absorbed them, could have swerved my life off its now advanced course when it came to my plight at the office. There, my story by now was long set in motion, and the complex apparatus at Poplar & Skeen, which charted what each individual got and what each didn't, wasn't a thing you outsmarted. There, in the world of productivity cycles and feedback loops, task-adjustment outcomes and up-to-the-minute evaluations, events abided by their own aloof set of imperatives.

So when we returned to the office that afternoon and I was intercepted abruptly in the brick hall by Marissa, there was no way to escape what was coming. "Yes?" I said.

"Uuummmm," she replied. It took her a big effort to get it out. Marissa had recently been promoted to work under Gerald, in a role they called "traffic coordinator," overseeing the flow of dailies and charts and subdivision invoices between our three departments. "Elaine," she started again. She was respectful but totally uneasy. Her navy dress pulled at her armpits, and her face was a tiny bit moist. "Mr. Cronin," she said, "wants to see you."

Another ten thousand dollars added to her salary and she too would have called him Gerald, I thought, but she would never get there; the system didn't allow for that kind of breakthrough.

"I mean, he wants to see you *now*."

I knew exactly what was happening. Back in my office I stalled, hung up my coat. I checked for mail from Scrivener, a gesture which by now was on the order of a tic or an addiction, and I chipped a bit of clear polish off a nail. Though outwardly I probably looked unruffled, there was a flash of chaos in my mind, when, standing perfectly still, looking down at my nails, I imagined an anonymous figure furiously twisting my arm up behind me and shoving me up against the wall. I wanted comfort so badly.

Gerald was pacing. I couldn't remember the last time I'd seen him up out of his chair. As he passed behind his desk, I watched the way his head obscured first the hawks then the set of leather-bound volumes—a history of the century, or at least up through the two wars—then the pewter figurines, the glass brick, the jug. To me, that backdrop reasserted, with each sweep he made past it, the presence and intelligibility of everything this man believed.

"Botsch," he said. He made a ticking sound with his tongue in between the words, as if to mark off the seconds passing.

For once, I had no impulse to act eager. Beyond the makeshift arrogance I'd erected, I was sickeningly afraid.

He went on: "Durbin says he's a full week short of dailies. Fine was forced to attend the Monday Morning with no Skeen totals. And Mr. Brill asked me a week ago for 0-6 forms I still don't have." His tone was level, almost robotic, as if more than the words' content, he wanted me to contemplate each phoneme, as if each individual syllable spelled out the gloom. Then he stopped and turned to face me, laying his hands flat on the corner of his desk and leaning in. It was the sort of pose an actor would use to sell aspirin. I was looking at the man, but I couldn't line up the words with the body, the looming implications for my fate with what the man said. He looked into my eyes. "*Seven days late on dailies.*"

There was a silence. At last in that gap I matched the words up with myself, with what could happen *to me* on account of their veracity. What I heard was a threat, in short. It was a reckoning of my recent past; it was an exegesis on my chances in the future. Immediately I knew there was only one doorway out of this cell, and it was restitution.

But just as my nervously nimble mind began studying the means to right things, Gerald's palm slammed down on the desktop. His voice at this volume had a timbre I had never heard. He was shouting. *"That's not acceptable!"*

I looked down at my hands, one gripping the knuckles of the other so they hurt. The only trope that could describe my emotions right then was to say that they were falling, pouring down all around me like rain. My heart was rattling like a storm against the glass. I didn't answer. I stared, stock-still, at the pen stand.

"That's not acceptable," he repeated, the volume almost normal now, but the enunciation just the same. "No further warnings will be provided. That's the bottom line."

And then came the oddest thing, the thing I didn't anticipate as I prepared myself to leave, my posture and my countenance, I knew, fully expressive of my remorse and my desperate commitment to change things. His business accomplished, his point made, Gerald nonetheless continued to speak to me. He'd begun again to pace. "Elaine," he said, his voice low and airy. It was as if he'd become another man. It was collegial, even warm, the way he intoned my name. Suddenly I saw that he *wanted* me to survive this. There couldn't be any other explanation. "Events," he said, stressing the word with great care, "will not slow down to wait for you. Nor will they leapfrog into the future on the force of whim. Concentrate, Elaine. Don't throw away what you've gotten."

And as he passed once more along the shelves, behind his aging, leather, high-backed chair, his footsteps muffled by the Mongolian rug, I realized that all Gerald's nostalgia—the hawks, the certificates and diplomas—was suffused with real gravity and sadness. What I'd always thought was conservatism in Gerald or just unoriginal taste was in fact a form of humility.


That evening, I did not log on to the board. Nor did I for a long time thereafter. Instead I wrote to Scrivener. I didn't care anymore if he answered. I knew he would at least read what I said, and I could feel in my own chest just how it would echo. I'd never sent him mail from home like this, and in a certain way I felt this was fitting. It was my attempt to integrate in my mind the roles that he played in my life: to retrieve him from the officialdom of the job and yet distinguish him simultaneously from the confusing masquerade, the shifting kaleidoscope of the bulletin board's identities. Via mail, rather than in the faceless real time, say, of room

1, I felt it would be just Scrivener and I, conversing in the manner that we always had. It was in this cleaner, simpler, more purposeful form that I would announce my plan to forsake him.

"Dear Scrivener,

"As I add it up tonight, it's four or five weeks now since I heard from you—that, after many years of daily notes. In those weeks nothing but the lousiest things have happened, to the point that I'm basically on probation at the only job I've ever had that I actually wanted and wanted to do well at. It's pretty rotten. Recently, as I've explained to you, I realized you might have something to do with all that. I have reasons to believe that you're the person I'd been having encounters with, which gave me such a sense of relief and serenity and confidence. I figured it out finally that it's not plain old coincidence that you disappeared exactly when Inez did. If it's the truth, then I guess I feel your just disappearing and rejecting me and withholding from me sexually even after all my explanations is pretty low.

"But the main thing I'm writing for is to say that I'm not about to keep this up. There's no point in waiting around and hoping. I feel dumb for one thing. It's pretty clear by now that all the searching and waiting I've been doing, and all the letters I've sent to you recently trying to reconnect, have done absolutely no good. Things for me have only gotten worse.

"So, I'm just writing to let you know that I won't be writing again. It hasn't helped me an ounce. Perhaps it'll be to my advantage to forget about it all—you, 'Inez,' the rest of it—and to try to just concentrate on what's in front of me.

"But I also want you to know that I have a lot of regret. Maybe you can carry the load of that with me. If you have it in you.

"Sincerely,

"Francesca/Elaine."

# 27

# THE

# HORSE

By the time the real ax fell I had already been through the grief. Several more weeks passed during which, constantly, I felt fearful and inadequate. Incident after incident, I felt thoroughly out of my depth. In a meeting with my Accounting counterparts, for the first time I didn't say a word. Whereas in the past months I'd been forthright and loquacious, now whenever a thought came to mind that seemed a worthy contribution, my heart would get loud and my skin would grow damp at the prospect of saying it aloud; never, throughout the whole unexceptional, rather monotonous conference, did there seem a lengthy enough appropriate pause in which to insert my immediately obsolete opinions.

Then later, for instance, when Charlotte appeared I suffered the same kind of paralysis. She'd ventured down to my office, a pocket in the hive she'd probably never seen, to track down the 0-6 forms I was to regularly update and send up the chain of command. Durbin and Gerald had already called me before them to inform me that my tardiness was plugging the pipes, but now Brill was sending his hatchet girl directly. She knocked on my half-open door. "Hello," she said, posing it rather as a goading question than a greeting, meaning, simply, Do you or do you not have a brain? "There's a *problem*." The inflection was tailored quite precisely for a restless pet or a child. "Our skeds go haywire, Elaine, every time those 0-6's are delayed. It's twice now." She wore a dark red dress over big breasts, firm hips, and thick, invincible shoulders. "I'll be needing, I'd say right about immediately, an accurate ETA."

I felt a mild churning in my stomach, my hand gripping my mouse. I could only barely recall the last time I saw her, when we'd circled each other, silently bargaining, in an economy of disdain and politeness that had fluctuated in the subtlest increments. This time, without question, the market was hers. "Yes," I said, "Charlotte," enunciating carefully, but the volume gone soft and my gaze fallen to the floor. This time I had no capital socked away, no scarce indispensable skills, nothing to leverage her kindness. "They're coming," I said under my breath, trying to swivel away in my chair, but too tense actually to turn more than a few degrees.

"I'm sure they are, Elaine—eventually. What I *need*," she enunciated, "is a reliable ETA."

It wasn't that I couldn't reproduce in myself that feeling of wielding professional assets or remember the timing of punches and feints you perform to establish, in conversation, your authority. Plenty of times alone in my office or apartment I was quite capable of recalling my old charisma or a sense of my hard-won expertise. It was just that I couldn't hang on to it. Like alchemy, the minute you put me in a room with another human being, who similarly had banked a quantity of worth, who reported to the duty of life with a sum of merits and who knew it, I instantly lost perspective. I'd feel hollowed out within seconds—impoverished.

So when it came time, for instance, to explain to Jean Fine why I'd given Brill that ETA if I couldn't have met it, I could come up with absolutely nothing to say. My face was burning. It felt as if it had grown not only pink but actually larger, my cheeks and forehead so hot from the rush of contrition they seemed to have inflated.

"You knew you had to get the weeklies to me first, but you committed to do the 0-6's simultaneously?" She seemed genuinely perplexed, not angry. She was seated before me, her elbows symmetrically propped on the desk, her fingers intertwined. I guess whatever it was that had made her feel we were peers had been siphoning away over time. That day, I can remember it still, she wore a brooch the size of a mussel shell and shaped like a knotted vine.

"Well," I said, "see it was early in the day. We had—or there was, I mean—a good portion of the weeklies were duplicates." I was lying. They weren't. My bun was pulling at my scalp. I felt the last dregs of our rapport trickling out. "I had Paul bringing me some of the back figures." I knew she could see my duplicity as plainly as she could see the redness climbing up from under the scooped collar of my black rayon blouse. Suddenly it occurred to me that this was one of the ways people develop asthma.

And each time I sat down to accomplish things, to finally plow through the accrual of tasks and get back on schedule, I'd be waylaid by a stream of jabbering thoughts about my worsening predicament. Sometimes I'd actually begin to chant in my head—the sort of murmur you strike up to keep yourself company on a deserted street where you should never have been walking alone—repeating words like "Almost almost almost" or "I'm home I'm home I'm home," as if such a rhythm could backhandedly produce the direly needed calm.

Then, failing to catch up with the workload, I stayed later and later at the office. At night, finally passing through the lobby at 8:15, too distressed to smile or even nod at the night guard, who eventually began to glare when I passed (later, he took up the passively hostile routine of dangling his pencil and flicking one end with his finger so the clack of his nail on the wood could be heard from the doorway all the way to the elevator), I would bypass the café altogether and eat canned minestrone or frozen potpies at home. My main objective was to get into bed as quickly as possible. Sleep was the relief, the asylum, that kept me safe from my own quietly persistent and insidious self-effacement.

So when the time came for the reckoning, in a way, I had already been through the hard part. I couldn't have felt a whole lot worse. I had given up entirely on hearing from Scrivener, though I was fully convinced he was the one. He'd been gone now for almost two months, and I'd have been naive to keep thinking he'd come back to me. And as far as finding a remedy at the hands of somebody else—Jacques, for instance, or "Daphne"—I was always emotionally thwarted by the recollection of too many discouraging attempts. Basically, there was no further down for my sunken spirit to plummet.

Materially, on the other hand, there was still plenty of havoc that could be wrought. Looking back from this perch, years later, I don't think I ever fully grasped this. I didn't realize how very easy it is for life to pick you up by the collar and plunk you down where it wants to. I arrived that day, as on all the days previous, a half an hour later than I'd meant to, barricaded in my overcoat like a hermit, and brazenly avoiding my hellos. I was under the illusion that the buildup of errors I'd committed functioned by now like a shell, that I was therefore, by some logic, exempted from the usual interactions. A senior from Marketing waved at me in the lobby, but I stepped into the elevator supposedly without having seen. I didn't meet the gaze of a single colleague passing in the brick corridor. As I walked through Billing, I uncoiled the long black scarf that I'd worn wound round my head and neck like a cowl, and I can remember still my own ignorance and simplicity in assuming that day would be just like the others. It wasn't.

"We've determined that it's in the interests of a variety of parties that we do some shuffling around."

That was how he started. How many times now had I sat in the forest green chair, my moist palms against the coarse upholstery? I was counting in my head the occasions that month that Gerald had called me in. This time I never even looked up at the hawks on the bookcase behind him. Almost from the moment I sat down, my eyes were focused on the floor.

"Several problems have arisen in other departments, unrelated to you or our affairs."

But this time Gerald's tone seemed different. This wasn't the way he'd begun the three meetings before this.

"Administration is expanding by four desks and absorbing staff from adjacent departments."

His tone was distant, quiet, as if he were letting the

words simply float out of his mouth rather than actually pronouncing them.

"This puts Operations down two assistants."

I circled my eyes around the faded swirls in the border of the Mongolian rug.

"Those positions are critical to the entire division's functions."

I was comparing the patches where the rug was well preserved and rich in color and where it was worn.

"We feel you'd be superbly helpful in taking up those tasks."

Then my eyes were still. It was doublespeak. I looked at his face for a split second, but only in action, not in spirit. I couldn't effectively see out, at that moment, nor let the image of him in.

"And frankly, Elaine, we feel we must decrease your duties. You and I both know your performance has been insufficient."

Now my eyes had shifted back down to the floor. It was the most tenuous form of denial. I stared at the rug, the night blue of it, the maroon.

"We believe the changes will benefit everybody."

At that point, there began a very long pause. Gerald was finished. I stared at the deep brown base of the desk. I stared at the tin antique waste bin with its chipping scene of a classical army, a cluster of helmeted soldiers, a goddess on a chariot whipping a horse. In me, something was beginning to crumble, as if my throat and my heart, the center of my spine, were turning to a very fine powder. It was the feeling you get when you finally acknowledge exhaustion.

Yet, I knew at the same time I had to resist what was

happening, that now might be my only chance to contest this turn of events. I knew I had to turn it around.

"Gerald," I said, shaking my head, affecting camaraderie and know-how. I began to gesture uncharacteristically with my hands. I know I must have sounded tipsy. "That's nutty!" I was speaking in an altogether inappropriate singsong. "No, really. That's a mistake. I mean," I shrugged, "Gerald, my *skill* levels."

I looked up at him. He was turned away, not answering. I fixed on the side of his face, the grayish, concave cheek, the eerily translucent skin. "But Gerald," I said, now suddenly crisply, emphatic, "Assistant?" By now I was quite sincerely incredulous. *"Operations?"*

And what transpired then—I sensed it even at the time— was probably the most complicated silence I've ever experienced. It lasted whole minutes. Gerald didn't move, his chair swiveled slightly away from me a foot or so from his desk, his elbows propped on the high leather arms, his head hunched oddly between the stiff raised shoulders of his suit jacket. Peering at the clean, square face, waiting, at once brokenhearted and querulous, for some reply, I saw again the ancient sorrow I'd seen in him three weeks ago. Again I saw how his stiltedness, his obsession with standards and codes, all served to shelter and contain the nostalgia he embodied for the rest of us. Gerald respected history and he hated it; he believed it would have the last word. He grieved the loss of time and the fixity of things that were over. He understood survival, how imperative and paltry it was. I saw all his knowledge vividly right then, or I heard it, perhaps, in his muteness. I knew that he wanted me to endure.

He lifted one hand to his forehead. The motion was

tender, it was felt. It was the gesture of another man altogether, someone who understood your wishes and your fail-
ings, someone who saw you as a friend.

"Elaine," he said. "This does not foreclose on other
prospects in the future should your performance warrant
them." His voice was just audible. "And I think it will. The
present decision, however, is final."

# 28

# T H E

# S N O W

That night it snowed. It was the heaviest snow of the season so far, though you wouldn't have classified it as a blizzard. It was the sort of snow that filled up the air not with its movement, not with the wind, but solely on account of its thickness. Each flake had its own density and stillness.

I left the office long after dark. I had managed, ironically, to accomplish more that day than I'd accomplished in ages, finally clearing two sets of dailies off my desk that had been stalled there for a week. But even as I was able to make some progress for once, every inch of the way had been labored. Filling out cells in a grid, matching figures, and tabulating losses had never felt so strenuous. Determining a single digit was more like moving a crate in the heat than hitting a few buttons on a keyboard, and by eight o'clock when I printed out hard copies of the now complete spreadsheets and graphs, my back and head were aching.

Downstairs the guard flicked his pencil, standing in front of the darkened glass doors. He was visibly taken aback, I saw, when I managed to work my pained and weary face into a friendly expression. It was a vestige, a meek and torpid trace of the motivation and pleasure, the sense of wealth and warmth of which I'd long been dispossessed. As I walked out into the ice-cold air and felt the snow against my face, that distant, gratuitous smile sank back inside me so far it was as if it had vanished forever.

The streets were extraordinarily hushed. Soundless, big, clumsy snowflakes landed on ledges, gathered in corners, and lingered on my sleeves. My hair grew wet as did my lips and my cheeks where I breathed an accumulating dampness into my black knit scarf. So much darkness and so much quiet, the way the snow's very substance filling the air created a feeling of enclosure, of matter taking up space in some sort of physical container—all of it caused me to imagine myself in the aisles of a vast vacant theater. I imagined the rows of empty seats and the high ceiling. I imagined walking down the aisle through scattered wrappers and other debris left over from a long-past performance as I shuffled through the new-fallen snow. Out there in the vaulted, vacated city, I had the deep, almost haunting sensation that some sort of raucous and dramatic event, filled with bathos and unrestrained oratory, was over.

I turned down Duane. At Jay Street I felt indecisive, even fretfully so, without really knowing what was so crucial, as I considered whether to take the long route or the direct one. I suppose the prospect of walking an extra quarter of an hour through one of the town's poorer neighborhoods—where the buildings didn't hide their decay and you knew there were people who, equating the devalued state of their surroundings with the cheapness of life in general, cared little for your individual existence—seemed soothing to me somehow, seemed a way to dull the significance of that day's unprecedented catastrophe. But I was torn: I was also gravitating toward Eddie and Vera's not more than eight blocks ahead along my usual path. I turned down Jay briefly but changed my mind and came back again, leaving two sets of cluttered footprints on the otherwise pristine sidewalk. I headed toward Reine Nadine.

By the time I reached the brightly lit storefront, I could feel the melted snow dripping along my hairline. The top of my briefcase had collected a small drift. But my pants and my blouse and the insides of my platform shoes had all stayed perfectly dry. And it was more than the snow on my toes at that point, around 8:45 at the end of the strangest, quietest day, that hadn't literally or figuratively soaked through to me. There was, of course, another more harrowing, more horrible form of precipitation that I still had not absorbed. So when Vera waved me in with her typically reckless gesture and exaggerated smile, it didn't have much of an effect on me. I hadn't revealed to anyone, including myself, the real proportions of the calamity I'd just suffered which Vera's human attention might have helped to cure.

She was positioned atop a stepladder at the right-hand side of the shop, wearing a dark shade of lipstick just this side of purple. Evidently, she was adjusting the huge blown-up photo that ran the whole length of the wall. It was a muted, grainy picture, shot in the sixties, of a dozen or so skiers—some in hats, some in turtleneck sweaters, some in belted jackets—lined up on the slope in a row. Vera laughed and raised her hand to her forehead when she saw me try the door and found it bolted.

"Come come," she said, seconds later, holding the heavy glass open. " 'Stás mojada, Girlie, give me your coat." Her broad hands brushed the snow off my shoulders. Her blunt-cut nails were painted bright orange. Then she stopped short and looked into my face. Even though I couldn't feel it myself, had no consciousness of how firmly my jaw was set and how stricken the look in my eyes, Vera must have detected it. The expression in her own cream-brown face, surrounded by the coarse, black hair that hung in waves down past her shoulders, turned to worry. One rush of the romance I'd felt toward her weeks back went through me, but mostly what brought the heat to my face and the tingle of release in my shoulders was just her earnest concern. "What what?" she was saying. She kept peering around my eyes and mouth for an answer. I had no idea what she saw. "Whaaat?" she said again. That's when I started to cry.

Vera didn't say anything to Eddie. Back in the office, carrying my wet scarf and coat over her arm, she just gave him a signal with her hand and a nod with her head and drew him seamlessly into the encounter. "My amorcita is soaked," she was saying, "and upset, and she's going to sit down with us and tell us whatever—the whole thing—that's the matter."

I sniffled and peered around, sifting anxiously through the mood of the room, and checking for strain or antagonism between them. Not that I could have held back any. The day's pain was already beginning to blast through the surface, and I probably couldn't have stopped it by then, even if I'd stepped into the middle of a dogfight. But it seemed I didn't have to. Eddie had swiveled around from the desk, and scanning his face for signs, I saw only the usual sanity and discernment in his typically receptive expression. The whole scene looked constant enough and welcoming.

So as Eddie leaned in with his elbows on his knees, as ready to listen as anyone ever can be, I started weeping, finally, uncontrollably. Days of ambition, months of labor and hope were collapsing, like rubble, tumbling, it seemed, on top of my lungs, so that my sobs had to heft whole stones of it off of me, forging a gap I could breathe through. For a good while Eddie didn't speak, and when he did, it was unsurpassably kind. "Cry," he said, "you can explain when you're ready."

Then at some point—I don't recall how long I'd been so ungracefully gasping—Eddie actually got up and took me in his arms. With one hand he held the back of my head, and with the other drew me into the most persuasive and palpable safety you could think of. His chest was a fortress. It had the same kind of hardness and corporeality, the scale, that makes architecture much more than an "art form." Who can argue that the design of a high-rise, in which thousands, maybe tens of thousands, of people take shelter and conduct lives, is on the same order as some miniature bronze horseman? And who could mistake the shape of Eddie's torso, the feel of my cheek against his chest and of my arms folded into his musculature, for an ordinary form of comfort?

"Tell us," I heard him say, and I was so relieved to hear him speaking for both of them. I could feel the rumble of his voice against my temple.

"Shit," I answered. "God damn it." There were many of these empty expletives before I said anything substantial.

"This has *got* to be about a man or the job," said Vera, directing me back to the chair, setting a cup of coffee on the file cabinet beside me.

"*Both*," I corrected her, moaning. "God damn it."

"I knew it, didn't I?" She was fairly pleased about her prescience. You knew she was speaking from experience, but there was an ease to her manner, as if the experience was behind her. "A man *at* the job," she said. "I'm right, yes? I know I am."

"No."

"Nooo?" she said. "A lover? A friend?" She was beginning to grow urgent and indignant at this point: she didn't like, one bit, whoever was responsible for this wailing. "What on earth did he do to you?"

"Left me." Still crying, I could only speak in these short, aborted monosyllables.

"Out the door? You didn't tell us. He *couldn't* have."

"Left me," I repeated.

She was covering her mouth with her hand, shaking her head back and forth almost sleepily. She didn't know the worst was still coming.

*"And then I lost my job."*

"Lost your *job?*" By now she was thoroughly incensed and also perplexed, both at the same time.

Meanwhile, Eddie was nodding. I heard him murmur, and though there were no discrete words, I knew the sound meant recognition.

Vera turned to him. "Lost her *job?*"

Again Eddie nodded serenely. He understood me. It was just this sort of secondary, underlying connection—between money and love, between professional standing and human psychology—that Eddie could always comprehend. And hearing his sagacious, unruffled affirmation, that little signal of wisdom that was no more than a vibration at the back of his throat, and feeling reassured that my Vera and Eddie were a team again, I started, fitfully, to speak.

The whole story of my nightlife and my sudden undoing welled up like a pool in my mind, hovering over a dam just opened. I didn't try to explain the electronic nature of it, or the slippery identities of the principal cast, but I spun the tale of how Scrivener, a longtime though secretive friend, had fed me a loving sort of punishment, delivered a deeply reassuring degradation that had given me a sense of my place. I told of how, having paid a metaphorical price with my body, I'd been strangely able to succeed, how, shorn of rank by this treatment and debased psychologically, I'd grown proportionately euphoric and confident. And I told them how all of that had changed when this nightly lover and daytime friend had left me. "Fled," I said, "without a single word, without the littlest scrap of explanation. And ever since then I've been useless." I threw up my hands like a widow, like a woman whose loved ones are gone or whose son has had run-ins with police on a few too many occasions. "I'm a basket case," I said. "I can't function. Every time you turn around I'm fucking up one thing or another. And now, after everything else that has gone wrong for me, well, now *this*."

Vera was holding me firmly at the back of the neck, while Eddie, seated beside the potted cactus with the white light of the monitor glowing on the desk behind him, continued at intervals to nod. When, a month ago, I'd told them I'd been passed over for the prized promotion, I'd said it cagily, off-the-cuff, giving them just the basic abbreviated information they'd pressed to know. But this time I said it all. I took the fullest advantage of their unified presence, that intermingling of their kindnesses that could wrap around you like a robe. This time, here in the back office, with the shop closed for business, I didn't hold back in the slightest. I described my hopelessness and shame without check. I told them that I wanted to quit my job completely and never go back to those offices. I told them I'd ceased caring about the "intricacies" and challenges of finance, that I detested the company from the bottom of my heart. And I told them I was ready, right then, no remorse, no second thoughts, for the grave. I said, "I have *no* interest in living."

# 29

## THE

## DOLLY

It's a good idea to talk out your problems. When in distress, if you attempt to articulate what's regrettable or odious about your life, as if to hold up your woes to the light, you're generally able to understand them more fully and hence figure out their cause. This often brings resolution. Often, on the other hand, it doesn't make any difference at all.

The following day, despite that extravagant, cathartic display in the back at Reine Nadine, I wanted nothing more than to stuff the whole of my long woolen scarf into my mouth and gag myself. If anything about my life had changed since my confession to Eddie and Vera, it was only that the appalling occasion of my demotion seemed even more real and the reassuring reconciliation between my two friends seemed less so. Most likely I'd imagined the new harmony between them simply to convince myself I'd have their full attention.

It was icy cold out, the sky brilliant blue. The sidewalks were cleared of snow for the most part but covered with sheets of thin ice in patches, which were undetectable to the eye and practically lethal to walk across. I might have loitered and stalled on my way downtown, rather than face the most explicit failure of my entire life, but the air was so frigid and the wind so brisk, I found myself unhappily punctual.

The first message in my box was from Jean. It was sensitive and motherly and mildly apologetic and included picayune instructions about how to proceed. I was to pack up that morning, make a "master list" of tasks still in process, call the deputy custodian and the team leader for Budgeting in IS, fill out a folder of forms for human resources, and report to Arnie Pall, my new boss. "You have much promise," Jean Fine wrote at the end, "and I have no doubt we'll be working together in other capacities later on. I'll look forward to that." Then the tone suddenly shifted, just as it always did, where she added dryly in closing, "Of course, you'll need to buckle down. Best of luck."

I plunged in. I began attending to the items on her list with a burst of my old efficiency. After all the tears of the night before, I had no interest in belaboring the facts of my condition. I only wanted to get it over with. Mostly I wanted to evaporate. Clearing off my desk, I felt a stab of elation and relief when I looked at the hard copies of spreadsheets spilling out of my in-basket and realized I wouldn't have to complete them. That lasted about five seconds.

I made two calls—left voice mail for the custodian, who, I knew from having seen him in action, would bring several coworkers and a dolly and transport my things in ten minutes flat, and made an appointment with the guys in IS. By 11:00 I'd gathered several empty boxes from around the Xerox machine, emptied my bookcase and file cabinet, and unstuck the Post-its from my walls. Then at 11:30, it was time to venture out of my refuge, which wouldn't be mine much longer, and head to Administration.

I dreaded being seen. All of my despair, all my self-loathing, seemed to have coalesced into this almost instinctual drive to disappear. I wanted to dissipate into nothingness in the biting and dry winter air. It was some kind of biological impulse almost, as if every cell of my body were recoiling. After all, what could I possibly say if somebody asked how I was? I knew that among my workmates—and even, in the back of their minds, my best friends—the news of my transfer would be no less than a declaration of my total decline, an announcement of all my deficiencies. How would I face their curiosity if they were to see me packing up? I couldn't even bear to think of it. The potential responses seemed foreign or opaque, any simple admission of fact impossible.

I took my hair down from its bun. It was a senseless attempt at disguise, at once exaggerated and laughably futile, that I executed in a meticulous stupor. All that morning there'd been a faraway, heartless, and exacting quality to the way I'd been behaving. I arranged my hair, stiff from the bun and trained in the wrong directions, then unrolled my shirtsleeves and loosened my blouse from my waistband, all in the same absurd attempt to hide myself. Then I headed through the brick corridor, down two floors in the elevator, past Investor Relations, and up to Personnel. The whole way, I kept my eyes on the floor, like a child who confuses not seeing with not being seen, and I experienced a pathetic sense of victory when no one en route said hello. Eventually, of course, the game would be lost. Why, after all, with my track record, would this little effort be different? But for several hours that morning, shrinking beneath my ghastly, spontaneous hairstyle and skulking around the halls, I managed to avert the miserable and inevitable moment of having to confront someone who knew me.

Back from Personnel, I started the last of packing up. Two more of my desk drawers still needed emptying when I ran out of cardboard boxes. I had no choice but to head to the supply room where fresh cartons you constructed yourself, I knew, were stacked against the left-hand wall. Miraculously, I made it out of my office corridor and past the desks of assistants without anyone raising their eyes, and I made it past the lounge area. But it was just beyond Jean Fine's open doorway that my luck started bottoming out on me. I had approached the door of the supply room. My fingers were folded around the stainless-steel knob. I was ready to slip into the welcome obscurity of the division's mini warehouse where cheaper items and relevant forms were labeled and stored by Acquisitions, when my hand sprang back and my heart surged simultaneously.

There was a noise, a pounding. I froze. The last thing I wanted right then was to linger at the door, stunned, in plain view of anyone passing; any minute someone could spy me and strike up a friendly conversation. I reached for the knob, glancing once to the right through my hair and over my shoulder. Again I heard the noises. There was something, surely, falling from a shelf, at first a clanging, then a thud. But here was the oddest thing: in the instant that I made my decision to go forward, panicking really, as I heard voices behind me, and carefully turned the knob, I heard inside the unmistakable hissing of breathing. Someone was murmuring and gasping. Was it a voice I knew? By now the door was slightly ajar, but I was completely immobilized. More noises: like the throb of a drum, then the slap of a shoe against a gym floor. I saw through the crack the end of the first row of shelving. It was swaying. Dark clothing, a black or dark green, no more than a slice visible through the gap of the door, passed at the far end. And just as I heard that breathing break open into a full-out moan—feminine, I was sure, but the pitch very low, hovering around some suspenseful edge between sex and mishap—I realized that whatever was occurring, I was just as much at risk of being seen from within as by someone passing in the hallway. My hand clenched around the knob and then let go of it. I heard a word—"haste" or "fast" or "yes"—called out, strained and muffled, as the door clicked shut. Barely thinking, I bolted back through the office, a new confusion clamoring in my mind, nearly drowning out my anxiety about answering genial questions. And only half-aware of the distance I'd traveled to get there, I ended up back in my hideout.

Now I had no boxes. Everything seemed more urgent than ever. It was as if the prowling, the need to pack up, and the queer sounds beyond the storage room doorway—everything seemed to exacerbate my already pressing need to hide. I'd lost all the morning's composure. I was willing to leave at this point, without even overseeing the custodians, without even waiting to exchange passwords and turn over my phone line to IS. But could I manage to fit the contents of my last two drawers into the cartons I'd already taped and stacked by the window? For some time—how long I haven't a clue—I paced, gazed distractedly out the window, or tapped my staple remover lightly on the sill. Finally, with a scissors I broke open both boxes. Pens, clips, stamps, pins, leads, erasers—I grabbed up fistfuls of paraphernalia and began spilling them into the gaps. And it was then that the day's game was over.

"Mary Jane."

I tried not to hear it. A stack of index cards and 0-4 forms, plastic forks and napkins—all of it went in a carton.

"Mary Jane, you there?"

What would I possibly tell him? I couldn't bear hearing him gasp when he heard it; I didn't want to see him cover his mouth; I didn't want to listen to him whip up some half-baked consolation about how Gerald was an asshole or how Budgeting, when you came right down to it anyway, was dull.

"Open up."

I waited while the knocking persisted. Of course, the first thing he'd see was the boxes, the first thing he'd ask is, What's this? And then—I couldn't stomach it—I'd have to explain to him.

"Open the fuck up." It was his special, ironic rendition of anger, a delicate twist he'd apply to profanity to give it a touch of fun and warmth. Clearly he knew I was there. He sounded a bit out of breath. The knocking got loud. "Fuck you, Hotshot." This too had the heightened correctness that made it an intimate joke. But then the tone changed. "Elaine, for real, there's something I badly—*badly*—need to tell you. *Get off it.*" He actually sounded slightly hounded.

"I'm in the middle of something," I mumbled. I was growing frenzied by now, dumping sheets of sticky labels and calculator rolls in any gaps I could find.

"Well, I guess I'm interrupting it then, aren't I?"

I didn't answer. I tested to see if one of the boxes would close. It wouldn't.

"Elaine." It was a complete sentence. Now he seemed frank and serious. There was no play to it, no song. I could still hear him breathing. "Elaine, I don't think I have anymore patience for this. Girl, you are *so* self-absorbed."

He was right. He knew just how to make me feel bad. Call me selfish, and you can pretty much own me for life. I can't stand it.

"For months, Elaine, you have been *so* stuck on your rabid ambitions, you've rearranged the whole fucking universe: there's no room for anyone but you in it. Well, hulloooo," he said icily, through the closed door, "there's a few more of us out here."

"Roberto," I answered, and I let go of the flap of the box, which I was still furiously trying to close. I opened the door, just a crack. "Please. I'm sorry." My voice was half-stubborn, half-pained. I wanted him to see the penitence in my face, but I didn't want to let him see *in*. "Please. I'm right in the middle of something."

"I need to talk to you." Now that he had me face-to-face, his voice dropped to a whisper. I could see he was slightly flushed. "What's going on?" he said softly. "You are completely unavailable. Really there's something *very* mind-blowing I've got to tell you. There is a *forest* fire right this minute in my psyche: you're not going to believe how— how outrageous this is."

It had been weeks since we'd met on the stairs, and I knew that's what he was asking for. But I glazed over. I just stared into the coarse weave of his black linen shirt, remembering all the times he'd worn the same blue-green tie and all the times he'd restored me from melancholy. "Not now," I said. It was cold.

"What?" He couldn't believe his ears. I don't think I'd ever said no to him, surely not when he'd expressed this much need.

"*Not now.*"

"OK," he said acquiescently. But it was artificial. What he really meant hadn't come yet. "OK." We stood there with the door barely open, as far as the width of my eyes, and then he stepped back, arms hanging. "You know, Cleverness, I think I'm catching on. I think I get the idea."

There was another pause. I didn't know what he was alluding to.

"I think that's about it. I'd say I've made my efforts. I've kept faith. I think it's time I just kept it without you."

Still I didn't fully get it, but I knew from his inflection it was definitive. Everything about his soft expression, the laxness around his mouth and the perfectly even pitch of his speaking, smacked of closure.

"Just one thing," he went on. I knew, I could feel it in my gut, he was going to launch into the religious stuff. "I think you basically lack perspective, Elaine. I don't think you understand that what you get in life is just your little fraction of love. It's a wealth, in proportion to your goodness, even if it's the tiniest slice of love on earth overall. The definition of an unhappy existence is the *squandering* of it." He was turning around. "All I ever wanted to do was help."

I panicked. "Roberto, I just said 'Not now.' "

"Right. 'Not now' since a month ago." He was already walking away. I knew that he loved dramatic endings; he'd told me about any number of them. But this didn't seem like show.

"Hold on, Roberto." I opened the door another tiny crack.

"You know what, Mary Jane?" he said walking away, his lean form nearly down at the opening of the narrow back hall, "eventually people give up." And he didn't turn back to me.

One hour later IS arrived, unplugged my computer and phone, followed ten minutes after by two custodians, who loaded my overstuffed, half-open boxes onto a bright yellow dolly, balanced my Galileo engraving on top, and rolled them out of my office.

# 30

# M O N E Y

From my perspective, of course, there was no way of knowing I was speeding toward the very last moments of my merciless and convoluted ordeal. Two months went by. As far as I knew I was just carrying on logically, taking my cues from whatever occurred and taking up professional residence in my empty new cubicle. I was trying to live in the wake of Inez as best as I could hope to.

Which is not to say I'd given up. I still had a will and an idea or two. I still contemplated, obsessively, my comeback, though by now whatever little plans I entertained most often ended up bobbing, elusive, half-afloat on the still swelling waves of my dejection.

And I insisted on going it alone. From the day I left Budgeting, I didn't see my old friends once. Roberto would have iced me anyway, though I never even attempted to meet him. The one time I ran into him by accident, near the vending machine, he was in the midst of giving a tour of the floor to some outside investor from Europe. This guy had his back to me—he was wearing the oddest mustardy-gray suit—and Roberto spotted me over his shoulder. In the middle of a sentence, delivered in that polished, heterosexual English he reserved for duties like this, Roberto caught my eye. There was no extra room in his face for communicating with me, so I had no idea what his gaze meant, but in the long run it left me with a feeling that whatever his message would have been, it wouldn't have been damning.

Kay, meanwhile, made every effort to preserve our long-standing friendship. She so much as told me I'd have her for good. "I don't really give a shit," she once E-mailed, for instance, "how long you ignore me, as long as you know I'll be here when you get back." But I avoided her messages till they eventually dwindled and stopped.

And even though I saw Eddie and Vera several times, I never again revealed anything to them emotionally. I was always half-leaving the minute I arrived at the shop, and whenever the suggestion of their troubles came up, I positively refused to stay focused. I figured if I'd managed to pay them a visit, and they were still there, together, that's how I'd just as soon leave them. I basically made it impossible for myself to find out where their relationship stood. And, similarly, I made it impossible for anyone in my life, not only Eddie and Vera, to find out the littlest thing about me.

From here, I can attest that this was not altogether intelligent behavior. Mixing sorrow with solitude can be a stupid mistake. It's a lot like drinking and driving: sometimes you make it over the bridge, but sometimes you don't; you crack up. Or sometimes you get pulled over, and then it just takes longer than you ever anticipated to get home again. With certain forms of unhappiness, though, it's extremely tempting to try it, especially when the pain comes from hating yourself. Some kinds of grief make you shrink away from contact, make you think, If humanity is the sole inventor of sorrow why not steer clear of it? And then things can really get worse. The further you go from social engagement the further you want to be. The more you desert your sympathetic supporters and the more you shirk obligations, the tougher it is to make up for it. Plenty of people have been known to go down this path and never, till death, or till some mental health professional intervenes, return.

It's not impossible. My own cousin's husband, Gabe Lehman, married to Melanie Botsch at the headstrong age of nineteen, flunked out of the Midwest's most prestigious college, and ten days later utterly vanished. It was that family's most tragic time. Melanie's mother, sympathetic from start to finish with Gabe's academic trials, his increasing agony and belligerence, mourned exactly as if he were one of her own. It was almost six years later that Phil, Mel's older brother, swore he saw Gabe in a park, wrapped up in a foul-smelling sleeping bag, wearing shoes much too big, and refusing to say even two words to him. The whole family roamed around that spot for months afterward, but no one saw him again. And you wonder where Gabe might be right this minute if he'd chosen fellowship over such deathly isolation.

In fact I'd been thinking about Gabe all winter. I'd had this nagging notion that there was an element in his story nobody knew about, maybe not even him. Gabe was paying his dues for something—that's how I put it to myself. Solitude for Gabe had a value, on the pages of an internal balance sheet. I just couldn't figure out what it was. Sometimes, I'd fixate on his father, a character I'd contrived in my head basically from scratch, save the one or two phrases I'd heard tangentially from Melanie, and ponder the possible debts he'd incurred metaphorically that he'd passed on tacitly to his son. I imagined the man might be wicked somehow, or at least guilt-ridden, unconvinced of what he deserved, and perhaps a painful sense of displacement or unworthiness had been his psychological legacy. Whatever it was, I had this suspicion that the guy had an ax to grind with history.

My interest in Gabe, however, was not a simple matter of identification. I didn't think I *was* Gabe, in short. Certainly, he and I had our resemblances, and no doubt I'd fantasized once or twice about disappearing into a park, gone in a cluster of trees, or about eternally forgoing my laundry, but I knew pretty clearly that the costs of my aspirations were considerably different from his. If I had to pay for advancement it was not nearly so dearly. My hopes, for one thing, weren't so high in relation to the status I'd come from. Under orders from his machinist dad, so I surmised, Gabe was climbing his way out of the depths of the working class, while I was only trying to ratchet up the honors of an already professional pedigree one more critical notch. A girl like me, with my kind of diploma, having watched a couple of *Nutcracker* ballets and having had my diction corrected over and over, was already primed for a life that families like mine, who didn't take luxuries for granted but *had* them, called "comfortable." I had just wanted to break into a social milieu considered one step better but still within range.

Basically I wanted to be approved of. And it was the people who were just out of reach of me who seemed to offer the real kind of love. I wanted Gerald to smile at me and take me into his confidence. I wanted Brill to wave his arm affably, beckoning me into his world, a world reserved for the Ablest and Best, all of them men, who would laud my entrance and confide in me. These analysts and specialists and executives, who'd known each other since college, were no longer obliged to *appreciate* those pleasures my family always harped on. These men just *had* things. Talking about them seemed obvious or boring. They just lived. It was a world where money was no longer a thing to gain or to save, it was a thing to be moved around.

But no kind of crossover, not Gabe's, not mine, comes without some amount of existential bribery: you buy it with pieces of yourself. The shape of power, snaking irregularly through the matrix of sociocultural life, doesn't just yield to your touch; it asks for recompense always. And that's why that winter, I frequently, sympathetically thought of him. Of course the richer you are the richer you get to be, so unlike Gabe, I had some automatic momentum behind me. But I could *feel*, when I landed at my new desk in Operations—not in the plush conference rooms, not in the junior executive suites—a huge pull, like gravity, surrounding me. It was nothing other than a sense of belonging.

The job was fitting. My cubicle was sufficiently roomy. Three of us, girls, clustered together, updated figures and percentages for Poplar's five subsidiaries and processed forms for protecting the company's trademarks. It was easy and quiet, and I was fully equipped for it. Of the three assistants, it turned out I was the second in rank, which, when you thought of my newly developed but adequate leadership skills and my particularly honed ability to follow, was appropriate. I knew how to take orders while simultaneously deploying enough personal initiative to perfect procedures on my own. I knew when to refrain from disturbing higher-ups and when to bring obstacles to their attention. All these were responsibilities I could handle with ease and still get plenty of sleep at night.

Of course, I didn't. I lay awake every night for hours. As weeks passed and my new position became steadily more familiar, rather than experiencing a growing acceptance, I was only more engrossed than ever in how I'd been success-fully pigeonholed. I grew confident that there was no further to fall, that the slot where I'd landed was totally apt for me, and that I wasn't going to fudge it. But I lay awake at night plotting a way to reverse things. Inez had kindled an ambi-tion in me that wouldn't fade. For hours in the dark, behind my closed eyes, I'd retrace the events that undermined me, rethinking the mechanics of how I'd gotten so close, how the status quo had sucked away my strength, and how I'd ulti-mately foundered.

Or I thought of her. I did not think of Scrivener. In my mind, I circumvented the revelation of his identity—associ-ated now with the slow climb in the elevator that bright, crisp morning, and with Jean on the sidewalk outside, sus-pended between love and malice. I simply bypassed the whole fact of Scrivener as I headed through time toward the sweeter regions of my memory. I'd slip on my Nepalese trou-sers and slip into bed and slip back into the months when she was her again. Inez was purely Inez. My feet were cold on the stone floor. There was something growing tight around my wrists. Hands in my hair, as I tried to rise up, yanked my head back to the pillow. Her voice was perfect, searing. My legs involuntarily stiffened. Then my breathing grew huge as I imagined her form lower over me, ungiving and vast in the dark.

I'd awake long before my alarm. Even with my drapes closed, to keep out the wintry morning light, I'd start stirring around 6:00 or 6:30. A recollection of Scrivener would come back to me, as if into the room, like some noxious oozing of remembrance, and I'd think of all the naive and ignorant notes I'd written him before I'd established his identity. His leaving felt deeper than an insult, colder than loss, and sometimes as harsh as ridicule. What was it about me, precisely—what gullible thing I'd said, what lame way I'd prattled on about my feelings—that had so permanently repelled him? What was it about Elaine, who was not the Francesca he thought she was, that had driven him to leave?

Weeks passed. I continued to avoid my friends. More and more frequently I took the long route home, bypassing Reine Nadine. And I schemed. I considered every sort of spiritual swindle a soul could concoct for transforming or redeeming itself in the world. I contemplated the ways you could buy your own worth.

Then once, I approached a prostitute. For years I'd passed by the whores along Arthur, usually one to a block, and occasionally I'd thought about their lives, who they did it with, at what price, what habits or family or what basic needs their earnings supported. But as that particular winter started to ebb and the job in Operations seemed increasingly trivial (who cared, after all, what I did there? who noticed?)—that's when I started to watch them for real. I started to see what they knew, and I realized they'd do just about anything a person might ask.

There was, for instance, a small woman in a short jacket and miniskirt, who hung around at the corner of Jay. Her legs were skinny as table legs, and she never for a second stood still. She was skittish and high, and the time it took to put out a cigarette was about as long as she could concentrate. When I saw her, she'd smile and look down, tap the ash on her smoke, flip down her collar, wipe her nose, turn around, and cough, all with the weird speed and deliberateness of a spy or a medium delivering a message in some sort of bodily code. Another wore a long down coat and flat plastic disks for earrings, sometimes lime green, sometimes yellow, and was more enigmatic than the rest of them. She never smiled at the cars that passed. She sized up every guy through the windshields. And she was the one I kept my eye on. Her own gaze was cool. It traveled quickly over surfaces, faces, but not out of fear. I slowed down whenever I saw her, watched her slide the down coat open, just an inch or so over a knee and a thigh, or I'd watch her warm her long hands. She'd pull them from her pockets, one at a time, raise them to her mouth, and blow on the backs of her narrow, feminine fingers.

So one night I approached her. It was a Thursday. From my perspective, I couldn't have known, of course, that it was the last Thursday of its kind, that a week later all my scheming, all these attempts—like approaching a prostitute for punishment—would seem wasted, that one more spin of the seven-day wheel would make everything different. There was no way I could have foreseen it. I walked down Arthur. It was prematurely warm out for March, and the whore had on her big coat, but open. She stared at me without registering for a second, not even a flicker, that we would speak.

She just stood there and watched me get nearer. Then I said it: "How much?"

"That depends." I could swear her eyes never blinked. She wore the lime green earrings, minty eye shadow, a half-open peacock blue blouse. "Depends what you want."

"Top me. Rough me up." I was forthright about it. After all, I'd been planning this for days. But in my mind I wasn't nearly so laconic: *bring me down, I beg you; make something possible, hurt me, take off my clothes.*

And that's when everything backfired. Not that she refused me. On the contrary—she looked at me steadily. A wave of distaste and fatigue came into her face, as if she felt in her gut this was the last thing she wanted to do, but she went ahead with it instantly. Her own appetites, she knew, didn't matter a scrap. What *she* wanted was irrelevant. I was the one with the cash.

"Fifty," she said.

In my pocket, my hand formed a fist. I was fiddling with a set of bills I'd stashed there several blocks back. A repugnance seemed to hang in her half-closed eyes, but she was trying to please me anyway. There was a pause, but evidently she couldn't wait. She said, "All right. Forty-five." She pulled a hand from her pocket to signal, as if to say "OK, you win," and I saw for the first time that her hands were chapped. Her pumps were soaked.

"Well, wait," I said. "Wait a minute." I hadn't signaled in any way that the price was too high. Suddenly, I couldn't ascertain who was asking for what.

She kept staring. She hated me, anyone could see, yet, much more urgently than that, she wanted my money. At once she was arrogant yet diminished; she was needy. We stood face-to-face, but I stared into the distance beyond her. A wind, all through the neighborhood, picked up.

Then she spoke again, too abruptly. "OK," she said, "forty. That's it." She gestured with her chin, just once, to cajole me.

And right then, the night air grew decidedly cold. I was ready, in every way, to go home. I looked to the right, up at a gutted building and beside it a row of glowing, yellowish windows. And the thought flashed in my mind that I'd never once stopped to consider if Inez had been rich or poor.

"No," I said to her, dismissively, almost gruff. "Forget it." What could I have been thinking? I was turning away. Buying your own ruin? *Purchasing* weakness? It's impossible.

"Then what?" she was saying.

It's like trying to learn the facts from a clown act. It's like going to jail for a dream or writing a book to change things.

"Forget it," I repeated one more time, though by then— paces, already, down the block—I don't suppose I was still within earshot.

The prostitute raised her voice. "Then you tell *me*," she was calling. "How much?"

# 31

# T H E

# C H I M E

Even now, I can remember the date vividly. Even now, the way you retain a recipe or a street name no matter how incessantly the years wear away its importance, I can remember it was March 17. It was Thursday, 5:27 P.M. I had just clicked on the spot at the top of my screen which toggled between the date and the time, and that succinct little inch of Helvetica has been affixed on my cortex ever since. And now I gazed meditatively at my message cue. The workday was pretty much done. A chime, sweet and soft against the hubbub of the department and the always inordinately loud baritone of Arnie our boss, had just rung. A beat or two after the audio alert, my mail memo icon lit up. A new letter had appeared in my mailbox.

I suppose it's inevitable with stories like this one that you ponder alternative scenarios, the endings that could have resulted if it weren't for a few key events. So, not unreasonably, I have often wondered in the years since how I would have fared if that March missive had never been sent to me. Specifically, I speculate about the durability of my ambitions. In less than two months I'd come to know how well I was suited for my new job, how pragmatic and manageable the department, and how naturally I could assume there an appropriate level of authority. It could have been that one or two months more in that environment—where I had to convince no one, including myself, of the validity of my membership or my talents—would have been enough to calm me down completely and teach me the folly of my drives. At what point does one cease to wish for change? Thwarted long enough, depleted of schemes and fantasies, I might have finally resolved to stay in a slot that, psychologically, socially, or otherwise, didn't cost me. I wonder now whether I would have eventually spurned the cutthroat marketplace of distinctions, the courtrooms of power where you plea-bargained your way to integrity, and stayed put. I wonder what would have happened if I'd never gotten that letter from Scrivener.

"Dear Elaine."

My hands were resting on the keyboard as if I'd forgotten them, like towels on the line left out in the rain. I was mesmerized. There is nothing like the unexpected to make familiar things—like feet and arms and sensations—suddenly seem inconsequential. Staring into the glow of that note was like living out some children's fairy tale where a princess passes through a doorway, a screen, leaving her ordinary being behind and entering a world that's magically unpredictable.

"I'm back just a day," Scrivener had written, "and spent a heap of that time reading your messages."

I read fixedly, as if in a trance. I knew, no matter how he spoke, he always stuck to the facts.

"It'd hurt me too much to think that's what you really feel about me."

Once again it was a voice I hadn't heard before, but that, in itself, was the same. It was just like him.

"So maybe I best start from the start. That's where the shock of it comes."

I was in it, this distant world of the thoroughly unanticipated.

"See I was first at the hospital of all the old friends, and second behind my sibling, and I felt the spirit of my mother sucked out of me, like a tree torn up by a mudslide, the minute I saw her in those bed linens. Jason—or Chairman—what we call my young brother—looked tall and bent like his regular self but the yellow film in his eyes was new. I thought: misery's the color of soured milk, it's like a skin that grows on your feelings."

Right there and then, as if a hand had parted the curtain, I saw the perfect truth that all this time I had doubted: Scrivener was just who he was. Scrivener was just that guy at the library, the one with the crazy flourish to his prose, and now—I knew it was true—the one whose mother had been dying.

"You see," said the note, "my brother Jason never left home. He stayed within blocks of my mother even when he took up with Alleen. Stopped in on the old woman daily. Spent nights there in the end. And when Alleen left him, gone off with the two girls and a month's rent, he never took it out on our mother. He drank enough to kill himself for six months, but once he was done with that business and started up visiting again, he never treated the old woman sorely. Could be my heart burst that day as much for the Chairman as for the bloated and ghostly look of our ma. See, Elaine, my mother was leaving, shipping out. Stuff was clogging all her chambers. Sound of her lungs was like chains. Arms the size of bed rolls and soft like dough. Still hardly a wrinkle in her face, though, hardly a fold.''

My hand closed spontaneously around my mouse. I had to hold back from hitting Reply before I'd finished reading. Even as my eyes welled up with sadness and sympathy for a human being's passing, I simultaneously wanted to rejoice—though I wasn't even sure, at that point, about what.

"Uncle Ric came next," the letter went on. "Sat at the bedside tireless, looking ten times older than she looked even on her very last day. Kept saying Shame and Ugly but otherwise just stayed mute. The man had a cap he'd hold by the brim and wave around like he was speaking, but the sounds from his mouth never came. Then on the tenth day he'd visited, Ric just up and left. Stood with his hands on the mattress, his cap on ma's knee, and muttered a few words none of us could catch, least of all the woman on her deathbed. Or maybe she did. Chairman said: Ric's just paying his respects, that's a language that doesn't need any alphabet. Suppose he could have been right on that.''

I heard a shuffling. It was my coworker in the next cubicle packing up. It's possible she even said good night to me, but I wouldn't have known. So much of my life all of a sudden was being rearranged in my brain that I had no room to pay attention.

"After five weeks," I read on, "we took her home. We watched. Little bedroom smelled of wheat. Always she had to have the curtains closed. Ma, said Chairman, the light'll cheer you up. But she'd wave her ballooned-up arm, blinking. Eyes wet. Puffed up from lid to brow. Must've been the sunlight burned them. But still my mother could weep. Tears

like shiny ball bearings would shoot down over her temples
and hit the pillow. While that face, facing up, didn't move.
She was leaving, and it was a long way to go. Looked into the
ceiling, the paint coming down up there like shards of cloud,
and must have seen away far-off where she was heading.
Took my mother three months to say good-bye. Took all
those long days for her crazy grip to loosen. I like to think
that's because my mother had a lot of good-byes for the
saying."

I swiveled to the left. This time for sure someone had
called my name. The letter, glowing like a ship's porthole
flooded with light, was still open on my screen: I looked up.
There in the now quiet department, passing by the wall of
my cubicle and looking down in, was Jean Fine, striding
through the broad passageway with an exec from New Ven-
tures and a VP of Sales. I had never seen her before in this
back half of Operations. I stood up abruptly, as if at attention, to respond. "Hi Jean," I said, and my own voice
seemed foreign, too sharp, too sunny, conspicuously Cauca-
sian.

"Where've you been?" Jean Fine said, detouring only
momentarily from the discussion she was in as the New Ven-
tures director paused to sneeze. She didn't wait for an answer. "You ought to stop in and visit." She wore a violet
wool suit with black buttons the size of hockey pucks, and
she waved with the faux warmth of a candidate. "Come
by," she added, "Let's catch up." It was just like Jean that
you couldn't tell if her words were a reproach or an invitation.

But it didn't matter. When I sat down again, my knees
bounced beneath my desk, my fingers tapping restlessly

back on the keyboard. I hadn't felt this expectant in ages. My message chime had sounded again, the little tone sweet, almost summery, with that softness like damp soil.

"Dear Elaine."

It was Scrivener again.

"Now that you've read of my loss and of the truth behind my prolonged absence, I hope we can resume our previous dialogue and renew our bond."

Yes, him—there was no question.

"You can imagine my distress upon returning at finding such enmity and worry, so many impassioned entreaties not opportunely addressed, such dismay untended in the letters you wrote during my sojourn. Hence, this second note, expressly to seek reassurance that all is forgiven."

Now I was only half reading. It wasn't quite clear in my mind what I wanted, or how I thought I'd proceed, but the way I was breathing so deeply, and the lightness I felt in my knees, the strange pressure I felt around my mouth that must have been an urge to start smiling—all of it arose out of the one conviction permeating my every perception: that I now had a second chance. Great doors of possibility seemed to have blown wide open for me. Then who *was* she? I kept thinking over and over. Who was Inez?

Again, the chime came.

"E, can we talk?"

But this time it wasn't from Scrivener. I heard the elevator closing at the end of the hall, a flurry of voices extinguished.

"I'm in the store. Please come."

I checked the "from" field. It was Eddie. The note was uniquely vehement. It wasn't like Eddie to make such a bald entreaty. I could tell without a doubt from the wording that he needed me to go straight to the shop.

But first, all in a rush, I launched into a reply to Scrivener. It was a long sputtering note filled with apologies and welcome and condolences and relief. It was a sloppy typewritten celebration over our shocking reunion, declaring more explicitly than ever how I prized our correspondence and conveying, I'm sure, in its excitement, this as yet unarticulated sense of hope, this feeling I had just then, with the department emptied out and all sound seemingly socked away in the long-sunken elevators, that my search for Inez and the boldness she'd evoked in me could still live.

# 32

# C U R T A I N S

Charged with purpose, possessed with curiosity and urgency and anticipation, I did not, that Friday morning, report to Operations. I went directly to the fifth floor. Half-formed passersby, mere extras in the crowd scene of my vision, seem to fall away into light motes or backdrops as I sailed along with a sudden, pervasive alacrity. A soft, natural light gave the halls a greenish cast, like a washed-out landscape speeding by as you pass full-tilt in a train, and I could actually feel the mildest little rustle of air I was creating simply by moving so purposefully. I wore my favorite checkered blouse that day, cut just right for your mother at the age of twenty-five—back when she wore kerchiefs and sunglasses and smoked cigarettes—along with a black miniskirt and a belted black leather jacket I'd bought at a particularly worthwhile rummage sale. It was about a month too early for such a spring outfit, but I'd chosen it quite deliberately. I think at that point I felt immune to temperatures altogether, or perhaps I was generating a private climate of my own. I was gliding past the lounge area, heading straight for my old department.

There are times when you know something without knowing you do. And it's even possible, at times, any number of them, that you know that you *don't* know that you do know. That is—a knowledge is latent, but you feel it. Like an old song whose first bars escape you, the thing is nevertheless present—you know it—and its journey from obscurity to the front of your mind is only a matter of time, maybe only a matter of minutes. All you need to do, when, say, you end up in the kitchen, having forgotten what in the world you came there to get, but knowing, somehow, you *do* know, is stand there in the presence of the many possibilities and wait for the right one to come forward. Which is to say this: when I woke up that morning I had the unwavering perception that if I were to *take* myself, simply, to the fifth floor of Poplar, stand myself there somewhere amid the assistants and hallways and office gear, I would know what I couldn't have known until then. I would know where to find Inez.

The hidden truth will come to you, I said to myself in the kind of coaxing whispers a coach might use on the sidelines; all the clues will come together and it will bob up to the top of your mind. Veering around one more turn, I felt so sure that the truth would appear to me momentarily that my thoughts were evacuated of everything else.

When I reached the lounge area, I stopped. The hallways of Budgeting looked frozen and plain as if existing in a single point in time, a point nearly three months back when I'd left there, not to return. They were at once far away and superbly familiar. Inherent *in* them, the carpeting, the walls, it seemed, were the days they'd been a home. Past the fax machine for a moment I panicked—what if my apprehension had been wrong?—but immediately I felt the certainty return again. There was the water fountain, the printer, the mail cart. Everything was right where it had been and everything goaded me on. It was as if the act of recollecting the place, recognizing every detail I passed, were further consolidating this perception that I harbored all the right knowledge. I seemed to know exactly where to go though I didn't.

"Hey Elaine!"

Across the way, on the other side of the photocopier, was Marissa. She covered her mouth, embarrassed. It was early in the morning, the place was hushed, and she'd blurted it much too loud. She wore her hair taut against her head like mine, hers in a ponytail at the back, and the dark brown skin of her face was powdered.

I didn't answer, just waved, still moving, like a runner who's just finished the race but hasn't yet fully slowed down. At the Budgeting desks, only two assistants were at their workstations, one reading a paper, several more yet to arrive, but neither of the two looked up at me. Then finally I stopped. I had approached the unmarked door—familiar, like your own mailbox or your wallet, a thing you'd open to find traces of yourself—that I'd entered so many dozens of times through the years and more and more frequently toward the end. It was the door to Gerald's office.

To this day, the expectations I felt at that moment remain remarkably intact, as if, put simply, I still *have* them. Even now, looking back several years, I'm filled with that sense of portent, verging on cognizance, which almost eradicates all the contrary conclusions that did, quite incontestably, come afterward. I stood listening, growing warm in my now open leather coat and black hose. A strain in my neck was a perfect metaphor for how, mentally, I was reaching, craning to locate the single bit of missing information that would make everything different. Without discerning why or how, still in the stupor that engulfs you as you fumble for the forgotten melody, I sensed that the solution to my life's most meaningful riddle was just beyond that threshold.

I raised my hand to push the half-closed door, ever so discreetly. I recall the look of my own hand, jutting in from outside the periphery of my camera-lens eyes, emerging only partially from the cuff of my too long jacket sleeve. I pressed gently. The door edged open a tad. I pushed gently some more. And as more of the carpet came into view, the antique wastebasket, the whip, the horse, I saw that no one was there. Gerald was not at his desk.

I turned. For a moment I felt suspended, hanging in the center of a sentence whose beginning you've forgotten and whose ending you therefore can't extrapolate, but I started moving again. It was as if I'd gotten a telepathic sign from some mental control tower I didn't know existed, and it was telling me I needed to continue. Jean Fine could be heard in the adjacent office, talking liltingly on the phone. A third assistant had arrived at his station with a steaming Styrofoam cup of coffee and was booting his machine. Without a trace of hesitation, with perhaps even more blinded certainty than before, I was heading further past the island. I was heading for my own back hall.

It was then, I remember, that I started feeling nervous, not less galvanized or less directed, but on top of the weird oblique assurance I felt, there grew a layer of fear. The little corridor was silent. All the safety and privacy it once represented now seemed long gone. But I knew I wasn't there for the sake of nostalgia. I was stalking a knowledge still deferred. Light, from my old office's doorway, cut across the passageway and fell against the opposite wall; it formed a radiant parallelogram across the carpet and a faintly luminous, more complicated geometry suspended in the air. All I knew was that I would find a clue here. And before I had understood any more than that, before I had any better grip on my own intentions, I was standing smack in the center of that stream of vivid sunlight.

"Elaine."

There it was again, my name. Only this time it wasn't Marissa. It wasn't Jean.

"What are you doing here?" I said. Everything seemed turned around. It was as if you'd arrived home one day and not just the furnishings but the rooms themselves, the very floor plan, had somehow been rearranged—the bathroom now on your right, the bedroom at the front of the building. It was as if you found out the month wasn't March at all, but June.

"Elaine." Again. It wasn't exactly a greeting or even an acknowledgment. The two syllables were flat and precise.

It was Kay.

"What are you doing?" I repeated. My tone was sincerely inquisitive. I was thoroughly at a loss, and I was open to explanation. I stared at her body, seated in my chair, her hands, hovering over a brand-new keyboard. Then I spoke again, still bewildered. It may have seemed to anyone else I was stating the obvious, but to me it wasn't obvious at all. "You're in my office," I said. "You're working."

And it was just after those few words came out that a wind seemed to blow in the valley of this consciousness. A fog, having lain dense and heavy there all morning, indeed for months, suddenly sailed upward on the briskest fresh current of air. Everything I had known, but *didn't* know, all at once appeared brilliantly plain in the valley's transparent atmosphere. The bars of the song flooded in. I was staring past Kay at my old plaid curtains, left on the windows when I moved. They were opened. Bunched up, like a waistline, pulled together and pinned to the wall, my curtains were tied and held open with a long red satin cord.

Quickly, Kay turned to see what it was that transfixed me. Then she turned back, but only halfway. She didn't want to look in my eyes.

I said the word under my breath—"Inez"—because like the very letters themselves suddenly flying together into perfect sequence, unscrambled, to spell out that name, a flurry of formerly unrelated facts in my mind was gathering to spell out the answers. I saw. I understood it. Complacent on the job for years, ever unambitious, contented, Kay, at night, had ascended. She had possessed powers, all those midnights. She had wielded a brilliance that made professional life, all the myriad daylight events, seem trifling. But only up until the day she'd left me. Without Francesca to own and demean, things for Kay had inverted. It was Kay who had later submitted to Jacques. It was Kay whose familiar voice I'd heard murmuring in the supply room, gasping and pleading with somebody inside who was forcing her to sexually comply. Somehow, Kay's role had reversed itself. And out of her new subservience had grown the sturdy, secure young woman who was sitting here now. I remembered her almost aggressive insistence on Christmas shopping. I remembered the suit she'd worn. I remembered her aplomb and confidence when she flirted with Vera's friend Jaime. Clearly when she'd left me, Kay had found her own special sexual captains, who'd changed her long-standing course in life, so that after all her many indifferent years and just in a few short months, she'd indomitably uprooted herself from Fulfillment and spun her unexpected surrender into a new career.

I said it over, "Inez," and I guess it made sense that my heart started pounding even harder than before, since when she finally turned around to look at me, took her hands off the keyboard and braced them against the chair and the desk as if to get up and come toward me, the look in her eyes was precisely the mixture of tyranny and lust, love and poison, hunger and audacity I'd pictured a million times over at night as I sat alone in the glow of our salacious adventure. I saw her long veined neck, the coffin pendant, the picket fence, the cool beautiful bones of her shoulders, the sharp authoritarian chin, and everything suddenly looked different. Once more I said it, "Inez."

And then she finally answered. She said, "Yes." But there was a meanness to it, a corruptness, and an aloof kind of love. "You want something?" she said. It stung. "You're going to have to ask for it."

"My god," I said vaguely. Then I repeated it again: "Inez."

33

T H E

E N D

A year or so ago, I got it in my head that I'd go back to school and study economics. I was really itching to get ahead, to make something of myself professionally. (So what's new?) It turned out to be a passing whim, though, not because I wasn't craving some kind of advancement zealously enough, but because I realized it wasn't monetary policy or money flow I was interested in. I wasn't necessarily dying to study the role of the Federal Reserve or the impact of national debt limits. Really, there were these *other* kinds of currencies and economies I was trying to understand—economies, for instance, of the heart, and the great invisible and overlapping economies of power.

It doesn't bother me, though, that I decided to forgo it. By now I've acquired enough wisdom to figure that professional advances and defeats have their own complicated rhythms and are subject to lots more social and psychological forces than just graduate school. A number of things make winning possible or unlikely.

For instance, I never got far at Poplar & Skeen. Sometimes I say it's because I jumped ship too soon, moved over to a competitor where I could have a clean slate and a good start in Receivables, before I'd given Poplar my best shot, but in my heart I know that's not the real reason I never succeeded in getting ahead there. In my heart I know the real reason why.

At Nickerson too I've had my ups and downs—just like you always do: that's life, that's economics. But my stint there began with a good enough rally to give me a head start on my new reputation, and eventually, at Nickerson, I broke through a glass ceiling or two. Those particular breakthroughs, of course, had much to do with Eddie. Vera eventually came back to him—the two of them, truly, share some kind of electricity that doesn't quit—but for a while there, she was on to other adventures, other men, and in those days, her leaving Eddie to his own rather lonesome devices had a considerable effect on my job life. Eddie had tricks up his sleeve you'd never have guessed at, an uninhibited grasp of his mastery that I wouldn't have ever known. I certainly didn't suspect any of it the day I got his urgent little note, the day when Vera officially announced she was leaving. That night he was completely distraught. But when things heated up much later and our long-standing relationship took a turn, I knew that it was Eddie, painstaking dominator, cruel graceful captor, who catapulted me so sharply up through the Nickerson ranks.

Scrivener seconded this analysis. Scrivener always agrees with my reading of the fluctuations and shifts of social positioning I've experienced throughout these years. "The exacting price of power," I remember he once wrote, "what you buy and sell in sex and love or self to win, comes in many forms and sizes. Friends," he said, "in this context, are really merely business associates."

Which wasn't meant, in fact, as a judgment; Scrivener was actually in favor of my life with Eddie. But perhaps in some measure it was intended as a lament. I've often wondered if it doesn't sadden Scrivener to know that he's "sold off"—to use his terms—so much of himself. Scrivener, after all, is a man whose "self" is pretty compromised. Or so some have claimed. Roberto, for one, told me that a person like Scrivener who spends so much time on-line and whose character is so elusive "has got to be psychologically afflicted." Of course, personally, I've always thought Roberto was one to talk—after all, a guy who slips from homo street slang to high-class German in a matter of seconds might just as readily be called fragmented. But besides, what Roberto doesn't see is how Scrivener's losses—of identity or personal history or of all those millions of class markers we call "style" and "taste"—is also his transcendence.

Anyway, I don't want to argue. Roberto, who eventually forgave me, has always had his troubles tolerating change. Roberto doesn't relish that imbroglio of identities, which can shift in the most intricate ways; he doesn't take well to the notion that it's not just good ol' *you* who determines who you are, that circumstance has something to do with it. Which is why after his little escapade with Kay he nearly went off the deep end. The fact that he could find himself desiring, even for a minor little interlude in the supply room, such a radically new role and such a different kind of seductress was more than he could handle, and you can bet my brainy friend Roberto will never have another sexual encounter like that one, rough or sweet, with a female.

But Scrivener understands those sorts of changes. He understood, for instance, all my ups and downs at Nickerson, and he knew the truth behind my fate at Poplar. No, it wasn't leaving the job prematurely that accounts for my never getting ahead, never excelling any less or any more— pleasing Arnie for what it was worth, but never earning the "entrée," the praise and power I'd been after. It was for reasons much deeper than that. In Scrivener's words, I was "a variable in the greater oscillations of the world." That's really what did it. "In any given relation (a:b)," he once wrote, "for which scarcity and inequity are conditions, a shift in one element (a) will provoke a shift in the other (b)."

He was referring, of course, to Kay. After he had returned from nursing his mother and was ensconced once again at his library job, Scrivener had made it his project to help me put the pieces of my situation together. So by the time Kay and I met up in the stairwell later that strange Friday morning, Scrivener had already been thinking over my plight. By then he had probably begun developing a pretty astute theory of what had gone on in my life, and in the years that followed he's been an invaluable source of perspective.

As always the stairwell smelled of autumn and bleach. She wore the usual liquidy dress, hanging from her squared-off shoulders, which looked to me especially solid that day, especially hard, and her hair had recently been trimmed. You could see the sharp resolute turn of her forehead at her temple and the rigid tendons on the sides of her neck. Below rolled-up sleeves, her arms were bare, and I noted, for the first time, they were much longer than mine were, and wiry. I wanted her to take me over.

At first, she didn't say anything. She saw me down below her from the top of the stairs and she checked once to see if we were alone. Then she stepped deliberately down the stairs toward me. Staring, bracelets jangling, dress running over her bones like water over rock, she took hold of me by the neck—pressure under my chin—and pushed me up against the lemon yellow wall. There might have been fear in my eyes, but if so, it was nothing but subterfuge—a meager attempt to slow everything down—since what was filling me up really, pervading the entire space of my experience so not a chink, not a crack was left for doubt or misgiving, was wanting. I was hungry. Her hand was solid, like metal, like chrome. When I struggled it was as if my energy only gave my longing more momentum. And when she did finally speak, that too made me want more.

"I told you," she said in a half whisper. I could hear the sound in her chest, which was rising and falling like that of a criminal, an outlaw who's just come up with a plan. "You're going to have to ask for it."

I was wearing that little shirt, I recall, and it must have been sixty degrees in the stairwell, but I felt the moisture heat up between her hand and my wrist, which she held clamped against the concrete.

I could only whisper. "Go ahead," I said. "Whatever." I think I was practically in tears. But it all happened so fast, I can't be sure of it, because before I even had time to shut my eyes and thrash, to protect my face, Kay opened her mouth and kissed me. No blow came down. Her mouth was a cavern. It was hot like your stomach must be on the insides, and though at first her tongue drove into me like a spike, an invasion, all in a flash it softened. At once the struggle between Kay and me, at the hot and charged point of contact, in the slowly revolving, dizzying outer space of a mouth on a mouth, produced a strange kind of confusion. It was as if whoever I was had become small and spherical and was twirling around in zero-g. For a long attenuated moment I couldn't make sense of the feeling. Then slowly, her hands running over my shoulders, dragging along my arms and my hips, Kay began dropping downward. Her grip was fast in my clothes. Her breathing was filling the room. She was kneeling down on the cold concrete floor. And I knew as I looked down at her gorgeous flushed face, her hair falling back at her temples, her eyes half-closed, exactly what she wanted me to do to her. For a second I experienced a new sensation—it was in my palm, like a tightening, an itch. There was a signal there, an impulse for contact.

But it passed. The silence in the stairwell exploded.

And I suppose it was in the very moment when that sensation entirely ceased, dissolved, really, into the driving resurgence of my other, older need, my longing for servitude, for debasement, so much greater than the palm of a hand could hold—I suppose it was then, when Kay had waited just long enough to understand my refusal and suddenly, acquiescently, dropped her head forward, that my status at Poplar—those finely tuned coordinates that Scrivener might well call $c$ and $d$, my fate, essentially, in the great scheme of influence—was simply and incontrovertibly decided.